Signs of Trouble

Signs of Trouble
Copyright © 2022 by Anna Alkire
All rights reserved.

No part of this book may be reproduced in any form or by any electronic or mechanical means, including information storage and retrieval systems, without written permission from the author, except for the use of brief quotations in a book review.

This is a work of fiction. Names, characters, places, and incidents either are the product of the author's imagination or are used fictitiously. Any resemblance to actual persons, living or dead, events, or locales is entirely coincidental.

Cover design by Ashley Santoro
ISBN (paperback) 979-8-9863881-4-4
ISBN (ebook) 979-8-9863881-3-7
ISBN (audiobook) 979-8-9863881-5-1

Water's Edge Publishing LLC
waters.edge.publishing@gmail.com

Signs of Trouble

Montgomery Brothers, Book 2

Anna Alkire

WATER'S EDGE PUBLISHING

SIGN UP FOR ANNA'S AUTHOR NEWSLETTER

Receive exclusive content, information about giveaways, coupons, and be the first to learn about Anna Alkire's new releases. Please, sign up today!

www.annaalkire.com

CHAPTER ONE

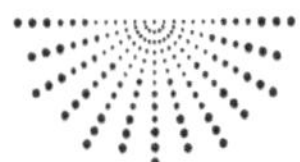

The muscles of Ellie's pelvic area rippled and squeezed, as if someone was yanking a belt too tightly around her swollen stomach. *Oh, no, please no.* She wasn't ready.

One of her hands reached up to grip the handrail next to her, and she closed her eyes, waiting for the fake contraction to settle down. *Think about something else.* She needed to decide where to live. Okay, maybe she had decided, but she didn't want to hurt anyone's feelings.

The pinching contractions tightened every muscle in her back. The old staircase squeaked underneath where she sat. She bent forward and put her head closer to her knees, breathing in short pants. *Crap.*

Her father-in-law had fried fish for dinner and the cooking fumes lingered in the row house stairwell. New Jersey was full of tall narrow houses, with each floor an apartment. It was only her pregnancy that made this one seem like a prison. She fanned her face, ignoring the buildup of saliva in the back of her mouth. At least after she'd gotten past her due date she could love food again.

The yelling continued inside the downstairs apartment

and what sounded like a fist slammed against a table. They were arguing about her again—something about bolting furniture to the wall before the baby was born. Well, also about her sister-in-law's unfaithful boyfriend coming over, but that seemed like a detour. Tempers ran hotter on the East Coast, judging by the Buckley household.

The Braxton Hicks contractions eased off. Ellie rubbed her belly with a shaking hand. "Mommy's okay," she said. It was a full two weeks before her due date so surely this was only a warm-up. Besides, being born on Valentine's Day would put way too much pressure on that holiday.

Technically, the contractions had started that morning and were getting stronger. *Don't think about it.* If Mitch was still alive, he'd be staring at her with those solemn green eyes and telling her not to worry. Stoic and generous, even after a surprise pregnancy and a shotgun wedding.

Her eyes filled up and her vision blurred. She sniffed, rubbing her nose. *Don't start crying, too.*

Ellie pulled out her phone and looked again at the listing for a vacation rental in Siletz, Oregon. All of her information was ready. The dates, July first to August thirty-first, and her credit card information had been part way through the checkout process for the last two months. She refreshed the internet page every day. Going back to Oregon meant leaving New Jersey and the two people connected to her husband, who fiercely wanted her to stay.

The door below her was flung open and her sister-in-law, Nora, stomped out. Her face was flushed, and her red hair pulled back tightly into a ponytail. "There you are—Jesus. How does someone shaped like an overstuffed shopping cart sneak around so well?"

"I don't sneak, I waddle."

"It's freezing out here in the hall. Come up to mine or go

back to Dad's. A chair feels a hell of a lot better than hard stairs."

"I know. In a minute."

"Ellie, are you okay? You're pale and you didn't eat anything but a few bites of salad."

"I don't know. If I say something, it might happen, and I'm really, really not ready for anything to happen."

Nora sat down beside her and took her hand. "No matter what, I'll be with you, and so will Dad. I mean, he'll be in the waiting room where he should be. But you can scream and cry and shit yourself or whatever and I won't even tease you about it for the next twenty years."

Ellie leaned her head on Nora's shoulder. "You're either a saint or a really bossy bully. Maybe both."

"I hope my niece is just like me."

Something was happening in her stomach again, and she swallowed. If she ignored it, hopefully it would go away. "Hey, look at this," she said hoarsely and held her phone out to Nora.

"A duplex in shithole Oregon? Don't give me that look—when the baby's out of your bump I'll stop cursing." Nora shoved the phone back in Ellie's hand. "Stay, Ellie. We really want you to stay here with us. You can live wherever you want in the house—you'll have a room downstairs with Dad and space upstairs with me. If you leave, I'll be super pissed."

The contraction hit so hard Ellie jerked forward and screamed out. Her phone dinged, the sound a distorted ringing in her ears. Her innards twisted around, rearranging themselves as she stared down at the scratches on the wooden step through the red haze filming her vision. She counted her breaths to sixty, conscious only of Nora rubbing her back, then started again. Another sixty. *Crap!*

"Ellie, hon, this seems a little serious. I mean, serious

good—you're going to get through this and be holding that little girl in your arms before you know it."

"I need to shave my legs." Fat tears plopped off her chin onto Mitch's old Stockton University sweatshirt that was barely big enough to cover her quivering stomach. She wiped her face on the sleeve.

"Okay, well, the first step is to get off these stairs."

Ellie stared down at her phone as the screen dimmed before it went into sleep mode. A message from the booking service said, "Congratulations your vacation awaits!" She blinked, then touched the screen to bring it back to full brightness. Sometime in the last few minutes she'd accidentally hit the "pay now" button.

"Come on now, Ellie," Nora said, standing up beside her and reaching out a hand. "Wait, what is that?"

"My water just broke." Ellie kept staring at her phone while Nora squawked and ran into the downstairs apartment to yell at her father. Accidentally paying for the rental was a sign, Ellie decided. She would go back to Oregon—at least for the summer.

Austin Montgomery walked into the dim bar that was decorated with bright green banners and signs for St. Patrick's Day. He glanced over at Chuck, the night shift bartender who'd called him.

"Get over here and drink a whiskey," Chuck shouted, his ridiculous shamrock-covered top hat listing sideways.

Austin took off his Stetson to run a hand over his head. The vein above his left eye twitched. He walked over to the bar and leaned on it, staring across the room as a dark-haired woman slumped over a table in the back.

"I'm not drinkin, Chuck," Austin said. "But one round's on

me for everybody up here." The twenty or so people at the bar cheered and Chuck got to work filling up shot glasses, a satisfied grin on his face.

Paying off Chuck for their arrangement kept the phone calls coming. It was his own form of self-flagellation, except with no perceived atonement in sight. He felt the gaze of the pretty blonde standing next to him who was trying to snare his attention.

"Cheers," Chuck said, taking Austin's credit card and sliding a shot glass in front of him. "This one's on the house. Hey, life's short. Even with your baggage passed out at the table over there, there's no reason for you not to start to move on."

No reason not to move on. Right. One reason was definitely Ryder, his five-year-old son, who woke up with night terrors every other night and had started wetting the bed again. He'd had to bang on old Mrs. McPherson's door tonight and beg her to shuffle over in her bathrobe while he ran down to the bar.

"Night, Chuck." Austin left the whiskey untouched. Someone would snatch up the free liquor before he'd walked across the room. He pushed away from the bar and made his way through the crowd to the booth in a dim back corner.

Becky sat there, slouched over the table, head on her arms, long dark brown hair trailing down her back. Her mouth hung open as she slept. An attractive firebrand, even with makeup smeared down her tan face and sweaty hair plastered to her head. Her clothes were covered in dust from riding in the arena. It was the start of rodeo season and she'd had a low score in the early qualification round.

Austin took a deep breath and stared down at his wife. He'd seen this coming, had known he'd have to come up with some reason that explained to Ryder why his mother didn't want to see him.

The last four days visiting her, staying at the apartment he'd rented in Pendleton for her to live in, had been bad. Socrates had written, "My advice to you is get married: if you find a good wife, you'll be happy; if not, you'll become a philosopher." Which showed, even 2,415 years later, relationships are a crapshoot.

"Let's go, girl." He checked she had everything in her purse.

"Austin?" Becky mumbled, blinking her eyes open. "What time is it? Shit." She rubbed her neck, no doubt sore from sleeping on the table.

"Time for bed. What I mean is, I'll get you in your bed and sleep on the couch, as usual. Ryder and I are leaving in the morning."

"I told you not to come."

"You did."

He helped guide Becky toward the door, doing his best to ignore her mumbled tirade about him shaming her, and not returning the sidelong glances of people as they passed.

Instead, the summer fishing vacation he'd been chewing on in his mind came into focus. Ryder's grandmother, Grace, wanted to see him, and Austin needed to talk through a few things with Becky's mother. He'd catch two fish with one net, so to speak.

Maybe Chuck was right. First thing tomorrow, he'd get Ryder back to the ranch where they both belonged. He helped Becky into the passenger side of his truck, gently pushing away her hands when they ran down his torso toward his belt buckle.

"Home now," he said. "It's been a long day." She turned her face away from him as he closed the passenger door.

He walked to the driver's side, heat in his face. That had been the first time she'd touched him all week. As soon as he opened the door, and forced himself to keep moving, he knew what was coming.

"I'm sorry," she whispered, tears running down her face. "So fucking sorry."

∼

ELLIE ROCKED BACK and forth on the swing of the playground set next to her vacation rental. There wasn't a better place to be in the world than the Oregon coast at the beginning of July. Kinley nestled against her chest in a sling, dozing after being fed. The silky red hair on her tiny head fluttered from the swing's motion.

Ellie let her eyes fall closed. She should go inside and lay them both down, but she didn't want to miss seeing her new neighbors. It was four p.m. and check-in time for the empty duplex next to hers.

The past five months had been a blur of exhaustion, worry, preparing to move, surviving travel with an infant, and finally landing. She'd been called insane more than once. She sighed. No one could lecture her out here.

She'd made it to her goal: a vacation. Pine and fir scented the air and insects buzzed next to a butterfly bush over-hanging the long driveway. The quiet duplex was surrounded by trees, out of sight of any other houses, and twenty minutes from the Pacific Ocean.

Her eyes opened to stare down at Kinley, whose little pink mouth puckered as she slept. She'd done it—brought her baby into the world and kept them both alive, fed, watered and cleanish, on about four hours of sleep a night. Every day was an accomplishment. If only she could make up her mind about tomorrow.

Her phone vibrated. She pulled it out of her pocket, looked at the screen, and sighed. *Not again.*

"Hi, Mom," she whispered. "Kinley just fell asleep—I really can't talk right now."

"I can't stop thinking about you out there, miles away from anything, with some stranger about to move into your house."

"It's a duplex, with a huge garage separating us. And there's a Dairy Queen three miles away. We're fine."

"Eleanor, you have a baby now, you have to be more careful."

"Mom, I can't talk right now…"

"It was so wonderful having you and that sweet baby girl with us last week. I know your brother has taken over the spare bedroom for his office—he really does study all the time, engineering is such a challenge—but I've been thinking about how we can all fit in. I'm going to talk to your stepfather about the family room downstairs. It's nice and big, dear. And the television could go in the sitting room instead. You stayed in New Jersey for the first five months of my granddaughter's life. You finally get back to Oregon and then only visit with me for one week? Eleanor, I worry about the choices you make. Who's going to help you? Also, your hair —I called my salon, and they can squeeze you in Tuesday next week…"

A massive pickup truck turned onto the gravel driveway, rolling slowly toward the house. The gray truck was new-looking, with one of those big dual cabs. A man was driving. She couldn't see anyone next to him.

She bit her lip. She'd really been hoping for a young family. "Mom, I'll call you later." Ruthlessly, she ended the call.

Kinley shifted around and Ellie started rocking again. The truck parked in front of the left side of the duplex, towering over her tiny Ford Focus parked on the right side of the driveway.

A small face smooshed itself against the back window of the truck's cab, a dark-haired little boy. He puffed out his cheeks and suctioned his mouth onto the glass. Ellie smiled and waved.

The driver's side door opened. A tall man emerged, blond hair cut short, wearing jeans and a T-shirt. He glanced at her over his shoulder. She waved, a smile from the little boy's antics still on her face. He gave her a jerky nod, stony-faced, and turned away.

Okay then. Her skin went hot. He clearly wasn't interested in being friendly.

The back door of the truck cab opened, and the dark-haired kid jumped out, dressed in shorts, a long-sleeved T-shirt, and a rainbow tutu. Ellie snorted a laugh, watching him jump up and down, pointing at the playground and jabbering a mile a minute at the tall, silent man.

Kinley burped, spit up, choked, and then jolted to screaming wakefulness. Ellie shot to her feet, shifting Kinley upright, head whipping around searching for the rag she'd forgotten to bring. She wiped Kinley's face with the fabric sling. The thought of what could happen in a few seconds with a baby twisted her nerves into jangled knots. Kinley grumbled but lay her head on Ellie's shoulder.

When Ellie looked up, the dark-haired boy was standing in front of her, his mouth hanging open. "Are you Strawberry Shortcake?" He grinned, showing a missing bottom tooth, and pointed at her hair.

"Hi. No, I'm Ellie, and this is baby Kinley. But I think strawberry shortcake, to eat, is an awesome idea."

"Yes. You're right." He turned back toward the tall man, who was unloading bags from the back of the truck. "Dad! We need to eat some strawberry shortcake with Ellie."

Ellie laughed. "I don't have any, I'm afraid. But Dairy Queen down the road might."

"Dairy Queen, Dad. We've got to go."

"Hang on, you just got here. Don't you want to see where you're going to be staying?"

"I want to go on the slide."

"Good idea." She nodded, smiling.

"Watch me, Ellie, I can go down backward."

"No way."

"Yeah, watch."

The boy ran across the cedar bark mulch to the other side of the playground, rainbow tulle fabric bouncing with each step. Ellie made open-mouthed surprise faces as he went down the slide. She swayed from side to side, holding Kinley against her chest. The boy went down the slide ten times, then launched himself onto a swing on his stomach, and finally hung from a bar one-handed.

Footsteps crunched on the ground behind her. Ellie turned around and caught her breath. At first glance the man standing in front of her brought to mind a young version of a blond David Duchovny wearing a cowboy hat, like when he was on *The X-Files* but with more muscle and a deep tan. He was hard-faced, spent a lot of time outdoors judging by his tan, and didn't smile much. The five-o'clock shadow on his face outlined a firm masculine jaw and a prominent chin with a dimpled cleft at the bottom.

"Ryder," he called out impatiently but without anger—the tone of a strict parent stepping into the same confrontation for the hundredth time. "Grandma Grace is waitin for us."

Ellie dragged her eyes away from him. The man obviously had no interest in talking to her, which was probably for the best since she would embarrass herself by trying to flirt with him. Really, though, she wouldn't be able to help it.

"Dad, I want Ellie to come."

She laughed, smiling back at Ryder, who was flashing his toothy grin at her. "Thank you, that is such a kind thought, but Kinley is sleeping, and my dinner is waiting for me in my fridge."

"What are you eating?" Ryder asked, stepping closer to her to examine Kinley.

"A sandwich."

"Those are for lunch."

"Yeah, that's what I had for lunch, too. But this time I'll have roast beef instead of turkey, so it will be different."

"What about strawberry shortcake?"

"Well—"

"Ryder," the serious cowboy interrupted, a little heat in his tone. "Take off the tutu and let's go see your grandmother."

"No! I won't take it off. I'm never taking it off."

"Hey, you found that thing on the ground at a gas station. I've told you not to touch trash, because it's covered in germs. Take it off. We'll run it though the washing machine—"

"Dad, no."

"Ryder, take it off."

"No. Never."

Ellie closed her mouth. Ryder burst into tears and ran over to her, sitting down on the cedar chips at her feet.

"Oh," she said, pushed a little off balance when Ryder shoved his face against her shins. She peeked up at the cowboy, who had his eyes closed, a pained expression on his face. "Things are happening fast around here today."

"I'm sorry you've been dragged into all this," he said. Then he opened his eyes and met her glance for a moment. A jolt of awareness shot into her. What was it with her and sad eyes?

"Don't worry about it a bit. I love kids." She realized he was staring at her hair, the same way he'd been glaring at Ryder's rainbow tutu.

Okay, the pink hair dye had turned out a lot brighter than she'd intended, more like a neon magenta. There had been a moment a month ago, before she'd left New Jersey, when she'd been looking in the mirror and couldn't stand her gloomy face for another day. Granted, changing her hair hadn't magically wiped away the bags under her eyes or the drawn hollow expression gazing back at her in the glass. Now, however, she could pass for an anime character at a Comic-Con. She'd compounded matters by giving herself a haircut with really short bangs and an attempt at dramatic layers, which actually appeared to be a badly styled mullet.

"Are you wondering where I paid for this fabulous hair style?" She smiled at him, brushing a lock behind her ear. "I'm afraid they're very exclusive about their clientele." They stared at one another. His eyes squinted. Ellie cleared her throat. "By the way, I like the tutu."

CHAPTER TWO

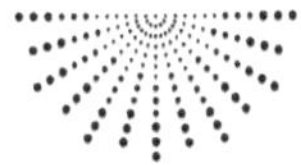

Saturday morning's dawn glowed above the mountaintops in the east, a streak of golden light. The brisk briny air tingled against her cheeks. Ellie's shoes crunched on the bark mulch as she paced around the little playground next to the duplex, patting Kinley's back, which was covered in a blanket, while her baby cried and cried.

The early morning had become an extension of the night before. Two hours of sleep wasn't enough. Kinley didn't have a fever, or a dirty diaper, or a hair wrapped around one of her toes. She had eaten fitfully and slept badly. Ellie blew out her breath, close to crying herself.

She walked back inside her duplex, ready to try again to get them both more sleep. At some point she would have to admit defeat, break down, and call her mother.

Two hours later, Ellie tiptoed out of Kinley's room, glancing over her shoulder to watch her baby's sleeping face. Hard knocks whacked against her front door. She froze. *Please, Kinley, please keep sleeping.* More banging knocks. Ellie hastily shut the bedroom door and hurried over to look through the living room window.

Ryder stood on the welcome mat, bouncing from foot to foot, staring forward. Ellie dropped the curtain closed, grabbed the baby monitor, and jogged over to her front door. She twisted the dead bolt and then jerked open the door, managing to swing it away from Ryder's fist before he banged on it a third time.

"Hi, Ellie. Where's Kinley?" Ryder said loudly.

"Good morning—let me step outside, thanks. Kinley is sleeping and I don't want our voices to wake her up."

"Oh." Ryder nodded, his eyes squinted together in thought. "Wait, don't babies sleep at night?"

"Yes, well, they learn to, but sometimes they have a hard time. And they do have to nap during the day because they need a lot of sleep."

"I don't need to nap."

"Yeah, you're a big kid now."

"Yeah, I am." Ryder scratched his head. "When do she wake up?"

"When does she wake up? Probably in about two hours. She's really tired, so I'm hoping she'll sleep longer, but I'm not counting on it."

"Okay. When is two hours?"

"Ten o'clock."

"That's my plan. You'll do my plan right, Ellie?"

"Um—"

"Ryder," shouted his dad, sounding very irritated.

"Uh oh—see you at ten, Ellie." Ryder took off for the driveway, mostly obscured by the garage jutting out and blocking her side of the duplex.

She yawned, walked back inside, and shut the door. Turning toward the couch, with her face watching Kinley's door, she tripped on a diaper bag. Groaning, she crawled forward the last few feet to roll onto the couch, her face smooshing into a throw pillow. Hopefully Ryder's dad would work out whatever plan his son was cooking up and prevent more banging on her door.

Ellie emerged from a dream of herself hammering down roof tiles—a strangely recurring dream since that summer she'd spent helping her stepfather reroof the three sheds in his backyard. More knocking. Ellie sprang up from the couch, then stared down at the baby monitor still clutched in her hand. Kinley shifted, moving her head on the crib mattress.

She stumbled to the front door and flung it open, cutting short Ryder's fist thumping against the wood.

"Hi, Ryder."

"It's ten, right? Time for the plan."

Kinley let out a furious howl. Ellie rubbed her forehead, her lips pressing together. The hope that a long nap would sweeten Kinley's temper died a whimpering death.

"The baby's crying," Ryder said earnestly.

"I'm going to go check on her."

"Yeah. She might have poop in her diaper."

Kinley coughed, then made choking sounds. Ellie dashed for the baby's bedroom, leaving the front door open. By the time she got to the crib, Kinley had cleared her throat and was back to full throttle, red-faced, wailing.

"Oh no, baby girl, Mommy's here." Ellie picked her up. Kinley's blue eyes focused on her, little fists flying out to thump against her shoulder.

Ryder popped up next to her. "It's okay, baby," he said, high-pitched and squeaky in an attempt at baby talk. He held out a stuffed lamb that rattled and shook it in Kinley's face.

Ellie blinked, gazing down at Ryder, groggily wondering what she should do next. The crying paused. Kinley was staring at Ryder too, a puzzled expression on her face.

"Hey, she likes me. Hello, you little cutie. Watch this,

Kinley." Ryder poked out his tongue and made raspberry sounds. Kinley stuck her fist in her mouth.

"Ryder, does your dad know where you are?"

"No. He's doing a poop."

"Oh, well, I think—"

A shout at her door interrupted her. "Ryder, are you in there?"

Ellie hurried out to the main room. "He's here," she called. "Come in."

Hands gripped her shirt, and she looked down to see Ryder hiding behind her back. "It's okay," she whispered at him, smiling.

Ryder's dad strode forward, a muscle twitching in his face. "Ryder, what the heck do you think you're doing? I told you not to leave our rental by yourself."

"Ellie's in our rental—she's on the other side of the house."

"Son, this is not okay."

"But, Dad, I told you, it's my plan. Ellie said we could do my plan at ten o'clocks. Then she needed my help with the baby."

"Well," Ellie said, suppressing a smile, "that's one version of what happened."

"Ryder, do not do this again. Let's go, right now."

"But my plan—I want Ellie to come, and she said she would!"

"I'm not sure what your plan is, Ryder," Ellie said.

"You're going to come with us, and baby Kinley too. We're going to a park."

"Ryder, what bug's gotten into you?" Ryder's dad sounded honestly baffled. "Ellie here did not agree to go to the park."

Ryder gripped her tighter. "Please, Ellie. You have to."

Kinley babbled down at Ryder. Ellie looked at Kinley's face, which was mellow for the first time in the last fifteen hours. Actually, she was a little tempted to get out for a while.

"Ryder," said his dad sharply, "no. Cut the crap, and get over here."

Wailing, tormented sobs burst out of Ryder. He threw himself down on the ground, clutched one of Ellie's feet, and bawled. Ellie glanced over at his dad, who had his eyes closed and was rubbing his face.

Even though she was an extremely new mom, she sensed the parenting code would frown on her interfering here. However, when worn-out-looking grumps were involved, better to ask for forgiveness rather than permission. She crouched down next to Ryder. "Hey, buddy, hold on a second. Will you listen for a minute? Let me think about this." Ryder gazed up at her, taking a shuddering breath. "Kinley and I can probably go to the park for a little while. I'll try to meet you there."

Ryder jumped to his feet with startling speed and hugged her. "You're the best, Ellie."

His dad cleared his throat. "We're going to his grand-mother's RV park."

"Yeah, Ellie—you're going to love it."

AUSTIN WATCHED the pink-haired young woman haul another bag out to her car, while still holding the baby. He shoved his hands in his pockets. Where the hell was the dad?

That was none of his business. Besides, it was easy enough to deduce the dad wasn't in the picture at the moment, even though she wore a wedding band around her finger. So did he, for that matter.

"Dad, I want Ellie to ride with us," Ryder said, for the third time.

"Nope. She's right about needing her own car. We might stay longer than she wants to, especially with the baby napping this afternoon."

The baby let out a howl. He couldn't sit there and watch her struggle anymore.

"Hey," he said, walking up to where she was bouncing the infant. "Let me help you a minute. Is she teething?"

The girl's big green eyes went round. "Teething?" she said, sounding like the idea had never occurred to her.

"What is she, about five months?"

"Yes, she is."

"Cutting in those two bottom teeth is rough on them. Does she take a binky? Or maybe a cold wet rag?" Jesus, he sounded like his mother. But he couldn't help himself. He'd seen her pacing around at dawn with the crying baby and figured, by the drawn, exhausted look on her face, that she'd had a long night.

"Oh, yes, I need to…" She started toward her car, then stopped, gazing down at her whimpering baby.

"I can hold her," he said, shocking himself. She stared up at him like a startled bird. "That bruiser over there was a fussy baby, so I've had some practice."

"Oh, yes. Thank you. She doesn't seem to mind strangers yet. Wait, I know this sounds a little odd, but I don't know your name."

"It's Austin."

"Right, okay, now I feel totally comfortable handing my child over to you." She smiled up at him, in what could be called a flirty way, and stepped closer.

He picked up the baby out of her arms, a scant fifteen pounds probably. "Come on, little red," he said, watching the baby's red scrunched-up face. She sniffed, one eye narrow as she glared up at him.

"Oh, my goodness, look at that," said Ellie. "I think she

likes you. Okay, give me three minutes—if you don't mind, I think I'll even comb my hair a little. Be right back. Wait, first I'll find that binky…" She stuck her head into the back of the car, still muttering to herself.

Ryder followed her around, his adoring puppy eyes alarming. Austin sighed. The boy was obsessed. After Ryder had spent ten minutes with the woman in the side yard playground, he'd latched on to her like an orphaned calf.

Ellie poured water from her water bottle onto a binky then popped it into Kinley's mouth. The baby blinked, a surprised expression on her face. Ellie ran off into her side of the duplex, Ryder on her heels.

He shook his head. Perhaps he should cut the whole thing short before Ryder got any more attached. Ellie was too damn nice to the kid, for a stranger. It wasn't her fault his son was starved for motherly attention, but he kept hoping she would become impatient with Ryder and say something sharp. The kid needed to back off a little. *I'm tired of being the bad guy.*

Instead, they both came out of her duplex laughing. She'd done something to her hair, pulled it back with some pins. Suddenly, she looked less like Strawberry Shortcake and more like a curvy, bright-eyed woman with high cheekbones and a pretty pink mouth. One dimple dented in her left cheek.

He swallowed, glancing down at the baby to distract himself. Kinley chewed on her rubber binky, eyes fluttering closed, her cap of bright red hair grown in a swirl around her head. Her mom always seemed to be smiling, or about to smile, with her little chin sticking up at a jaunty angle. It sidetracked him.

Ellie took the baby from him, her hands brushing against his arms. His body responded. Fresh apple and a little female musk wafted off her body. He turned away quickly to round up Ryder and get them both in the truck. The whole setup, single parents stuck side by side in a vacation rental, was a hook-up cliché waiting to happen. He wasn't that guy.

With Ryder buckled in, he drove the truck part way down the driveway then parked, waiting for Ellie to pull up behind him. She was too sweet for him. Too young. Too messy. Hell, he didn't want to deal with anyone's drama, and a vulnerable young mother on her own would be chock-full of land mines. *Might as well call her Trouble.*

"Dad," Ryder said, "Ellie said Kinley's daddy died. Died means dead right? Do you think he could be a zombie?"

"Died means dead. Zombies are not real."

"Kinley doesn't have a daddy."

Austin inhaled, looking in the rearview mirror at his son, trying to work out the right thing to say—truthful, but not too hard. Ryder, though, was already absorbed in his tablet, playing a video game with his eyes locked on the screen.

Ellie waved at him from the driver's seat in her little commuter car. She was a widow. He shifted to drive, and their two-car cavalcade drove out onto the coastal highway, between trees stretching out their branches to reach above the road.

Morality comes from within. There was Kant again, fresh in his mind. Yes, he agreed that we are responsible for our choices. He'd been reading about the categorical imperative, the philosopher's ideas about creating deep moral programming of the mind. It all boiled down to "Tell the truth, the whole truth, and nothing but the truth." Regardless of the consequences, never lie. He sniffed. Kant must have been a hard man.

Ellie's car swerved, teetering close to a steep drop at the edge of the road. The baby was probably crying. Her car straightened out and he sucked in a breath.

Ryder was turning out to be a fearless manipulator.

Reminded Austin a little of his own brother, Buck. Yesterday, Ellie was a stranger that didn't know his name, and he'd had no intention of spending time with her. Now, she was his son's best friend, on her way to meet his wife's mother. He rubbed the top of his head. If he was being honest with himself, he knew drama was barreling down the road at him like a semitruck with busted brakes.

ELLIE FOUND a parking spot in the crowded lot up by the entrance to the RV park. Above her, a row of cute little wooden cabins faced out over the grass lawn that sloped down to the wide river and the forested slope on the other side. O'Malley's RV Park appeared to be the busiest place in Siletz, between the tent campers, cabins, boaters, and RVers stretched across many acres. Anglers lined up along the shore of the river, their fishing lines cast out in the slow-moving water.

She was back, on the West Coast. An osprey plunged down from the sky into the river after a fish, its massive wings tucked into its sides. Ellie smiled. Between the barbecue smoke, salty marine air, and tantalizing aroma of deep-fried fish, the place had the feel of a laid-back festival.

Kinley had dozed off in her car seat during the drive over, after wailing for a solid five minutes. Ellie leaned back against the car, next to the open door, and closed her eyes. One bad night with the baby had torpedoed her into questioning her entire life. She was so in over her head.

"Hey," said a low voice next to her.

Ellie startled but knew before she opened her eyes that a tall, solemn-eyed cowboy stood next to her car. Austin, the baby whisperer. How did he become better looking each time she saw him?

"Hi, Ellie," said Ryder, bouncing on the balls of his feet. "Where's baby Kinley? I want to show her my fishing pole."

"Hi, she's sleeping, poor little pumpkin."

"Oh." Ryder shifted from foot to foot. "Is she done yet?"

"No, it's only been about five minutes. I'm thinking I'll hang out here for a while and catch up with you guys later."

"What, no—Ellie, you have to come with me." Ryder's face was scrunching up, as he took in big heaving breaths.

"Ryder, calm down," Austin said. He took off his hat and rubbed his head. "I could haul the baby in her car seat up to the park. Find a shady spot with a good chair. If you'd like."

"Really?" She had thought about doing that herself but decided she was too worn out. "Um, yeah, that sounds like an excellent plan. Her seat pops out of the base. I'll get all the gear and find a cotton blanket to drape over the top to keep the sun off her face…"

"I can help you, Ellie," said Ryder, following her to the trunk of her car.

"Oh, my goodness, that would be so great. Here you go, can you carry this picnic blanket for me?"

"No, I want to take the big bag."

"Wow, okay. But you'll give it back to me when you're tired right?"

"Yeah. But I won't get tired. I'm like Spider-Man."

"Right. Thanks, buddy. Just let me know when you want a break."

By the time she emerged from the back of the car, with Ryder carrying the backpack-style diaper bag on his back, Austin had the baby carrier extracted from its car seat base. A blanket covered the top, and a conked-out Kinley snoozed soundly inside.

"You know what?" she whispered at Austin. "You're a miracle worker. The last time I tried that, she woke up screaming."

Was that red on Austin's cheeks? *Oh my.* She held in a giggle and flashed a thumbs-up at Ryder. He grinned back at her.

As they trooped across the parking lot, all she carried was her small purse, slung over her shoulder, and a water bottle. Giddiness bubbled up inside her. Being part of Austin's little family wouldn't last long, probably just this afternoon, but about thirty pounds had been lifted from her shoulders —literally.

They walked up a dirt road toward the central compound, which was a general store inside half of a manufactured home with a big deck built onto the front. A path from the store led down to the water. Along the dock was a line of shacks where anglers cleaned their fish and could rent out boating gear. Many wooden docks poked out into the water, lined up like the fingers on a hand. Big trees dotted the area, providing shade for the picnic tables tucked under their boughs.

A woman looked up from sweeping as they approached, a big smile breaking out on her face. She reminded Ellie of Susan Sarandon but with dyed black hair: big eyes over round apple cheeks topped by a shag of loose curls.

"Ryder, there you are. Come give your granny a big hug." She held open her arms, crouching down, and Ryder dutifully walked forward to give her a stiff hug.

"Hi, Grandma Grace. Are we gonna catch some fish? Wait, I need to show Ellie the playground first."

Grace stared at her, then Austin, her eyebrows drawing together. "Hi," Ellie said, walking toward Grace. "I'm Ryder's new neighbor, Ellie. He decided to adopt me for the day and show me what he says is the best park in the world."

"Well, okay." Grace stood up and dusted off her pants in a preoccupied way.

Ellie snuck a glance at Austin, who stood impenetrably

still, holding the baby carrier. Awkward moments made her want to ramble, or ask questions. She bit on her bottom lip.

"Morning, Grace," Austin said. "Ellie's baby is sleeping in this carrier. Where can I put her down?"

"Oh, is that Ellie's baby? Silly me, of course she is. I get so distracted sometimes. Well, why don't you all come over to the back patio. Don't worry, Ryder, we'll get going in a minute. Let's get your friend and her baby settled in first."

Following Grace, they walked through the little store, stocked with fish bait and gear, T-shirts, soda, chips, and candy.

"Dad, I want an ice cream." Ryder leaned over a chest freezer that had a paper picture taped on the top showing different ice cream flavors.

"Maybe later."

Through the back door was a cement patio, shaded by a tall pine, with a round table in the corner and four lounge chairs set in the middle. "This is lovely," Ellie said, staring out at the light sparkling on the water.

"Okay," Grace said to her, "I'll be back to check on you in a bit. For now, let's get this boy doing."

Ryder's restraint snapped and he took off, running toward the playground in the middle of a big square of sand. Austin set down Kinley's carrier next to her then walked off with Grace.

Ellie stretched herself out on a lounge chair, luxuriously covered in thick cushions, and gazed up at the blue sky, clear except for a few streaks of high white clouds. Dogs barked and children shouted. A boat motored by on the water.

Austin had appeared shocked and put out when Ryder had invited her to go with them. She probably should have had mercy on him and backed out, considering he was visiting Ryder's grandmother. Selfishly, she was glad she hadn't. She let her eyes drift closed.

Also, invading Austin's dome of remoteness was…exciting. Little butterflies in her stomach took flight every time he came near. Teasing him was oddly satisfying. However, the man might still be married, for all she knew. At some point, she'd remember to look at his ring finger.

Like a bird let out of a cage, she wanted a little freedom after the last year of being cooped up in the row house in New Jersey, mourning Mitch. She'd loved him. Mitch had loved her. There had been so much potential there and a happy life around the corner—after they'd saved enough to get into their own home, after he'd finished graduate school, after they'd both settled into their marriage and stopped feeling like strangers to each other. Then he'd died. A sudden brain aneurysm had killed him while driving back from a job interview. He'd had time to pull over, probably with a crushing headache. They'd lost him.

Ellie rubbed her temples. Even though their marriage hadn't lasted long, she'd felt overwhelming grief after his death. She missed Nora. Mitch's sister had stepped in and helped in every way she could. Her father-in-law too. After Kinley was born, he'd cooked when he was home from work, and shopped, and done all the things necessary to keep a roof over their heads. How was she going to do this on her own?

CHAPTER THREE

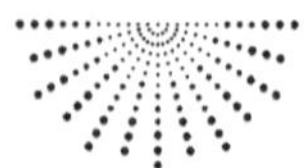

Austin sensed Grace preparing her questions. He stood still, giving her time, watching Ryder chase around another kid.

"So, Ellie is your neighbor?" Grace pursed her lips. "How long have you two been, um, friends?"

He knew how it all appeared: Grace couldn't help but wonder if he'd brought his new girlfriend along on the vacation. His back stiffened up, fed up with not being allowed to be young, or have a life outside of his role as father and jilted husband.

"Not long," he said, then stopped and tried to swallow the edge out of his voice. "Grace, I'm hopin we can talk about a lot of things while I'm here. Becky and I, we haven't been together in years. She lives in the apartment in Pendleton, and I'm out on the ranch. I know she's not waitin around... It's time. I have the divorce paperwork ready."

Grace sighed. "That girl came out crazy, and with a one-track mind. Rodeo fever. I don't think her head's going to clear till she wins her golden buckle. I'm sorry it didn't work out. You've put up with more than most."

"A baby didn't fit into her plans for herself."

"Mark my words, she's going to regret it once she realizes what she's lost."

Austin blew out a breath. "I can't do this anymore."

"No, you can't."

They stood together and watched Ryder dig in the sand surrounding the playground structure. His son had become the most important person in his world. The truth was, Becky didn't have any patience with little kids. He thought he'd stuck with his marriage so long because he wanted to give Ryder and Becky a chance to find a way with each other. But every time he got them together, they both suffered. He didn't understand it, but it was just the way things were.

Hopefully, when Ryder was older, he would connect with his mother. Becky might do well with a teenager.

"Ellie's good with Ryder, isn't she?" Grace said.

"So far."

Grace nodded her head. "If she's right next door, I think that's a great opportunity for you."

His sex-deprived body went in the wrong direction with that thinking. "She has her hands full with the baby."

"Yes, but a little distraction would do her good. Why don't you see if she'll babysit for you a bit, in the mornings, so you can get in quality fishing. They'd all be welcome over here. In fact, it'd be good to have her around to help keep an eye on Ryder. A little easy nanny work for her."

He grunted. One thing was certain, his son would be enthusiastically in favor of the idea, at least for a couple days. The downside would be everyone getting closer.

His control was stretching thin. He crossed his arms, trying to rein in imagining all the ways things could progress between him and Ellie. How could he explain, honestly, that he didn't want any strings attached? Just that phrase alone was oblique and selfish.

He and Ryder had two and a half more weeks on the coast. What he wanted was to go home and not feel guilty. His burden of wrongdoing was already too heavy. No, starting something with Ellie would not be simple. And there were always strings attached.

ELLIE AWOKE from a doze with a start. Kinley babbled excitedly from beneath the blanket she'd pulled down over her face. Ellie jumped up and freed Kinley's face. Post-nap breastfeeding and diaper-changing took up the next half hour.

Ryder ran by and waved at her before skipping down to the dock with his dad and grandmother. Ellie stared at the array of gear laid out on a lounge chair, her foggy, sleep-deprived brain insisting she had forgotten something. Babies required a lot of decision-making: what to wear, what to buy, when to do this or that vitally important thing…

Kinley did her squeaky pre-crying protest. The time to dither was over. Ellie picked her up and then spent the next twenty minutes trying to figure out how to use the front-facing baby carrier she'd brought along, for the second time. The first time she'd used the thing had been while traveling and Nora had been there to help her strap it on correctly.

With her baby finally loaded into the harness strapped to her chest, and a yellow sun hat velcroed to Kinley's head, they both walked down the gravel path to the long wooden dock where Ryder was fishing.

"Ellie, watch me," Ryder called out. He reeled in his line then managed to cast a few feet into the water.

"Very nice. Somebody is back at the fish-cleaning station with a really big one." Ellie glanced back toward the open shed she'd walked past on her way down the dock.

"Seventeen-pound salmon," said Grace. "I took his picture for our Facebook page."

"Wow. No wonder this place is so popular."

"Ellie, do you want to try?" Ryder held out his pole.

"I do." She took Ryder's kid-sized fishing pole out of his hands. "I'll hold it for a quick minute. Kinley has grabby hands."

A suddenly energized Kinley darted out her hand toward the pole, kicking her feet, and managed to snag the fishing line on her fingers. The dock rocked under Ellie's feet as she startled. The fishing pole made a wheezing whirl and unbelievable amounts of clear line pooled on the ground at her feet.

"Woah." Ryder chortled, pointing at Kinley and laughing.

"Wait, hold still for a minute," said Austin, stepping in close to untangle the line from around Kinley's hand. Ellie glanced at his face, placid as ever. He smelled like tangy man-soap.

"Wow," she said, holding the pole stretched out as far away from Kinley as she could reach. "I'm sorry, Ryder. I thought I was prepared for the grabby hands but was tricked again."

Austin took the pole out of her hand. He stepped away and an absurd pang of loss pulled at her. She swallowed and forced a smile on her face.

Actually, he was the last man she wanted to get involved with, even for a fling—too obviously withdrawn, uncommunicative, and emotionally unavailable. No, she was a mother now, and had to be picky. No more flings.

"It's okay," said Ryder. "I'm done fishing."

"That girl looks just like the Gerber Baby, but with red hair," said Grace. "What a cutie."

Ryder walked over and leaned in close to Kinley. "She is such a little cutie patootie, squishy wishy." He reached out a hand to tickle the baby's tummy. Kinley grabbed Ryder's nose. "Honk," he squeaked.

Ellie and Grace laughed. Ryder flapped his arms like a chicken and waggled his bottom, dancing around with his tongue hanging out. Even Austin cracked a smile.

Austin took her and Ryder for a short ride in the small aluminum fishing boat Grace was lending to him while he stayed in the area. The little gas motor puttered them around on the wide, placid river that opened up to a bay.

Grace had stayed on shore to mind the store since her husband was away on a supply run. Austin's silence was somehow relaxing in the back of the boat, his attention seemingly fixated on the pole he was fishing with. Ryder, on the other hand, kept up a steady flow of chatter. They played I Spy and watched for animals. Kinley babbled happily for the first ten minutes, then abruptly became fussy, probably sick of her baby carrier, and started reaching up her arms to be held. Austin turned the boat around and headed back toward the dock.

By the time Ellie stepped out of the boat, Kinley was crying in earnest. "It's okay, pumpkin, give Mommy a minute."

"Is she okay?" Ryder's face was scrunched up.

"Maybe this carrier is pinching her leg a little—I'm not sure what's the matter. I get a little nervous unstrapping the harness when she's wiggling so much."

"Here," said Austin, stepping in front of her. "Can I lift her out of there for you?"

"Yes, but watch out, she has a mean right hook when she's angry."

Ellie undid a few buckles. Austin pulled Kinley up and out of the harness in one smooth motion. He put her, tummy down, over his shoulder and patted her back. Kinley burped. The crying slowed to snuffling, and Austin moved her lower against his chest. Kinley put her head down on his shoulder and sighed.

"Wow." Ellie realized her mouth had been hanging open. "That was pure magic."

"Come on, Ellie, let's go get some lunch," Ryder said.

"Thank you, but I have to head home now. Kinley didn't sleep well last night and needs a nice long nap in her crib. This was such a good idea, Ryder, thank you for inviting me."

"But you can't go, I want to be with you," Ryder said, his bottom lip sticking out.

"Hey, don't worry, I'll see you at the house later."

"Ryder," Austin said, "go check on your grandma. Then we'll help Ellie with her things. Go on, we'll wait for you."

Ryder sniffed. "Okay," he said, glaring at his father's face. "Don't leave, Ellie, I'll be right back." He ran up the path toward the store.

Austin sighed. "Hey, Ellie, can we talk for a minute?"

"Of course."

"Thank you for being so kind to my son. He's a little fixated on you at the moment." Austin paused, squinting.

"He's a great kid. I'm really honored he wants to be my friend."

"Grace came up with an idea. I'm not sure it's a good one, but thought I'd see what you think. Don't hesitate to say no if this doesn't work for you." He stared intently at her.

"I won't."

"Well, I could use a part-time babysitter for the mornin. Paid, of course. That way I can get out fishin before Ryder wakes up. Be back by lunch. We'd have a slew of details to work out but that's the gist of it. Is that too tough to handle with the baby? I know infants are a lot."

Ellie blinked, biting her lip. She'd really like to make a little money to offset the frivolous drain of the vacation rental on her meager savings. Also, being by herself all the time was harder than she'd imagined.

"Let's try it. I'd like to help out and, frankly, I could use the company. And I am up early these days—a bit shocking, after being a night owl all my life." She pulled out her phone. "Can I have your number? I'll send you a text so we can figure out the details. Oh, there's Ryder back already. Do you want to tell him or should I?"

"Go ahead. Hand me your phone, I'll type in my number for you."

"Ellie, Grandma Grace made us sandwiches for lunch—there's one for you too. She said if you're leaving you can take yours in a doggie bag. I think she meant a lunch bag, since you don't have a dog."

"Wow, I can't wait to try her sandwiches, how thoughtful of her." Ellie smiled, her stomach reminding her that she was half starved. "Hey, Ryder, listen to this. Your dad is wondering if I can hang out with you in the morning tomorrow until about lunch, while he goes fishing. Does that sound okay, if I'm in your house when you wake up?"

Ryder frowned, glaring at his dad suspiciously. "Dad, you're going to take me fishing still, right?"

"Yes. We'll take out the boat again when we visit Grandma Grace."

"Okay." Ryder reached out and took her hand, gripping it tightly. "I can't wait to show you my toys. You'll play with me?"

"Yes, I will." Apparently, Ryder wasn't letting go of her hand anytime soon.

The little boy turned and gave her a hug, squeezing tightly. "Ellie, I want to spend all the vacation with you."

~

THEY DECIDED Ellie would let herself into Austin's around six, Sunday morning, shortly after he had left to go fishing. The door was unlocked. Ellie stepped inside Austin's side of the duplex, hauling Kinley, in her sling, and the diaper bag.

His duplex was decorated differently than hers. Where her duplex was beige and linen, his was brown leather and oak. The scent of coffee and pastry pulled her toward the long kitchen bar to her left like she was a fish on a line. A note was taped to the counter that said, "Help yourself."

She smiled, surprised he'd thought to feed her. A flaky croissant was melting in her mouth before she'd taken another breath. Her fridge and pantry were sparse compared to the feast of choices spread out around this kitchen: cookies, bagels, brownies, golden fresh bread, crackers, a tower of fruit and more.

An infant high chair sat incongruously in the corner of the kitchen. She walked over in a daze, blinking, wondering if it was real. It was exactly what she'd been desperately wanting ever since leaving New Jersey.

The note taped to the high chair said, "Grace remembered she had this in storage yesterday and thought you could get some use out of it." Ellie held the paper to her chest then crouched down to examine how the tray slid out. The lingering smell of spray cleaner clung to the old but solidly built plastic surfaces.

"Kinley, you are in business for some solid foods. Bananas for babies, beautiful nanas for bubbly babies."

Kinley stared up at her with her mouth open, perfectly ready for a culinary adventure.

Five minutes later and Kinley was strapped into her high chair harness, smashing banana chunks on her tray. Ellie pulled out her phone to dictate a text to Austin.

Ellie: Thank you so much for the high chair. Last

night I was considering which overpriced option to have shipped here because I was desperate. This is perfect! And thank you for breakfast as well. I'm making serious inroads into everything. Fair warning, I love all the foods. Speaking of, what does Ryder like for breakfast?

His response came within a minute.

Austin: You're welcome. Cereal.

Ellie huffed, and resisted the urge to text him again. The man was not interested in conversation, or her for that matter, and teasing him would be rude at this point. She tapped her chest then stood up and went about finding the cereal and bowls.

Ryder woke up at seven, shuffling out of his bedroom with his brown hair sticking up on one side.

"Morning, Ryder. Kinley and I are in the kitchen."

"Hi, Ellie." He blinked sleepily. "Where's my dad?"

"Fishing for a couple more hours. I'm here to hang out with you, just like we talked about yesterday."

"Oh." He walked over to her and wrapped his arms around her middle, pressing his face into her side.

She hugged him back, startled by how quickly he was becoming affectionate with her. In her experience, usually five- and six-year-olds were slow to warm up to a stranger.

"I've gotta pee." He pulled away from her and shambled off to the bathroom.

Two hours later and Ryder was asking to go to the beach every ten minutes, while running laps around the room.

"Kinley is napping right now," Ellie said, reminding him again. "When she wakes up, if there's time, I'll call your dad and see what he thinks. How about we go out to the playground again for a while? Then we could play a game of Candy Land."

"Yes, yes, yes."

While Ryder was occupied with rolling his Hot Wheels car collection down the playground slide, Ellie called Austin. He didn't answer and the call clicked over to voice mail.

"Hi, Austin, this is Ellie. I'm wondering about taking the kids to the beach—I'm thinking Old Nye Beach in Newport. Ryder really wants to go and is pretty restless. But Kinley is sleeping at the moment, and I want to make sure it's okay with you before I make any plans. Okay, I'll try texting too. Bye."

Cell phone reception was spotty in the coast range mountains and he'd probably driven, or boated, deeper into a wilderness area for fishing. Ellie tapped her foot. She'd like to get over to the beach.

Discreetly, she started preparing the diaper bag and a beach bag. When Ryder pointed out his box of brand-new sand toys, going to the beach was feeling like a forgone conclusion. Except, Austin still hadn't texted or called her back.

"Please, Ellie, please," Ryder begged once Kinley was up and getting her diaper changed. "Please, can we go to the beach?"

He'd worn her down, and she was totally swayed by his big brown eyes and hands clenched together in earnest supplication. "Will you hold my hand when we're next to the street?"

"Yes."

"Will you stay close to me the whole time?"

"I promise I will."

Obviously, she was a horrible babysitter. No way should she be taking Ryder out to a public place without his dad's consent. Irrationally, she was a little put out with Austin for being unreachable—it was her and Ryder's vacation too. They wanted to do things.

"Okay, put on your shoes and find a hat. We're going to Newport."

She left a note for Austin, and tried calling and texting one more time, leaving messages explaining the plan when he didn't respond.

Getting both kids into the car, plus all the stuff, took longer than she'd imagined it should. *But we're on our way.* She adjusted her sunglasses and grinned at the passing fir tree forest through the driver's side window. Her leg was bouncing, and she could have laughed out loud. She cleared her throat—she had to get out more.

The drive to Newport was only twenty minutes, but once they pulled onto the main road through town there was a wall of traffic. "Oh my gosh, Ryder, I forgot about the holiday."

"Holiday?"

"Tomorrow is the Fourth of July. This place is jam-packed with tourists. We might not find a parking spot." Ellie glanced at Kinley in the rearview mirror, who kicked her legs and threw her teething toy on the floor.

"It'll be fine," said Ryder, not raising his face up from his tablet video game.

Twenty minutes later, she considered giving up. She had been circling endlessly, looking for a parking spot in walking distance of Old Nye Beach, along with about a hundred other cars. Sweat trickled down the back of her neck. Kinley started whimpering.

A narrow spot opened up in front of her. Immediately a car going the other way slammed on its brakes and started to U-turn toward the parking. "Oh no you don't," she muttered under her breath, accelerating forward while letting out a quick honk.

"Go Ellie," Ryder shouted from the back seat. Kinley started crying in earnest.

She got to the spot first. Then she stopped traffic behind while she relearned how to parallel park in a spot barely bigger than her car.

"Phew," she called over the baby's wailing, parked at last, "we made it."

They had an eight-block march to get to the public beach, with multiple bags and no stroller. "My feet are tired," Ryder complained, dragging his sand bucket on the ground.

"Almost there, buddy, and I mean it this time."

When they turned a corner and the beach came into glorious sight at the bottom of a steep downhill sidewalk, Ryder took off running. "Ryder," Ellie yelled, forcing her trembling, overburdened body to move faster, "wait!"

Ryder kept going, stumbling once but managing not to trip and fall on his sprint downhill. He paused long enough to kick off his shoes when he got to the sand then took off for the crashing waves.

"Oh no, oh no," Ellie muttered to herself over and over. Kinley bounced in her carrier and gurgled, hands waving.

Panting, she stepped onto the sand, moving forward even while her heart leaped into her throat. She didn't see him— there were too many bodies.

"Ryder!" she shouted, tears burning her eyes. Why, why was she such a stupid idiot?

A brown-haired boy carrying a red bucket caught her eye. It was Ryder, already dumping sea water onto the sand. She let out a sob.

Kinley reared back against her chest. "It's okay," Ellie croaked. Kinley started crying. The closer they got to the ocean, the louder Kinley screamed.

Ellie dropped the bags in an open spot of sand then took Kinley out of her carrier, all the while keeping a sharp eye on

Ryder. Facedown against her shoulder, Kinley clutched her shirt, unhappily sobbing. Ellie walked forward again. More screaming.

At last, she made it to Ryder, who was playing in the spongy wet sand at the edge of the water. "Ryder," she shouted at him until he looked up at her and waved. "Kinley is afraid, we have to move back further."

"Don't worry, I'll be fine."

"No, Ryder, we have to stay together."

"Okay, okay, give me a minute."

Ellie bounced Kinley and rubbed her back, while all the people around them shot sidelong glances at the mom with the terrified baby. "Come on, buddy, let's go have a snack."

After more coaxing, and he'd filled up his bucket with water, at last Ryder was ready to walk up to drier sand and the spot where she'd left the bags. Ellie put out the picnic blanket and Ryder was willing to sit for a minute to eat a cookie. She loaded Kinley in the sling and started breastfeeding, covering Kinley's head with a blanket. Kinley snuffled but settled down. Ellie dug out her phone.

There were four missed calls from Austin. She stabbed at her phone.

"Hey," he said, picking up after the first ring.

"Austin, I'm so sorry about all this—I forgot about the holiday and Ryder really wants to be in the water but Kinley is afraid. Um, this is a little tougher than I thought it would be."

"Hang in there," Austin said, calmly. "I found parking. I'll be down there in ten." He hung up.

Ellie put away her phone, ignoring the pile of messages she needed to respond to, and sagged. If she was lucky, they'd all survive another ten minutes.

CHAPTER FOUR

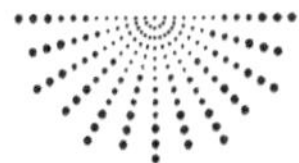

Austin spotted the pink hair right away on the crowded beach. He marched across the sand, boots on, not sure what he was going to say to her. The muscle in his cheek hammer-spasmed, vibrating his face.

His son sat in the sand, next to her picnic blanket, digging industriously with a shovel. Ryder laughed at something Ellie said. A little of his anger crumbled.

"Daddy," Ryder shouted, waving at him. "Look at my mud pie Ellie taught me to make."

Ryder had on the damn flashy rainbow tutu skirt again. *Damnit.* He'd convinced him to put the thing in the washing machine, and then left it hanging to dry in the backyard. He'd meant to hide it in the laundry room. Instead, it poked out of the ground while Ryder buried himself in sand.

"Are you the mud pie? Son, you're shivering. Time for dry clothes. It's barely sixty degrees out here today."

"No," Ryder yelled, dragging out the word into a wail.

The baby started fussing and Ellie pulled her away from her chest. Austin caught a glimpse of pink nipple without wanting to. *Damnit.* He should have known better than to look while she was nursing.

"Austin," Ellie said over the caterwauling of the children. "I'm really sorry about this."

He kept his eyes firmly on the water. "Yep."

"What, Ellie?" Ryder sniffled. "Why are you sorry, Ellie?"

"I'm sorry that I took you to the beach without your dad's permission, Ryder. It turned out to be a little dangerous since you ran away from me when you saw the water."

"I was excited."

"Also," Austin said, "Ellie didn't have your car seat booster."

"Oh, my gosh, I didn't even think of that." Ellie covered her face with her hand. "I'm so sorry."

"Dad, we'll use the car seat next time."

"There isn't going to be a next time, Ryder."

"Noooooooo."

And then both kids were screaming. Ellie stood up and bounced the baby, walking a little distance away, probably to give him a chance to calm down Ryder. After five minutes of getting nowhere, Ryder ran away from him and put his arms around Ellie. Austin took his hat off and rubbed his head.

"Hey," Ellie called, walking over, holding a still-crying Ryder's hand. "Austin, can we switch for a minute? Kinley is frightened of the ocean. I was thinking you could stay up here with her, and keep your boots dry too, while Ryder and I run down to the water and rinse off some sand. Then Ryder will put on dry clothes. Sound okay?"

"Fine," he said, sounding like a disgruntled asshole, which possibly summed him up at the moment.

She handed over the baby and her blanket, then ran off toward the water with a now-cheerful Ryder. They jumped into the water, laughing and chasing waves. He sat with

Kinley, the other grump. Kinley sighed and grabbed his chin with her hand.

"I'm not big on salt water either," he said to the baby. She scratched his neck with a jagged fingernail. "You know what? Your mama is too stinkin nice. I'm gonna hold it against her."

ELLIE SHOOK out the picnic blanket while Austin stood with the kids. She bit her lip, holding in a smile. He was pissed—and she was sorry about that. But the smoldering, intense way he stared at her was…it sent shivers down the back of her neck.

She stuffed everything in the backpack, taking the opportunity to turn her back on him for a moment. The man had some fire in his belly. At first glance, you might think his nose was too big and that his chin stuck out. Also, he was quiet and seemed to try to disappear at times. But angry—his eyes snapped at her, his body tense, with the musculature in his shoulders and neck defined. She liked angry. Obviously, there was something very wrong with her.

Bags on her shoulders, she stood up. He nodded at her and started trekking toward the promenade where there was a stairwell up into the old town. Ryder ran around Austin, wet tutu dripping on his dry clothes, while Kinley grabbed at Austin's hat. He lowered the baby down into a football hold, which made her giggle, and kept walking.

Ellie sighed. For a few more moments she could pretend they were a little family and she had a partner, making life five hundred times easier. The back of her eyes burned. *Crap.*

Ryder ran back to her, circling around her like a collie herding sheep. "Come on, Ellie," he shouted, racing forward again.

She caught up to Austin at the stairs. He took the tote bag out of her hands without a word. "Thanks," she croaked.

"Dad, I'm hungry." Ryder bounced up and down on the balls of his feet.

"Yep, lunchtime," Austin said.

Ellie's stomach rumbled. She cleared her throat. "See you guys later. I'll wash up Ryder's swim stuff and leave it all on the laundry line." She held her arms up for Kinley, who leaned back in Austin's arms to smile at her upside down.

"What? No, Ellie, you can't go." Ryder gawked at her like she'd just suggested murdering kittens.

"That was super fun, Ryder, thank you for going to the beach with me. I'm going to head to my car now."

"No, Dad, I want Ellie to come with us."

Austin looked up at the sky, still holding Kinley. "Hey," he said, "can we get you lunch? I made reservations at that fish and chips place just up the sidewalk."

"Oh, I don't want to barge in…"

"Come on," Austin said, and he started walking, taking her baby with him. Ryder flashed a grin at her, fist pumping against his side like he'd just won a tennis match.

"Well, okay then." She followed Austin up the sidewalk to a steamy café where they magically jumped the long line of people waiting and were seated immediately.

Ellie leaned over in her chair and whispered at Austin, "How did you do that?"

"I tipped the host a fiver to text me when our table was ready." The corner of his mouth turned up.

"Wow."

"Ellie, can I sit on your lap?"

"Oh." She glanced at Austin, whose face tensed up like his gut was clenching. "Um, for a little while." There was just something about Ryder—she didn't want to say no to him.

The little boy settled onto her lap, a solid sixty pounds

she thought, and immediately zoned out into his tablet video game. The kid was a big five-year-old.

"Hello, everybody," said a smiling server wearing a cute yellow dress uniform with a Crabby's logo on the chest. "Aren't you all just the cutest family ever. What can I get ya?"

Ellie smiled, her face hot, and glanced at Austin to see what he would do. He raised an eyebrow at her. "Fish and chips for me," she said.

"Three fish and chips platters, and a couple of bowls of chowder." Austin shifted Kinley to his other shoulder. "I'll take a pint of Pelican lager as well. Ellie?"

"Lemonade." Oh, for the day when she wasn't breast-feeding and could freely imbibe again. For now, she was on the clock.

"You got it," said the server, then hustled off in a businesslike fashion.

The screen on Ellie's phone flashed with an incoming text. She glanced down at it on the table. Two missed messages. One from Mari, her best friend. The other was from Todd, the guy she'd been in a situation-ship with, before Mitch. Less than two years ago, unbelievably.

Ellie tapped a finger on the table but didn't pick up her phone. Todd lived in the area. Or at least he had a big pot-growing operation nearby, one of several he was involved in, and spent a chunk of his time guarding his greenhouses and living in a trailer out in the woods. The potential for seeing Todd was one of the reasons she'd landed in Siletz. And yet, now she didn't know what to text him back.

She glanced at Austin, who sat entertaining Kinley with a spoon in his hand. He peered over his shoulder at the server walking back toward them, their drinks on a tray. A man like Austin would never pick her. She was sweet, and silly, and was passed over for the challenging and sultry women every time.

The lemonade was cold and soothing on her dry throat. Todd wouldn't be right for her. Her problem was that a big part of her was still convinced she was a young and single twenty-three-year-old, free to enjoy life. It wasn't that she was done mourning Mitch, or that she was ready to move on, it was that being alone was killing her.

"You're quiet," Austin said, startling her out of staring at her napkin.

"Oh, yeah, I guess I am. It's guilt, probably. Here I am, having lunch with you, thrust into your life, somehow, and you didn't choose any of it. So, on top of being the world's worst babysitter, there's that too."

"What?" Ryder looked up from his screen.

"Hey, my legs are hurting now. Can you grab your chair again, Ryder?"

"Sure, Ellie." Ryder slid off her lap. He scooted his chair close to hers before sitting down.

"What you called 'somehow,' is sittin next to you. The force of nature there is spoiled, if you can't tell." Austin shook his head at his son, but Ryder was too intent on his game to notice.

"He's great."

"That skirt he's wearing is going to cause a big stir at home on the ranch. I wish I knew what to do about it."

"Do about it?" Ellie felt her eyebrows come together.

"It's a conservative community."

"Okay," Ellie said, blinking in thought, surprised by how disappointed she felt. "Well, if it were me, I'd show him love and support no matter what."

Austin grunted. "I'll be at his wedding, or whatever, no matter what." He took a sip from his pint. "Gettin bullied isn't good for any kid. And part of this is I don't want the attention."

"You're shy."

He sighed theatrically. "Yeah, I guess I am."

She smiled. "Does it hurt your eyes when you see my pink hair?"

"That's more than pink."

"Mellow is for wimps. Ryder and I know how to have fun."

"Yeah," said Ryder.

She looked at Austin with her eyebrows up. He shrugged. You never really knew when kids were listening.

The food came and they focused on their plates with hungry intensity. Ellie made it halfway through her platter. Kinley grunted, rubbed her eyes, then started her turn-into-a-grumpy-pumpkin routine, beginning with a messy diaper.

Ellie realized there would be no stopping at the store for bread and diapers if she didn't hurry there immediately. She stood up, grabbed her things, hugged Ryder, and waved goodbye to the solemn-eyed cowboy on her way toward the door.

Lunch had been nice, and her heart stuttered when she made eye contact with Austin one last time, but she was glad to have created a wobbly barrier against her little infatuation with him. She understood Ryder a lot more than Austin.

Austin stood in front of Ellie's door at five in the morning, raised his fist, and knocked softly. Her light was on, and he could hear dishes clattering inside. He shook his head at himself, disgusted he hadn't been able to say no to Ryder.

He hadn't said yes either. But as the evening had worn on, and Ryder had chattered on about Ellie, he'd realized he didn't have the strength to be a hard dad at the moment. *Am I afraid?*

Her door swung open, and Ellie stood there in a ripped,

oversized T-shirt that was hanging off one shoulder. And no pants. The bright light behind her shone through the T-shirt, highlighting every curve. Austin swallowed, his mouth dry.

"Mornin," he said, turning his body away from hers and fixing his eyes on the window frame next to her door. Jesus, he was ready to pin her against a wall.

She yawned and his eyes darted back to her long enough to see her cover her mouth. "Good morning," she said. "Am I supposed to babysit? I can't remember anything these days."

Austin rubbed his head. What the hell had he decided to say to her? "No, we didn't have anything planned."

"Oh, okay."

He glanced at her, and she was smiling at him. Damn woman. Was she doing this on purpose? The heat of his deprived and desperate flesh was cooking his brain. He should probably get the hell away from her and cancel his plans.

"Would you like me to watch Ryder again today? I'd love to. Looked at my phone this morning and realized it's the Fourth of July and I don't have any plans. Kinley and I really like her high chair you brought back for us, by the way. What a sanity saver. I thought I knew what to do with an infant, from babysitting and nannying jobs, but I'm learning a new lesson every single day. Okay, I'll be over there in about fifteen. Luckily, I still have a bag mostly packed from yesterday. Have a nice morning, Austin."

The baby babbled and then something crashed to the floor. Ellie turned around and ran toward the kitchen, leaving the door wide open. A moment later and Kinley shouted cheerfully, while Ellie chattered back at her.

Austin reached forward and closed the door. He stood for a moment, staring at white paint. What the hell was wrong with him? Her pink-haired hot-mess of a self was not his type. The last two years without sex were making him crazy.

He got into his truck and shut the door. There were women he could be dating. All kinds of normal women, who fit into his life and had done things like show up at his house with a hot casserole and a thin reason for being there. Every time that particular hot-dish-making gal had tried to talk to Ryder he had cringed and run away.

The truck roared to life, and he backed down the driveway. If he was being honest with himself, he'd have to admit nobody had stirred him up enough. Well, he was ready for them now. The days of being wary and gun-shy were over—as soon as he got back home.

ELLIE STARED at her phone where another text message from Todd lit up the screen. She bit her lip, spacing out on the small pile of dishes in the sink while the kids ate a snack. Her foot started to jiggle.

"Where are we going today, Ellie?" Ryder licked peanut butter off his fingers. "Daddy put my car chair over there." Ryder pointed at the booster seat propped up against the wall by the garage door.

"Oh, I don't know. Your dad and I didn't talk about it, and he was pretty upset about yesterday." She glanced toward the window. The weather forecast was predicting a little heat.

"It's fine." Ryder gulped down half the milk in his glass. "He drew a picture for you over there."

Ellie walked over to the round kitchen table in the dining room, with a shaggy area rug underneath it. The kids ate in the kitchen above the scrubbable floor, whenever she could help it.

Her picture was a note from Austin with a hand-drawn map below a few scrawled sentences. He'd written, "If you feel like getting out, I'll meet you at Moonshine Park. Bring water gear."

An hour later, she pulled into the state park tucked into a forest by the river, not far off the highway. The big grassy lawn, dotted with towering fir trees, was a busy hive of parents and children. Picnic blankets and floaty tubes dotted the green next to the wide shallow swimming hole in the river.

Ryder helped her to haul their gear to a clear spot on the lawn, and set up the picnic blanket. He bounced on the balls of his feet, rainbow tutu fluttering. She put Kinley in her carrier and applied sunblock to everyone. When a ball rolled onto their blanket, Ryder picked it up, then shot off with a group of kids.

For the next hour, she trailed Ryder through the park, Kinley gazing around with wide eyes or kicking her feet happily in the cool river water as they waded in. Ryder ran to her for quick hugs and cold juice boxes. "This is the best day ever," he said, resting on the blanket for a moment with a cookie in his hand. "Where's Daddy?"

"On his way. He's picking up lunch for us." Ellie glanced over at the parking lot, not spotting the big gray truck. She adjusted her bikini top under the tank cover-up dress. The man might be made of stone, for all he noticed half-naked women parading around in front of him. Her cheeks warmed up. Opening the door that morning, barely covered, had been one of her wacky ideas that came out of nowhere. Like a psychotic lust-crazed alien had taken over her body.

Kinley kicked her foot, her heel landing in the soft, still bulgy, tissue around Ellie's abdomen. Ellie grunted, adjusting the baby's breastfeeding position, reminded yet again of her altered post-pregnancy body. She used to jog. On a good month she'd even popped into the gym a few times. Now she jiggled. No doubt the cowboy wanted a woman as lean and toned as he was.

"There he is." Ryder leaped to his feet and ran off across the grass.

Austin strolled toward them from the parking lot, straight and tall, wearing his tan cowboy hat. Did he notice the heads that swiveled his way? He seemed to stiffen when he saw Ryder wearing the tutu. Ellie sighed. Gorgeous or not, he wasn't perfect.

Kinley finished breastfeeding as Austin walked up to their picnic blanket. "Pizza for lunch? Smells amazing, thank you." She glanced up from rearranging her clothing to smile up at him, only he was crouched down with his back to her. Was he screening her from being seen as she shifted her clothing underneath the scarf she'd dropped over her chest? She'd never been particularly modest but she didn't think anything shocking had been visible...

"Yeah, Dad, thanks for the food," Ryder said, plopping down next to Ellie with a slice of cheese pizza in his hand.

"Your Grandma Grace has been calling," Austin said. "She's making us dinner and has a few surprises. You're invited too, Ellie."

"Oh, that's so kind of her." Ellie met Austin's gray-blue gaze, which turned the dial of her brain to haze and static. She looked down at Kinley's half-lidded, blinking eyes, then turned the baby over her shoulder and gently patted her back.

"Wait, I don't want to go over there yet, Dad. There's no place to go swimmin."

"Well, son, we're having lunch here."

They ate, and Ryder extracted a few sentences from Austin about his morning fishing, which hadn't netted any monster fish. Kinley faded fast, yawning and exhausted but unable to fully fall asleep. Ellie sighed. She should have left an hour ago, but sticking to a strict routine defeated her nearly every day.

"Give me your car keys," Austin said.

"What?"

"I can rig up a napper for her with the car seat."

"Oh." Was a short nap in the park better than a later but better-quality nap that would push back bedtime? *I don't know.* "Okay," she said, mostly because she couldn't stand going back to the duplex and spending all afternoon moping around inside.

Five minutes later, Austin walked over holding Kinley's car seat and a windshield sunshade, which must have come out of his truck. Kinley went into her seat, eyes drooping closed. Austin draped the crinkly sunshade over the top in one smooth motion so that it tented up over the car seat, supported by the wide plastic carry handle. They were already under a tall pine tree, so Kinley's rigged-up napper created cool dark shade. She settled into it without a fuss.

"Wow, wow, wow," Ellie said. "You're a little magic." She smiled at Austin and their eyes locked together. Her breath caught. *Oh. Boy.* She wanted to lean in so bad...

"Ellie, come swimmin with me," Ryder shouted, running up to the blanket from where he'd been playing in some sand. Kinley's foot jerked.

"Sure," she said, "if it's okay with your dad."

"Go on. I'll guard the baby fort."

Ellie smiled, leaning a little closer to him to grab her towel and catching his leathery, grassy scent. His forearm muscle flexed when her fingers brushed his hand.

"Come on, Ellie. Wait, I've got to pee. Will you walk up to the toilets with me?"

"Yep." She slipped on her flip-flops and followed Ryder toward the squat building with public bathrooms. Austin had a big innertube waiting for them by the time they made it back to the picnic blanket.

Ryder kept her in the water for the next hour, pushing the tube upstream to the little waterfall then floating back across the wide eddy of water. When she glanced over at the picnic blanket, Austin was there, reading a book next to the sleeping Kinley in her car seat.

Ellie kicked her legs in the cold water, weaving Ryder on his floaty through the crowd of swimmers constantly in motion. She blinked a splash of drops out of her vision, the bright sun bouncing off the surface of the river and blinding her eyes. *I'm living. I'm here.* A rebirth, giddy and effervescent, bubbled up inside her—maybe it would only last for one day, but the shell of grief around her had cracked.

CHAPTER FIVE

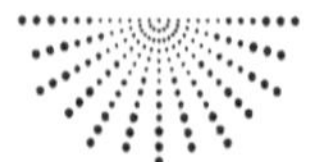

Austin checked his phone again, then scanned the parking lot for the dinky little commuter car. *Why the hell am I worried?*

"Where's Ellie?" Ryder asked for about the fifth time. "I want to show her my surprises."

"Ryder," said Grace, her eyebrows pinched together, "come and paint the bike with me. Everything's ready by the shed."

"Grandma, I have to show Ellie. The bike is the same as her hair." Ryder rolled back and forth on his bright pink bicycle, rainbow tutu barely high enough to avoid getting shredded by the chain.

"Come on, son," Austin said. "Let's do another lap of the RV park. Watching so close for Ellie might make her jumpy."

"Like a frog?"

"More like a rabbit." Now, why the hell did that thought turn him on? Ellie seemed so soft and ready—he cut off that thought. The situation was already too complicated to throw anything more into the mix.

Ryder rolled off on the bicycle and he followed. Grace

went back into her kitchen to check on the food. Everywhere he looked were small families, standing around grills with grandparents, spreading out food on picnic tables decorated in bright cloths. He'd wanted that for Ryder, and for himself. What he'd gotten instead was five years of guilt.

A ball rolled in front of them. Ryder jumped off the pink bike and picked it up. He confidently walked over to the pack of rough-looking boys and said, "Can I play?"

One of them shrugged, eyeing Ryder sideways. An older boy sniggered but Ryder didn't notice, blithely picking a side and wading in. Austin stayed back, sitting down on a big log, longing for a panel of parenting experts to tell him what to do. One minute into the soccer game and the tutu was pulled on, then partially ripped. Austin stood up, his chest tight. In the next second, Ryder was rolling on the ground with a boy that outweighed him by twenty pounds, crying, but still swinging and kicking with all his might.

Austin pulled them apart by the backs of their shirt collars. "You're done. This is over." A parent was running over but he didn't feel like sticking around to talk it out. He picked up a sobbing Ryder in one arm, and the bike in the other, and walked away.

"Dad, he called me a p…p…"

"I know, son. That kid was acting like a jerk."

They turned a corner and Ellie was there. He paused, taking in the red, white, and blue clothing and matching big blue bows on Ellie and Kinley's heads. A bag dropped off Ellie's shoulder, plunking on the ground and spilling out a small pile of new diapers.

Ellie glanced over and saw them. She smiled and waved, even though Kinley appeared to be thrashing in her arms. "Hey," she said as they walked toward each other, her face turning from sunny to concerned. "What happened, Ryder? Are you hurt?"

"That boy made me cry, Ellie. He pushed me on the ground." Ryder stumbled away from Austin to throw himself on Ellie. She managed to put an arm around him while still struggling with Kinley.

"Here, I'll take the baby," Austin said, stepping forward and picking up the red-faced girl out of Ellie's arms. Distracted by flying through the air, Kinley stared at him with her mouth open.

"Oh, no," said Ellie, squatting down and putting her arms around Ryder. "I'm so sorry that happened to you. What happened next? What did you do?"

When Ryder didn't say anything, Austin said, "Ryder tackled the kid to the ground and punched him. You got him back, son."

Ellie looked up at him through her lashes, her mouth turned down. "Well," she said, "if somebody hits you first, you defend yourself. And if that boy tries to touch you again, I will be talking to his family. That kid is out of line."

"Yeah," said Ryder, sniffing, a little smile turning up one corner of his mouth.

Austin felt the smile on his own face. Pink hair and big blue bow on her head, Ellie still managed to seem a little fierce. Kinley grabbed his nose.

"Come on," he said, dropping the baby down into a rocking hold that had her burbling, "let's get some dinner."

Ellie and Ryder walked beside him, holding hands, toward the big, manufactured home where Grace had her store and living quarters. Did Ellie know what she was doing—was she like this with everyone in her life? What the hell was he going to do when Ryder had to say goodbye?

After finishing dinner, Ellie watched Austin walk off toward the parking lot with all of her bags over his shoulders. The constant chivalry was done with such ease, never seeming to ask for anything in return. *I'd put up with some rough edges for a man like that.*

"Ellie, honey," said Grace, "I want to ask you something."

"Sure, Grace, anything. Did I tell you how delicious that Jell-O salad was, with the pretzels in it? I used to eat three Jell-O cups a day while I was pregnant. Can I have the recipe?"

"Of course, and I'm glad you liked it." Grace glanced over at the kids. Kinley was sprawled out on a blanket on the floor, happily gumming on the frozen celery Grace had given her, while Ryder built a wall of blocks around her. "Did you say you're staying through August, dear?"

"Yes. That's flexible, though, because I'm still deciding what to do next. Finishing my college degree would be nice, but I didn't get a spot in the student daycare center for Kinley. I'm on the waiting list."

"Oh, I see. Well, I've been thinking lately I could use a little help out here, especially this summer during the busy season. Would you like to hear more?"

"I would. But you know I'll need to have Kinley with me —regular childcare is out of my budget, and I don't have anyone helping me."

"Right, I figured you'd have her with you. I'm thinking you can mostly sit in the store, or at least be in the house where you can hear the bell when someone opens the door." Grace smiled at her.

Ellie nodded and leaned forward. Being on her own all the time, without anyone else that could speak that is, had been shockingly difficult for her. *Should have realized...*

"When it's time to clean those cabins," Grace continued, "I'll stay with the kids. Kinley might be napping during that time—checkout is at eleven and then I have until three in the afternoon to get it all done. We have plenty of toys and things around here, even a little playpen for naps. My husband, Ned, had four children with his previous wife, and they all have babies now themselves. Anyway, what do you think, dear?"

Ellie reached forward and gave Grace a hug. "I'd love to. I have a few plans with friends and family but otherwise I'll be here every chance you give me."

Grace's big blue eyes, a little watery, blinked at her. She patted Ellie's back. "I'm sorry you lost your husband, dear. Life is so unfair sometimes. But I'm glad you and Austin have each other right now—a little fun will do you both a world of good."

Ellie's cheeks went hot. "He's the best neighbor I've ever had. And such a good dad."

Grace sniffed, squinting at the door Austin would walk through at any moment. "He's too serious for his own good."

"I like serious people. But they can tell, from a mile away, that I'm not one of them."

Grace patted her hand. "If everyone was serious all the time, we'd all die of boredom. Austin takes his time with things, but he'll come around."

Ellie adjusted her bright red tank top, not sure what else to say. Austin stepped into the room, ducking his head as he came through the doorframe to avoid knocking his hat off. His eyes met hers and her breath caught. Was he maybe thinking about her a little?

"Ready, Ellie?" His somber eyes seemed to retreat even as she gazed at him, becoming remote and distant.

She sighed. "Yep. I'd better get that pumpkin over there home. She really hates fireworks."

They'd all retreated into Grace's house after dinner, to give the baby a break from the explosions. It wasn't dark yet, but O'Malley's RV Park was alive with blasts and pops, a blanket of gray smoke hanging over the asphalt roads and grass lawns.

"Come on, little red," said Austin, bending over to pick up Kinley from her blanket on the carpet. "Let's get you out of here before the big bombs come out."

"Goodnight, Ryder," said Ellie.

"Night, Ellie." Ryder stayed focused on his blocks, totally absorbed in creating a tower. "See you tomorrow."

She thanked Grace and couldn't help giving her another hug, promising to be there tomorrow to help out. Making a little money would ease away some of the tension she carried around like an overloaded backpack. *Where am I going at the end of the summer?* She really didn't want to move into the family room at her mother's house.

Austin held Kinley as they walked down the gravel path toward the parking lot. Her phone buzzed in her pocket. She tried to look forward to a long evening, by herself, returning messages and calls. Austin stared straight ahead. She began rattling on to him about working for Grace, filling the loaded silence between them with words.

At her car, Austin effortlessly loaded Kinley into her car seat, tightened up her harness straps and then put a binky in her hand.

"Thank you, Austin, really, for everything."

"Glad you could make it." He took off his hat and rubbed his head. "We won't be here long. Ryder goes to bed early."

"Oh," was all she found to say. Was he thinking of seeing her later? A jolt of electricity zapped up her spine. She stood up straighter, examining his face.

"Watch out for that pothole by the entrance, on the right side." He returned her gaze for one electrifying moment, then turned and stalked away.

Ellie drove back to the duplex in a daze, tapping the

steering wheel. Firework blasts exploded in the distance. Kinley made it through the drive, eyes droopy, unconcerned with the far-off noise.

Hauling the baby and the inevitable pile of gear, most of which she hadn't used but still needed just in case, back into the duplex was its usual back-pinching chore. Finally, she collapsed in the chair set up for breastfeeding, getting Kinley started before she'd put anything away, and reaching up to rub the back of her neck. Austin was spoiling her. Here she was, feeling sorry for herself, after an hour away from him.

She pulled out her phone to see if she'd missed any emails about her university applications. Not likely on a holiday, but she pulled open her spam folder in case something had gone in there during the last week. Nothing. The hard reality was that if she didn't get the subsidized student daycare for Kinley, she couldn't afford to go back to Oregon University and finish her degree. But if she did miraculously get a spot, she'd be completely on her own: no family within ninety miles.

With a swipe of her finger, she switched over to look at her text messages, hoping to see something from Nora in New Jersey. Nora wasn't talking to her. Every week, Ellie sent photos of Kinley and updates to Mitch's family but, so far, only her father-in-law had responded. The last night Ellie had been in the row house in New Jersey, Nora had finished a box of wine by herself then demanded that Ellie not take her niece across the country. That was the last time Nora had spoken to her.

Another text message came in from Todd while she was reading the last two he'd sent that day.

Todd: Babe, I really miss you. Where are you? I can be there in twenty.

She huffed, then paused to shift Kinley to the other breast.

"Todd, you're such an fboy," she muttered to herself.

He was not a serious person, at least about his hookups. Growing pot and making money were sacred to him, and that was about it. She liked his basic cheerfulness and casual physical affection—he'd usually slung an arm around her shoulders and squeezed in close when they sat together. Plus, straightforward horn dog sex was his style, and he cared about her getting there. They'd been on and off for years, never exclusive, more like a couple of magnets that bounced together whenever they weren't attached elsewhere.

Kinley finished and Ellie moved her to her shoulder, patting her back gently, and managed to send off a quick, badly-typed update to her mother along the lines of, all is well, we're still alive. Not visiting this week. Luckily, the long drive kept her parent from coming to her, not to mention her mother's intense nursing management job. She loved her, but only in small doses.

Her best friend, Mariana, who everyone called Mari with the Spanish pronunciation, had sent a message about going to the country fair. She was excited, had bought the tickets, it was happening and that was that. Ellie smiled. Mari was a bull. The kind of person you wanted on your side, and also extremely decisive. If Ellie did go back to school at least Mari would be there, ready with marching orders whenever she needed them.

Ellie stood up, glancing at the clock. Off schedule again. She sighed and walked into Kinley's bedroom to put on the little girl's pajamas and a night diaper. Holding Kinley tight for another moment, she kissed the top of her head, breathing in the flowery scent of baby lotion. She laid her down inside her portable crib. Ellie knew she was a screw-up accidental mother, but she loved her girl with every cell in her body. Whatever it took, she had to make a better life for them both.

An hour later, she put the baby monitor in her back pocket and slipped out of the door. On the back side of the house was a long deck, connecting both sides of the duplex, divided by a lattice wall. Below the back deck was a little grassy lawn, surrounded by forest, with a firepit set a small way from the house. Austin sat in a chair by the fire, reading a book.

He looked up as she walked across the grass. "Hi," she said. "Mind if I join you?"

"There's a seat there," he said, pointing at a log. He closed his book and put it in his pocket. "Everything alright?"

"Yes, Kinley's sleeping." She pulled the baby monitor out of her pocket and showed him. "This little spy camera has been the best gift I've ever received. Otherwise, I'd be creeping in there to check on her every hour—and probably sleeping in the same room. Well, I do that most of the time anyway, but at least she's not sleeping with me." Good grief, she was rambling. And talking about sleeping. Maybe the alien would take over her body soon and rush this along to the good parts.

"Yep, those are nice," he said, laconically. Did he have to pay for each word, compensation for sins in a past life?

"You're so good with babies. What was Ryder like as an infant?"

"Colicky. A little anxious. He wanted to be held all the time. Eventually I kept him strapped to my chest. Till he got too squirrelly."

Her lips parted as she examined his rugged, serious face. He was such a good dad. She hadn't had that until her stepfather had come along when she was in middle school. Her own father leaving had left her with a few issues. *Kinley needs someone like him.*

She took a swallow of her apple juice. Talking about babies wasn't taking her where she wanted to go. "It's been great, spending time with you and Ryder. Going swimming today was the highlight of my summer."

He glanced at her. She hoped he was thinking back to that moment when she'd emerged from the river earlier at Moonshine Park, dripping wet in her bathing suit, and met his eyes. He'd been watching her. It had felt like a spark.

"I'm glad," he said, and stood up. "I'd better head inside. Goodnight, Ellie."

"Night," she said, not meeting his eyes. His footsteps padded across the grass, then creaked onto the deck, until finally a door opened and shut.

Ellie bit her lip, blinking her eyes. Her nose stung. He was a serious person, no doubt making the right choice. *Why does it have to land like a slap in the face?*

She pulled out her phone and opened up the text conversation with Todd.

Ellie: Maybe on Wednesday. I'll see if I can find a babysitter.

AUSTIN SLEPT BADLY. His body burned, his groin a pulsing viperous rod of resentment, despite his usual methods of dealing with it. She swam through his thoughts and appeared in his dreams. Why the hell did she have to tease him? That pink-haired yo-yo had no idea what she was messing with.

In the morning, he didn't knock on her door. Instead, he pulled out his laptop and fired off some emails. Helping his parents run the ranch was a whole lot of business, which they dumped on him every chance they got. He didn't mind, really. Using a computer and cell phone was just another thing he did to make work easier. His father, however, broke electronics when he inevitably lost his temper because "the piece of shit was screwing with me."

The work distracted him, while he drank coffee and waited for Ryder to wake up. A day away from Ellie would be a good thing for everyone. He'd take Ryder over to the aquarium and whatever else kid place they could find. Tonight, at dinner, he'd finally have the conversation with Ryder he'd been dreading. And putting off for years.

"Hi, Dad," Ryder said, walking out of his room in his pajamas. He stopped, rubbing his face. "Where's Ellie?"

"Morning, son." Austin stood up and went into the kitchen. "I'm not going fishing this morning. I want to take you over to the big aquarium in Newport today, and do a little sightseeing."

"Aquarium?"

"Yep. They have a big collection of sea creatures to see and study."

"Oh." Ryder sat down on a stool at the counter. "That sounds okay, I guess. As long as Ellie comes."

"It's a father and son day. We'll stop by and see Grandma Grace too."

"What about Ellie and Kinley? I want to see them, Dad. I'm going over to her side of our house after I eat breakfast."

Austin put down the jug of orange juice and turned to face Ryder. "Hey, listen to me now. Ellie is our neighbor, not part of this family. We're going to say goodbye to her next week."

"Ellie is my friend, Dad." Ryder pushed his plate away. His lower lip trembled.

"She's a…vacation friend. I want you to keep this in perspective, son, and not get too attached."

"You're too attached," Ryder gasped, a big gulping sob exploding out. He wiped his running nose on his sleeve, glaring at Austin across the counter, devolving into full-on crying.

Austin let his head sag down. After a minute he pushed away from the counter. He focused on tidying up the kitchen, giving Ryder the space to calm down on his own.

Five minutes later Ryder croaked, "I'm goin over there, Dad."

Austin rubbed his head. He was spoiling his son. Yet, the kid had been through a lot. If the Ellie experience was going to leave a gaping wound no matter what, he might as well wait till the end to get it over with instead of starting early.

After a deep breath, Austin said, "I'll text first and ask if it's okay with Ellie."

"Fine. Text her now."

"I need you to promise me you'll think about what I said, Ryder."

"Okay, geez."

Twenty minutes later, Austin stepped outside and watched Ryder run over to Ellie's door. The door squeaked open and he heard Ellie's bright, "Good morning." Austin leaned against the garage door, crossing his arms, not willing to risk another sighting of her in her pajamas.

When Ellie's door snapped closed behind Ryder's excited babbling, he levered himself up and walked over to his truck. He removed Ryder's booster seat and put it on Ellie's car. On a whim, he tried her car door handle and it opened easily— completely unlocked. *Of course.* He set up the booster chair then closed up her car, leaving it unlocked in case she'd dropped her keys inside the cab.

With a couple of hours free, he picked up fresh groceries, gassed up the truck, and made a few phone calls for the ranch. On horseback, or gloved up to repair a fence, his father could outwork any man he'd ever met. Finance, however, his father liked to pretend didn't matter.

Around noon he parked at O'Malley's RV Park to pick up Ryder. When he walked up to where Ryder was standing by the playground, laughing with Ellie, there were honest-to-goodness flutters in his stomach. She was dressed in the style of Rosie the Riveter, a handkerchief over her hair and her shirt sleeves rolled up. He swallowed, not sure what he wanted to say to her.

He didn't get a chance to say anything. Without meeting his eyes, she gave Ryder a quick hug while he was still walking over, then turned and hurried away. Kinley stared at him over her mother's shoulder, mouth open in a surprised O. His stomach sank.

"Where's Ellie going?" The words came out of his mouth without his brain's input.

"She's doing work for Grandma Grace. For money. But Ellie said she didn't care how much she made. And then Grandma Grace said she had the wrong ideas about working. I didn't think that was very kind of Grandma, but Ellie laughed and hugged her. So, I helped Ellie put more candies out in the store. Then she bought me a Tootsie Roll—those are really good, Dad."

The rest of the day they bounced around to different sights on the Oregon coast. As they walked through Ripley's Believe It Or Not, a museum full of creepy wax statues under flickering yellow lights, Austin wondered what Ellie would make of it. He snorted, disgusted with himself. Ryder's infatuation might be contagious.

He took them to Mo's Chowder House for dinner—a big, crowded warehouse of a restaurant. They were seated at a small corner table in the steamy interior, surrounded by rambunctious families and the clatter of dishes. Austin ordered their food, then took a minute to drink down part of his beer.

"Ryder, I need to talk to you." He patted Ryder's back and waited for him to turn off his tablet.

"Yeah, Dad?"

Austin cleared his throat. "Son, it's about your mother."

Ryder frowned. "I don't want to talk about her. She doesn't like me."

"That's not true. She loves you." Austin blew out his breath. "The truth is, she's a professional athlete and needs to focus on her job right now."

Ryder sniffed, his lips sticking out in a pout. "She's mean to me, Dad."

Austin put his arm around the boy's shoulders. "She's strict. Because that's the way she grew up. Son, like I've told you before, she's going to be a better mom when you're older."

They sat for a minute, leaning on each other. Anytime Becky came up they had to go down this road. Austin rubbed his head, trying to gather his thoughts.

"Is that all? I want to play my game."

"No, hold on a minute. Your mom and I are getting a divorce. That means we won't be married anymore."

Ryder's eyebrows furrowed together. "How are you married if she don't do sleepovers?"

Austin held in a smile even though it was a grim reminder of what his life had been for the last three years. "Well, that's part of the problem. Sometimes people don't want to be married anymore, so they get divorced."

"Then what happens?"

"A few things. If they have kids, then the kids spend some time with their dad and some time with their mom, usually." Austin paused when Ryder's eyes got big, his mouth opening to protest. "Hold on, don't worry, nothing is going to change. You're going to be with me just like you've always been.

Unless you want to go visit her. You'll want to someday, and we'll figure it out then."

"Dad, I want to stay with you." Ryder sniffed, his chin trembling.

"Me too, son. Hey, don't worry—come here." He hugged Ryder into his side with one arm. When Ryder grabbed his tablet after a few moments, Austin let him. The kid needed a break. Talking about his mother was always a trigger straight to the tears.

The food came and they ate, Ryder watching his tablet while Austin read on his phone. When the server came by and asked about dessert, Ryder asked for an ice cream sundae on his own. Austin smiled and nodded.

"Dad," Ryder said around a mouth full of whipped cream, "if you make a divorce, does that mean you can get a new wife?"

"Yes, that's pretty much what it boils down to. You can only be married to one person at a time. But I'm not—"

"Wait, I have to finish my question." Ryder took another bite from his bowl. "When you get a new wife, then she's going to sleep over and be part of the family, right?"

"Yes." Austin took a deep breath. Ryder's train of thought needed to play out, even if he had an uncomfortable premonition where this was going.

Ryder scraped the last bit of ice cream out of his bowl then slammed his spoon down on the table. "Dad, I want you to marry Ellie. She'll be my new mommy, and I'll get a baby sister. Ellie would sleep over, Dad. I know she would."

CHAPTER SIX

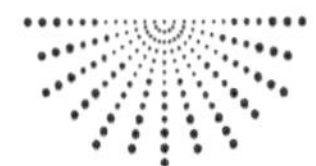

Ellie avoided speaking to Austin again Wednesday morning. They texted each other, in a businesslike manner, about the logistics of Ryder spending the morning with her, and that was it.

She let herself into Austin's duplex in a daze. Kinley clapped her hands, seeming to look around with recognition and approval. Tonight, Todd would arrive for a date. Like an angel from heaven, Grace had volunteered to babysit when Ellie had asked if she knew of anyone she'd recommend.

Crap. Ellie dropped the diaper bag on the floor. She needed the darn high chair. After ten minutes of wrangling Kinley into the baby carrier, she went back to her side to haul over more gear.

Theoretically, she should be extremely excited about an evening out. All she could summon up were stiff shoulders and a pinch in her empty stomach. She was a new mom, a widow, a directionless mess temporarily living in a vacation rental, unsure where she was going next, and she was going out on a date for the first time since her life had shattered.

With Todd. Possibly, she hadn't really thought it through. *Like everything else...*

Back in the days when large quantities of alcohol were involved, Todd had always seemed like a not-bad idea. He had given her more to drink. They'd spend an hour together in the back of his truck, on a mattress, with the old aluminum frame canopy providing some illusion of privacy. Then she'd pass out for a few hours, or wander off sooner to find a bathroom and go home, by herself. To say they'd ever "dated" was a brittle stretch of the imagination. They'd stumbled over to the all-night burrito stand a couple times, with a group of friends. One time he'd asked her to babysit his dog. She hadn't been able to, because of work and class, but had found someone else for him that could.

What was wrong with her? Why had she ever thought she wanted to see him again? *Stop.* Getting out there again would take a little practice—and maybe Todd would surprise her.

She set up the high chair at last, over the washable floor in Austin's kitchen. Kinley banged her hands down on the plastic tray, cooing when one of them smooshed into a piece of ripe banana. Ellie glanced at the clock. Hopefully Ryder would be able to get a little more sleep...

"Mornin, Ellie," said Ryder, stumbling into the kitchen rubbing his eyes.

"Good morning. I think Kinley's banging woke you up early. Sorry, bud."

"Yeah," he said, dumping cereal in his bowl. "She's really loud."

Kinley grunted and tossed banana on the floor. "Well, we're both happy to see you. Would you like to check out the local elementary school playground this morning before we go to Grandma Grace's?"

"Sure."

They all settled into eating. Ellie sipped orange juice,

considering what she would wear that evening. Something casual. Clothing that said, "Hey, I'm here to catch up with you and maybe flirt, if I feel like it. But that's about it."

"Ellie?"

"Yeah, bud?"

"Can you keep a secret?"

"I can. But I don't want to hear any secrets that might get someone in trouble."

"Okay." Ryder looked at her, scrunching his mouth around. "The secret is I'm Spider-Man."

Ellie smiled. "Wow, Spider-Man. You're a good guy that helps a lot of people."

"Yeah, I am." Ryder leaned forward across the counter. "I was bit by a radio action spider and now I can shoot webs out of my hands. Also, I'm really strong."

"A radioactive spider. Yes, I saw your movie, the first one. That green goblin guy was pretty creepy, but you did a good job handling him."

"Thanks." Ryder popped a blueberry in his mouth. "Ellie, it's me again, Ryder."

"Hey, bud."

"I want you to be my new mom."

Ellie blinked, gazing over at Ryder. She stood up from wiping banana off the floor. "Ryder, wow, thank you so much. I'm really honored that you think that." She sniffed, the tingling behind her nose and eyes blurring her vision. "That's about the most amazing thing anyone's ever said to me."

"Yeah." Ryder smiled at her. He took a big breath, clasping his hands together in front of himself. "But, Ellie, I want a lot of mommy hugs."

"Would you like a hug right now?"

"Yes."

Ellie wrapped him up in a tight hug. "Ryder you're the best, kindest, most wonderful boy I know."

"I love you, Ellie."

She huffed, wiping her face with a napkin. "Thank you. I love you too, Ryder. But, buddy, we have to talk about this a little more. Unfortunately, kids don't get to choose their moms. But you do get to choose your friends. You and I are friends."

"But Daddy's going to make a divorce. So now a new mom can sleep over and be part of the family. And I really want a baby sister too."

Hand on a roll of paper towels, she halted. Austin was, technically, not in a relationship. Not that it mattered to her since the man barely tolerated her as a neighbor. "You are amazing. Whoops, Kinley is rubbing banana in her eye." Ellie ran over just as Kinley started crying. Ryder slid off his stool and walked over to his toys.

She was trembling a little, and smiling. Ryder picked her. Austin didn't like her, but at least somebody did.

AUSTIN DIDN'T SEE Ellie at all in the morning or afternoon on Wednesday. That evening, he crossed his arms, standing by the front door of the duplex, waiting for Ryder to put on his shoes. *Why am I so wound up?*

A truck pulled into the driveway. He leaned forward in the doorframe to get a better look. It wasn't anyone he recognized. Then Ellie was there in a tight T-shirt and jeans, smiling at the smug-looking guy behind the wheel. She hopped in and they were off. Without the baby.

He walked out until he could see her front door. Grace's car was in the driveway, parked behind Ellie's little commuter. He whipped out his phone. Grace answered on the second ring.

"Hello, Austin," Grace said. "Did you finally notice my car out there?"

"I did. Guess you're babysitting?"

"That's it. I'm hoping to see both of you boys. Kinley is sleeping, and I have this baby monitor, so why don't I meet you at the playground? Is Ryder going out again?"

"Yep. See you there."

Ryder ran out to the duplex's playground and Austin followed.

"Grandma Grace." Ryder ran over and wrapped his arms around her waist, making her step back hastily to catch her balance.

Grace waved to him then played with Ryder on the playground for the next twenty minutes, pushing him on the swings and ferrying cars up to the top of the slide for him to send down.

He paced back and forth on the bark mulch. Ellie was on a date? Who the hell with—some idiot from the internet?

"Want any dinner?" he asked Grace when she had a chance to walk over.

"Oh no, thank you, I ate already. Will you come chat with me after Ryder goes to bed?"

"Yes, at the little firepit in the backyard. We can hear both of the kids back there."

An hour later, after Ryder was in bed and had dropped off to sleep, Austin carefully opened the back door and slipped outside. He texted Grace then started a small fire in the stone and gravel pit.

Grace came out with a glass of wine in her hand and took a seat by the fire. "Well, that poor girl is finally out doing something fun."

"Who's the guy?"

"An old friend of hers. She was at Oregon University at the beginning of last year. Might be back there soon."

"Huh."

Grace took a swallow of her wine. The fire crackled as Austin put on another log. "Becky won big in Reno last weekend," Grace said, sounding proud of her daughter but also resigned.

Austin grunted. "That's good. She'll have a chance at the finals now."

"Yep." Grace sighed. "Might finally get her golden buckle. Then she'll realize what she's given up."

Austin took off his hat and rubbed his head. "Hey, I don't hold nothin against her." He stared at the fire. "I sent her the divorce papers."

"She sign yet?"

"Nah, I doubt it. She's travelin too much. Rodeo won't give her a break for a while."

"She'll come to her senses after you really leave her."

Austin poked the fire with a stick. Sparks flew up and smoke puffed out of the flames. Becky wanting him back was…terrifying. She usually got what she went after.

"I'm asking for full custody of Ryder." He glanced over at Grace's gloomy face. "When they're both ready, things'll be different."

Grace blew out her breath. "She won't like it, but I'll do what I can for you. You're a good dad."

"Ryder and his mom, they have a hard time. She told me once that she just can't handle little kids. Seems like they never bonded, the two of 'em."

"Well, Becky's father's a real son of a bitch, as you know. For some reason she's convinced being hard, like him, is the best way for everything. It doesn't help that Ryder is a little emotional, and sensitive. Don't get me wrong, I wouldn't change a hair on my grandson's head."

"Me neither. But, especially lately, he suffers after a visit with his mom. Clings to me, wets his pants, cries a lot more than usual. Even throws up. Ryder needs a break and I'm going to do what I can to give him one."

"I see." Grace stared down at her empty glass.

"Hey," he said, reaching out to pat her knee. "Ryder and I aren't going anywhere. We'll be out to see you in the summer. Once Ryder is older, and a little tougher, he'll find a way with his mother. I don't talk bad about her."

She squeezed his hand, then wiped under her eyes. "Okay."

They sat in silence, watching the flames eat down the wood. Going over the divorce wiped him out, knocking open pits in his chest made of old regrets. At the same time, the air went in and out of his lungs easier, like now some of the lead weight he'd been carrying around had disappeared. *It's going to be done.*

He glanced at Grace bent forward over her knees, shoulders hunched. "You must be tuckered out. I'll take that baby monitor and let you get home. I'm here anyway and will tuck that thing in the back door when Ellie's home."

Grace looked at him, one eyebrow up. A half smile cocked up one side of her mouth. "Been a while, son?"

He snorted. "Go on, we'll be fine."

"Well, what does an old woman like me know." She stood up and dusted off her pants. "But a little pokey would do you both some good."

His face went hot. Grace turned around and walked off, a satisfied smile on her face. *Interfering old biddy.*

ELLIE STARED at the densely packed growing crop of marijuana buds filling the semitruck-sized cargo ship container. There were maybe fifty plants inside the long rectangular room, growing in black plastic pots, the fat cylindrical buds on top glistening with sparkly resin. Her nose tingled. She sneezed into her raised elbow.

"Sour bubblegum diesel, baby," Todd said, nodding his head like a proud parent at a sporting event. "Let's trim these badasses down to size."

Ellie forced herself not to touch her itchy eyes. "You want me to trim bud with you? What about dinner?"

"Babe, I've got you. There's snacks everywhere, and a couple pizzas in the freezer. I'll get us set up out here while you cover starting dinner in the trailer."

Seriously? "Todd, I don't understand what's happening here. I thought we were going on a date."

"Hey, give it a chance. We're going to give all these sweet buds wicked haircuts. I want you to feel life with me, get to know my rhythms. I missed you. Had me thinking how much better life would be with a partner, babe. Just you, me, the dogs, and the bud."

Wow. "And Kinley."

"Who? Hang on, we need music. I'll be right back." Todd disappeared out the door.

Ellie stared at the card table set up in a corner, littered with trimming scissors, an ashtray, and a glass pipe. Two saggy lawn chairs sat side by side. She turned around and walked out of the cargo box. Bozo, Todd's dog, ambled over to lean lovingly against her side. He licked her hand while she petted his bristly pit bull head.

She looked up at the dense layers of stars overhead. Todd's property was down several dirt roads, in the middle of the woods. An owl hooted nearby. It had taken them thirty-five minutes to drive out to his place from Siletz, after a stop at the grocery store, where he'd bought beer.

"Bozo, you're a good dog."

The dog sat back on his haunches and panted at her, his tongue hanging out one side of his mouth.

She'd let Todd kiss her, after he'd turned off his truck in the Safeway parking lot. A tingly flush had swept over her, like her body was coming to a sputtering start. Todd was a good kisser, patient and slow and smooth on the lean-in timing. It had been nice.

On the drive out into the coastal mountain range, he'd slung an arm behind her head and had smiled at her while he drove, chatting easily about his plans. Ellie sighed. His chin-length wavy blond hair, framing his handsome Nordic face, had always attracted her like a sugar trap left out for ants.

Now she was in the middle of the woods, without her car, standing next to cargo containers and greenhouses full of pungent reeking marijuana, without cell phone reception. Todd had disappeared inside his camper trailer, where he slept on a twin-sized mattress surrounded by piles of junk. Ellie put on her phone's flashlight and walked over to the camper, Bozo prancing at her side.

"Hey, Todd?" She stuck her head inside the camper. A dim light was on, but the tiny space was empty.

"Babe," Todd said, appearing behind her. Ellie jumped, covering her chest with a hand. "Just me. Portable speakers were in the far greenhouse where I cropped last night." He leaned in closer to her. "Damn, you look good. Want to go mess around?"

Ellie took a step away from him. "No. I have to go home. My baby needs me."

"Now?" His face scrunched up as she nodded. "Shit, Ellie, we just got out here. And I don't show many people my grows. Babe, I've really missed you."

"Thanks. And this is all very impressive. But I can't do a work session tonight. This is better for you, to drive me back now, before you get going out here. I'll go wait in the truck."

It took Todd another twenty minutes to prepare himself to drive her home. She kept her phone in her hands, waiting for reception. What if something happened to Kinley and no one could reach her? Todd turned the music up, nodding his head to the beat as he drove. She didn't think he'd be texting her again.

At last, her phone vibrated with incoming text messages. Ellie scanned through them, barely comprehending, skimming the words for "hospital" or "emergency." She blew out her breath. Apparently, Kinley had survived for three hours without her. The messages said Grace went home and Austin took the monitor. Kinley had woken up and Austin went inside and dealt with a leaked diaper. After that, Kinley had gone back to sleep and Austin went on the back deck, where he could hear either of the kids if they started crying.

Ellie slumped back in her seat, biting her lip. She would need to go and thank Austin. The man should stay away from her because she wasn't doing a good job of distracting herself. The lust alien might release a trigger.

Todd pulled into the duplex driveway and parked. He tapped the steering wheel while he glanced at her. She opened her passenger door. "Thanks, that was…an adventure. Bye, Todd, I'll talk to you later."

She didn't wait for him to respond, jumping out of the truck and then closing the door behind her. He reversed fast, then whipped the truck around and took off, dust billowing behind him.

Her front porch light was off, the path to her door dark. Of course, yet another thing she forgot to do. Ellie drooped. She could use a shot of chocolate, straight in her veins, to help her forget what a wreck her life was.

"Hey, Ellie."

She shot two feet sideways, a garbled squeak coming out of her throat.

Austin took a step back, putting his hands in his jacket pockets. "Sorry I startled you. I heard a truck peeling out up here and came to see if everything was alright."

Ellie huffed. "Hi. I'm fine. A little shell-shocked after the worst date of my life. But one thing is now clear to me. I do not want to be a pot farmer. It feels good to have cleared out that fantasy."

"Huh," Austin said, one corner of his mouth turning up. "Profitable crop, if you have water rights."

She took a deep breath. "Thank you, a bazillion times, for keeping an eye on Kinley for me so Grace could go home. After the blown-out diaper, I think we're even on the babysitting exchange—considering that I like having Ryder around and enjoy the company."

"We're not. Here's your gadget." He reached out toward her. She stepped forward and took the monitor, blue light flickering from the screen, letting her fingers linger on his.

"Thank you, really."

"Ellie, I was wondering…" He rested his shoulder against the house siding next to her front door.

She stayed where she was, close enough that the flap of his jacket brushed her stomach when he inhaled. Austin swallowed. She wanted to lean forward and put her face on his neck.

"I'm wondering if you want to spend time with me." He reached out and traced a finger over her cheek. She jerked, her lips opening, a pulse of heat jolting to the base of her spine. "But I need to do the right thing. We're both…"

"Vulnerable," Ellie gasped out. She took a breath. He was right, and she needed to focus and think with her brain, for once. But when she glanced back up at him her nipples hardened, and she inhaled male sweat and woodsmoke and something that was rum and pine.

"Yeah, I guess that's it. I'm leaving next week for the far

southeastern side of the state, eight hours away. You're headed back to school."

"Am I?" Her restraint broke. She tilted forward and pressed the front of her body against his. "I'm glad somebody knows what I should be doing."

He shivered, his hands landing on her waist. "Hey, I…"

"Austin."

"Yeah?"

"I want you, so much."

CHAPTER SEVEN

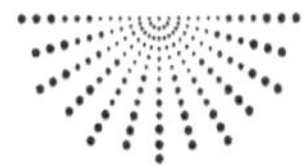

Austin leaned forward and pressed his mouth against her full pink lips, his body rigid and aching. His ability to think burned away, the desire tearing through his veins like dry sapwood bursting into flame. She thrust forward and slid her arms around his neck, one of her legs sliding up to hook around the back of his calf.

He reached down and put his hands on her full round butt cheeks in the tight jeans, yanking her up higher. There was something off about his reaction—he was quaking, almost out of control, so tight and thick with need he was panting. She shivered, humming a low note.

Groaning, he lifted her up. Hands gripping her ass, he swung around to pin her against the side of the house. Her legs were wrapped around him, her mouth as hungry as his. She pulled the back of his shirt up and her hands slid up his skin. When her hips pumped against his he shuddered, seconds from tearing off her pants or coming in his own.

He yanked back, bracing her off him and forcing her to slide to the ground. "We have to stop. I don't have a damn condom."

She crossed her arms, slumping back against the house and looking up at the sky. "Right."

He paced down the path, putting some distance between them. Breath rushed in and out of his chest like he'd just raced his brothers across five miles of rough terrain. Her door squeaked open, and he turned around to see her hunched shoulders silhouetted in the doorway.

"Ellie."

She paused, glancing back at him over her shoulder. "Goodnight, Austin."

"See you tomorrow?"

Her mouth twitched and she stood up straighter. "You'll see me if you want to come to the country fair in Veneta. I'm leaving at nine."

ELLIE HANDED Austin another bag to load into his truck. Kinley babbled in her other arm, a little starfish hand reaching out to pat her face.

"Hey," he said, "I'll get all this stuff, you don't have to haul it out to me. Would you unlock your car though? I'll move that infant seat over."

"Sure," she said, still stupidly shy around him. She cleared her throat. Really, he didn't deserve any nasty surprises— even if he had left her highly frustrated the night before. "Austin, listen, like I tried to tell you earlier, this is an alternative hippie fair with, like, mostly naked people dancing around. Are you sure you're up for it?"

"Do you think Ryder will have fun?"

"I do, actually. It's you I'm worried about."

He hadn't touched her again all morning, but when he turned around and smiled at her, a warm flush swept over her chest and face. She smirked back at him. Maybe he'd get inspired and take his shirt off today…

"I'll handle it. Come on now, girl, get a wiggle on. We've got some road to cover."

She grinned. "Wow, you're a turn on when you talk. My wiggles will be on display today, fair warning. There's a lot of pale pasty skin under these clothes."

"Don't wind me up when we can't do anything about it." He took a step closer and leaned forward.

"Dad," Ryder shouted, charging out onto the driveway, his face red. "Where is my magic rainbow circle? Are you hiding it?"

Austin took a deep breath, his eyes squinting. "Laundry room, Ryder."

Ryder ran back into his side of the duplex. Ellie sighed, heading inside to find her keys. Austin probably was hiding the rainbow tutu from Ryder every chance he got.

She couldn't put it off any longer. After getting Kinley started breastfeeding, she pulled out her phone. Her best friend needed a heads-up.

Ellie: Hey, Mari, I'm bringing along my hot cowboy neighbor and his kid. You're welcome.

Mari started typing back immediately.

Mari: I was just about to text you to hurry up and not be late, so do that. Is the cowboy for me? Pretty please?

Ellie: He's a nice guy, not an escort. Also, I'm hoping he isn't that slutty.

Mari: Wait, are you telling me you found a cowboy hookup?

Ellie: I better go. I don't want to be late.

Mari: Ellie!

Mari was a workaholic business major, already started on her MBA. They'd been friends since high school. While they were opposites in many ways, and Mari would probably never understand why Ellie couldn't get her life together, Mari was also the friend that had your back no matter what.

Ellie stared down into Kinley's drooping eyes, smoothing the fan of red hair over her forehead with one finger. She had to be strong now, and smart, for her girl. Letting herself fall for someone who was leaving next week wouldn't be good for either of them. *I'll keep it under control.*

She bit her lip, glancing up toward the door. Kissing Austin the night before had been like sticking her finger in an electrical outlet—except it hurt, horribly, when he stopped. Her and Mitch had had chemistry like that. She closed her eyes and took a deep breath, pinching her nose to stop the tingling there.

Before long, Ryder ran in to see if she was ready yet and then they were all clambering into the truck, the kids in the surprisingly roomy back seat. Austin drove easily and cautiously, going with the flow of traffic.

"Thank you for driving," she said. Her seat was very comfortable. Amazingly, she was actually going to arrive for a long day of hiking around the fair not already an exhausted mess. And, assuming she didn't totally screw up, he would drive her home too. *A minor miracle. I'll take it.*

"Glad to, Ellie," he said, turning toward her long enough to wink.

The man was becoming less grim by the moment. "Well, don't mind me over here, doing my hair and makeup. I have a lot of missed sleep to cover up for."

"You don't need that stuff."

"You say the sweetest, most oblivious things." She snapped open her makeup mirror, facing away from him toward the passenger door.

"Son," Austin said, "put your headphones on. The baby's trying to sleep."

"Okay, Dad."

They were all quiet while Kinley blinked, her head dipping sideways then popping back up as she tried to keep herself awake. Ellie exhaled a long breath when Kinley finally closed her eyes.

She pulled open the rearview mirror and went to work on a loose double-bun style—braided by her temple, half down in the back. Then she went to glitter town: thick streaks through her hair that complemented the brushed-on gold glitter over her eyes, lips, and chest. She tucked a few silk flowers into her hair, pinning them in place.

"Looks good," Austin said softly, grinning at her when she turned toward him. *What is happening?* How was this gorgeous man driving her around and acting like the partner she desperately wanted? *Leaving next week, Ellie, don't you forget it.*

They turned off the highway onto a narrow forest road, dense greenery surrounding the asphalt. Fanciful hand-painted wooden signs directed them to a large field that had been recently mown. Austin parked next to a long row of portable toilet stalls labeled "Honey Buckets."

Ellie stepped out of the truck, stretching her arms above her head. Kinley still slept in the back of the truck cab. Austin followed Ryder as he darted for a toilet.

"Hey, you're late."

Ellie spun around and Mari was there, grinning at her. She wore a metallic gold one-piece jumpsuit, sleeveless, with a deep V collar and matching back. Garbed for the fair, Mari appeared a bit like a punked-out Selena Gomez.

"Yeah, by ten minutes," Ellie said. "The black belt against the gold cloth is killin' it. You're fabulous."

"Oh snap, look at that pink hair—I freaking love it!" Mari threw her arms about Ellie and they squealed, jumping up and down. "Damn, girl, I am so happy to see you. Wait a minute, where's the babes?"

Mari crawled into the cab to see Kinley, whispering oohs and awws. They moved back out onto the field. "She's amazing," Mari said.

"Best thing I ever made," Ellie said, her voice cracking.

"Ahh, honey, I'm sorry about your man. The dead one. Don't laugh at me—you know what I mean. Geez, what are you smiling about? Get your gear on. I know you're not going to wear that ugly ass T-shirt into the fair."

Ellie dug around her stuff in the truck until she found her beaded halter top with a fringe that draped down over her stomach. It was a glorified bikini top that left her back bare except for a string tie. She whipped it on while crouched over by the truck door. With her little linen shorts and strappy sandals, she was as gussied up as she was going to get.

"Girl, I brought some Molly." Mari held up a pill bottle and rattled it, her eyes open wide and a toothy grin on her face.

"You have MDMA—wow, you're making me a little jealous here." Actually, she'd never thought the comedown was worth it.

"What? Let's do it."

Ellie took a deep breath in and out. She could really use a dose of euphoric energy at the moment. "You know, for someone with genius-level business intelligence, you're pretty goofy sometimes. Someday, probably in about two years, I'll be so ready for, well, lots of alcohol actually. I'm filling out this top rather nicely because my tits are loaded with Kinley's lunch. Take your damn pill and have fun."

"I will. It's legal now, you know."

"It's decriminalized in Oregon, if you have less than two grams. Here comes Austin and his son Ryder."

Mari swallowed her pill and made the bottle disappear. She said hello to the guys then went back to her car to finish getting ready.

Ellie watched Austin's gaze, which was a deliberate and slow perusal of her from head to foot and back again. Heat coiled in her stomach and between her legs. The thing between them was happening, soon. While Ryder had his back turned, Austin leaned in and kissed her on the mouth. "You look real good," he said.

"So do you." She grinned up at him. "It's getting hot out here—are you sure you need that shirt?"

"It might come off later."

"Kinley's awake," Ryder shouted. "Can we go now?"

Austin insisted on taking Kinley in the baby carrier, and also carrying the backpack diaper bag. "Austin, you're too good to be true," Ellie said, slinging her purse over her shoulder.

He stared back at her with his solemn eyes. "I know what it's like, doing this alone. I'm glad I can help you out, while I'm here."

Her bubbly excitement popped. Yet another reminder that he was leaving soon. Her chest squeezed. Someone like him didn't pick a girl like her.

Ryder grabbed her hand and pulled her toward the curved wooden gates into the fair. Ellie and Ryder walked through a rainbow twelve-pointed 3D star that was a towering twenty feet tall. They showed their tickets at a booth then walked toward an enormous horned dragon head, where the information booth was inside its gaping mouth. Ellie pushed away the sadness and grief of what was coming, and what had been, and let her eyes feast.

The winding path, under a forest canopy, snaked around a village like something out of a fantasy novel, except with vendors selling tie-dye and the whir of blenders mixing up high-level smoothies. There were hundreds of different kinds of food and every kind of handcraft, homeware, and body care item you could think of. Everything was gorgeous. "Love love love," said a blue, orange and purple flag waving from the second-story balcony of a tree house shop. A troop of folk musicians, dressed up like Victorian performers wearing fairy wings, picked out a jaunty tune in front of her. Art installations like bird statues and blooming flowers, sculpted out of twigs and moss, popped out of roofs and under awnings.

"Dad, I want wings," said Ryder, pulling Ellie toward a stall.

"We'll see," said Austin. "Keep hold of Ellie's hand."

"I'm getting these," said Mari, holding up shimmery black fairy wings.

"Ellie," whispered Ryder at her, "I really really want some."

She couldn't say no to that desperate face. "Okay," she whispered back. "Pick something fast and I'll buy it for you."

Ryder emerged from the stall wearing orange pixie wings, the same shade as in his rainbow tutu. He raced off down the path with Mari, who was twirling in between great skipping hop leaps. *Oh crap.*

Austin raised an eyebrow at her. She bit her lip. "Come on," she said. "The kid village is that way."

They speed-walked down the path. "I'm gonna pay you back for those," he said.

"No way, dude. My present to Ryder."

"They'll still be that."

After turning a corner, they found the kid village. Ryder waved, already exploring a climbing structure. Mari stood near him, dancing in front of a ring of xylophone players. Ellie blew out her breath, the clenched knot in her shoulders loosening. She took Kinley from Austin and sat down on a shaded bench at the edge of one of the stages to breastfeed. Kinley waved her arms, too excited to settle down, her face full of surprise as she glanced around.

"See," Ellie said to Kinley, "aren't you glad we left New Jersey for a little while?"

Ellie was glad to be out of the city. She'd been too pregnant and sad to really explore the East Coast—mostly stranded in the row house while everyone else worked. It had felt too fast-paced for her out there. Kinley frowned, seeming to suddenly realize she was hungry, and got down to business.

After a while, they hiked further into the fair to shop for lunch, finally settling on Peruvian bowls for her and Austin, and a waffle plate for Ryder. Mari wasn't hungry but slurped down a berry lemonade like it was the best thing she'd ever tasted. She wandered off while they ate.

"What's tempeh?" Austin was staring at a menu board nearby like it was written in an alien language. He took her hand under the table.

"Um, a kind of spongy cake made from soybeans. I like it better than tofu."

"Huh."

"Dad, I want to find the circus parade."

"Well, I'm going to get Ellie a slice of cheesecake because she's been talking about it all morning. Want some, son?"

"Cake made out of cheese—gross. I hate cheese."

"I bet you'll change your mind about that," Ellie said.

"Someday you might even like cheese cereal and cheese ice cream. Cheese juice? What about cheese frosting on your cheese brownies?"

"No way."

"That's cheesy," Austin said.

Ellie grinned at him. "And salty." Their eyes locked together, his the color of storm clouds. Her breath caught. She'd never fallen so quickly before, infatuated from almost her first glimpse of him. Then charmed by every layer of his personality revealed—well, almost. He wasn't perfect but she liked him better for it. Not hiding himself behind a facade. His fingers smoothed over the inside of her wrist.

"Be right back," he said and stood up to get in the short line.

Ryder bounced in his seat. Then he jumped up and started running around the table. Kinley fussed as soon as Ellie got her back in the baby carrier. She should have changed the diaper first.

"Come on, Ellie, let's go." Ryder increased the size of his loop around the table, getting further away with every pass.

"Okay, as soon as your dad is back. We'll bring the cake with us."

"There he is," shouted Ryder, triumphantly. Then he turned around and ran.

"Ryder!" Ellie paused to grab her phone then left everything else on the table before dashing off in the direction Ryder had run, already out of sight in the masses of people. "Not again," she muttered, bracing Kinley to keep her from bouncing too much as she dodged through the crowd as quickly as she could. There was a fork in the path. She stopped, panting, then shouted Ryder's name. Kinley caught on to her distress and started wailing.

Ellie flagged down one of the fair staff members who was glancing at her. "Lost child," she gasped out. "Five-year-old boy with short brown hair, wearing a rainbow tutu and orange wings. Please help me find him."

"We're on it," said the woman, pulling out a handheld transceiver and talking into it.

Austin appeared at her side. "Austin, I'm so sorry, I'm not sure which way he went," she said, her vision blurring.

"Okay." His eyes never stopped scanning the crowd. "I'll go right and you go left. Check in after five minutes on the phone." He took off.

AUSTIN SPENT a familiar five minutes of agony, teetering between wanting to pound sense into Ryder and being willing to sacrifice parts of his body to see the kid safe and whole. His phone rang in his pocket.

"Ellie?"

"I have him, Austin," she said, her voice shaky. "We're in the kid village on the climbing structure."

"I'll be right there."

After he'd hiked halfway across the fairgrounds, he found Ellie slumped on a bench with her head in her hands, while Ryder patted her shoulder. His son peeped up at him, a nervous smile stretching across his face.

"Daddy, I'm really sorry," Ryder said. "These wings made me too excited. Ellie's heart is hurting her."

Ellie glanced up at him, wiping at the streaks under her eyes. "Today has been too exciting for me."

"Group hug?" Ryder held open one of his arms.

Austin walked forward as Ellie stood up. He put an arm around her back and the other arm around Ryder. Kinley squinted up at them as she was squeezed in the center of their circle.

"Ryder," Austin said, glad he'd had a ten-minute walk to

calm down, "thirty-minute time-out when we get home tonight. And we're going to talk about runnin off, a lot."

Ryder stuck out his bottom lip.

Austin turned and kissed Ellie's forehead without thinking about it. Stepping back, he let her go. "Come on, Ryder, let's go see what was left at the lunch table when you ran off. We'll meet you back here, Ellie."

Thirty minutes later, they found Ellie sitting with Kinley, her friend Mari next to them on the bench. Mari had an arm slung around Ellie, leaning her head on her shoulder.

"Get your shit together, Ellie," Mari was saying. "Come back to school—I'll help you, I promise."

"Thanks, Mari, I know you would. But even if I had a spot in the daycare, I don't have anywhere to live. I bet all the rentals are already taken."

"Yeah, dang, that's true." Mari rubbed her forehead.

Austin set down Ellie's cheesecake at her elbow. She looked up at him and smiled. He wanted to lean over and kiss her. Somehow, they'd gone from total strangers to something like a couple in a matter of days. He put his hands in his pockets. The less he led her on, the better.

"Ellie," Mari said, slapping her knee, "I'm going to find somewhere for you to live. I have a few ideas already. Or maybe I'll murder my stupid roommate that never does her dishes and leaves the door unlocked."

"Not worth it. I'll leave dirty dishes too."

"I love you, chica." Mari hugged Ellie tight. "Get your ass back to Riverside."

"I'm working on it."

They were quiet on the drive back, to let Kinley sleep. Ellie stared out the window, her shoulders slumped. He thought about holding her hand. *Don't be a jackass.* Somehow, physical affection was tempting with her in a way he hadn't experienced in a long time.

He pulled into a drive-through for take-out dinner. Kinley woke up and started howling. Ellie moved to the back seat to sit next to her for the rest of the drive. By the time they were back at the duplex—dusty and streaked with mud from the fair, piles of gear to put away and cranky children to get in bed—he could tell Ellie was exhausted.

"Goodnight, Ellie," Ryder called as he ran inside to play with his toys before bed.

"Goodnight, buddy," Ellie called, while loosening the straps around Kinley.

"I'll get her," Austin said. "And the bags. Head on inside."

"Thank you." She hesitated, then dug around in her purse. "I bought you a thing today—just something silly to remember your first visit to the Oregon Country Fair." She held out a hemp necklace, the rope thick and knotted with a few green and blue beads. A rainbow fish pendant hung in the middle.

"Thank you," he said, taking the necklace out of her hands. Kinley grumbled, crying in a halfhearted but soon-to-be-furious way, so he tossed the necklace over his head and then got to work extracting her from her car seat. He caught up to Ellie in the driveway, where she was digging around in her purse again.

She pulled out a set of keys, sighed, took a step toward her car then turned around again to face the duplex. He managed to lean over and kiss her, while bouncing the baby in his arms. "Thank you," he said again. "I like my hippie neck rope."

"You should wear it tonight, when you come over."

His body jerked, coming to rigid life. He groaned. "Damnit woman, you're too tired. Stop teasing me."

"I'm not."

"Tomorrow." He kissed her, his tongue sliding into her

mouth and his free hand gripping her hip. She melted against him.

Kinley cried out, a cranky and furious howl. They went inside. Ellie disappeared into a bedroom to change the baby's diaper. Austin sighed, fantasizing for a moment about moving them all into one side of the duplex. He'd discovered, while babysitting yesterday, that Kinley's baby monitor fizzed out inside his duplex. It only worked in part of the backyard and half the driveway. And he wouldn't leave Ryder alone in his duplex either.

He turned around and walked out. Sleeping with her was a selfish thing to do in any case. Maybe tomorrow he'd find some willpower and do the right thing.

CHAPTER EIGHT

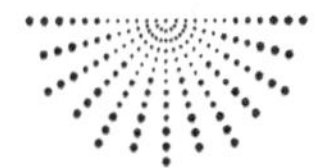

Ellie had every intention of texting Austin that night, but she passed out on the bed in Kinley's room instead. A good thing since Kinley woke up an hour early, with a rash on her bottom.

That morning, Austin had plans to meet up with one of his brothers to fish and Ellie was scheduled to help Grace at the RV park. Ryder wanted to go with her and show Grandma Grace his "fire wings." The mild sunny day crawled by while she cleaned and fed children, sat in Grace's store and sold fishing bait, and generally zoned out every chance she got to consider Austin.

Late in the morning, she opened the door behind the shop counter that opened into Grace's living room and peeped in. Kinley was asleep in her pack and play. Ellie sat back down on her stool behind the counter.

Austin came across as stoically calm and unshakable when they were out and about with the kids. When they'd kissed, it was like a hungry wolf took over his body, wound up and ravenous. Heat simmered between her legs. He was rough, and hard, and forceful. She wanted to push him over the edge.

Blowing out her breath, she pulled out her phone to distract herself. He'd felt the chemistry too, at least enough to want to sleep with her. At the same time, he struck her as withdrawn and not able to care deeply for anyone but his son. Was he a Grinch, with his heart ten sizes too small?

Ellie opened her email app and then sat up straight. She put her phone down on the counter and stared at the unopened email. The subject line read "Application for subsidized daycare." Like her hand was moving through water, she gradually reached out and pressed on her screen. She covered her mouth with her hands.

The third time she read through, the email still said the same thing, and the acceptance began to sink in. She had a spot. Kinley could go to a daycare while she finished the last year of her bachelor's degree. She put her head down on her arms and closed her eyes.

After a moment, she sat up again and reread the last paragraph of the email. Her "spot" in the daycare would start August first, and if she didn't accept right away, they'd offer the opening to the next person on the waiting list. Take it or lose it. They needed an answer in the next four days.

Grace walked in with Ryder, back for a snack after a trip to the playground. "Hey, Ellie." Ryder grabbed a package of cookies off the shelf. He dashed out to the back patio.

"That boy," said Grace, resting a hand against the wall, "is a pistol. He loves to run. Use the cash in the cigar box under the register to pay for his cookies."

Ellie reached down slowly and pulled out the old cardboard box that was full of coins and one-dollar bills. She stared at the pile of money, wondering if Kinley would take a bottle while at daycare then go back to breastfeeding at home...

"Are you alright, dear? Did something happen?"

"I'm…in shock. I've been offered a spot for Kinley to go to the on-campus daycare center at school. It's thrown me—I didn't think I was going to get a spot."

"Well, congratulations. But you don't seem happy. This is good news, isn't it?"

"I mean, it's a good option for me, I think. There are just so many things to figure out. I don't know, Grace. I'm really awful at making decisions."

Grace walked over and patted her shoulder. "What does Austin think about it?"

"Austin?"

"Yes, you should tell him. He doesn't say much but he's got a good noggin on his shoulders. The way you two look at each other, I thought you'd be going back to the ranch with him."

Ellie blinked, the idea making her vision go blurry. "He doesn't want that," she croaked out.

"Humph. He's too angry at life to know what he wants. You should both listen to Ryder. Kids know things. You'd be surprised."

"Austin," said his brother Buck, managing to prop his crossed feet up on the side of the raft, "this is a damn fine stretch of river."

"Yep." A smile tugged at the side of Austin's mouth. Buck was grinning at him, as usual.

"We're gonna talk, brother. Do I need to put coins in you for the words to come out?"

"I came to fish. But you can talk all you want and forget about landing a steelhead." It was pointless to argue, but he did it anyway out of pure stubborn cantankerousness. Buck always had an agenda.

"Fish love me. I'll lull them closer with the sound of my voice."

Austin huffed. "Randi might love you. Everyone else is just stuck."

Buck snorted. "She won't set a wedding date. I'm hoping a baby comes along and puts some fire in her belly to tie me down."

Austin shook his head. "You don't know what you're talking about." Babies made everything a hundred times harder, in his experience. When Becky had found out she was pregnant with Ryder, they'd both been shocked. Then she'd hated him for it, half the time, and the rest of her pregnancy she'd been miserable.

Buck handed him a beer from the cooler. "Is Becky winning at rodeo this year?"

"She is." Austin took a long swallow. "I served her with divorce papers. Hopefully it'll be done before Christmas."

"Good man." Buck reeled in his line. "You made a great kid with her. The rest of it wasn't in the cards."

"What's your story?"

"Well, I'm finally moving my girl east this weekend. She's done with school and packed up, ready for a glamorous life in a trailer on a construction site. Permits for the road and sewer are in, it's all getting torn up next week. Poured foundations for a few of those little A-frame vacation cabins I told you about. I'll be hauling you out there to help with the framing before you know it."

Austin grunted. "Yeah, I'll lend a hand. When I can get a babysitter."

"Luckily, you live next to one."

"Ma likes her weekends to herself," Austin said. His mother had already done too much for him. Having his home next to his parents was the only reason he'd been able to manage as a single father. "With a lot of notice, I can find somebody."

"How's Dad?" Buck glanced at him, his mouth turned down. "Has he been back to the doctor yet?"

"Nope, won't go. He's dead set on toughing out his heart problems by working even harder. Blows up when anybody tries to talk to him."

"Jesus." Buck cast his line out into the river. "We could tie him up and call it an intervention. Take him straight to the hospital cause he'll be mad enough to burst a vein."

"Hey, I live in a barn on his property and have to work with him every day. When Chase gets back from Vegas, rope him into your crazy plan."

"Our brother's not coming back from Vegas. Looks like he's going to flip houses out there and start a construction company."

"Well, damn, he's doing it. Been talkin a long time."

Austin turned and found Buck squinting at him. "What's that thing around your neck? Is that a twine necklace with beads on it?"

Austin shrugged, trying not to grin. Buck was staring at him like he'd just licked his boot. "Yeah, it is."

Buck sat up. "Hang on, you're telling me you bought yourself some hippie jewelry? This from the man that thinks the color red is too flashy?"

"It doesn't have any red on it." Well, apart from the rainbow fish pendant.

"Come on now, spill it."

Austin took a sip of his beer. Saying anything would be a mistake because Buck had a memory like an elephant. Strangely, though, he wanted to talk it out, a little.

"My son decided he found a new mommy."

Buck's eyebrows shot up. "Well, damn. Who is she?"

"A pink-haired single-mother student with a five-month-old baby, living in the duplex next to ours. Ryder likes her because she reminds him of Strawberry Shortcake."

Buck leaned back, his mouth open, his eyes alight with wicked amusement. "Must be real sweet if Ryder likes her."

Austin huffed. "She's been babysitting for me, in the mornings. Then she met Grace, and that old dragon likes her too. Gave her a job."

Buck took a swallow of beer, his pole dangling forgotten in his hand. "So, then what happened?"

"She flirted with me a little and now I'm making an ass of myself. Went to a big hippie art fair with her yesterday. She bought Ryder fairy wings and me this necklace."

After pinching his mouth together, Buck snorted. "Okay, hold on. You're a single father, not a saint. It's okay for you to have some fun with another consenting adult."

Austin shook his head, staring out at where the river disappeared around a bend. "I'm no fuckboy."

"Yeah, you're too damn mean for that."

Austin's eyes narrowed. Something about that had him clenching his jaw. He didn't like many people, and preferred to spend a lot of time alone, but he'd never thought of himself as mean. More like brutally honest. "Yeah," he said, finally. "I guess I am. Sweet girls are too soft. Becky was about what I deserved."

"To hell with that. Letting Ryder choose might be the way to go. A little shortcake would do you good."

ELLIE WATCHED Austin set up the grill on the driveway by the playground. They were all back at the duplex and Austin had offered to make burgers. Earlier, he'd picked up Ryder from Grace's, and had wanted to take them all to the beach, but

Kinley had been too fussy. She'd gone back to the duplex on her own. After a stop at the store.

Buying condoms from the pimply teenage boy at the cash register of a big-box store had been an experience to make her brain bleed. He'd studied the condoms, he'd looked at the baby, then he'd stared at her chest. Smiling, he'd nodded at her with a smirk on his face. Kinley had started crying at exactly that moment, as if in protest of whatever that jerk had been thinking.

After getting back to the duplex, she'd indulged in a little female primping. If the kids had a good night, she'd, hopefully, be getting some action for the first time in over a year. Her skin tingled. Nervous twinges made it impossible to stand still.

"Can I do anything, Austin?" she asked again just to break the intense silence between them. He seemed more wound up than usual. She wanted to touch him, badly, but kept her hands in her pockets instead.

"No, I've got it."

He did have it, whatever it was that made a man irresistible. He caught her staring at him and she smiled, biting her lip, even as her face went red hot. His eyes narrowed, staring back at her in an almost angry way. Gawd, she loved it.

Once the burgers were done, and the tater tots baked in the oven in Austin's duplex, they all sat down at the picnic table on the front lawn by the raised garden beds. The air was cool in the shade and alive with buzzing bees and flapping butterflies. Ellie put her bare foot on Austin's leg then grinned when he startled. He glared at her. She leaned forward and slid her instep up his calf.

"I want to watch Spider-Man, Dad," said Ryder. He pushed his empty plate away.

"Yep. Let's go." Austin got up from the table, pulling away from Ellie's exploring foot.

"What about ice cream?"

"On the floor in front of the TV tonight."

"Oh yeah."

They moved the kids and food inside. Ellie put a blanket down for Kinley and settled her on the floor next to Ryder with some toys. Austin dumped a large bowl of ice cream in front of Ryder then started the movie.

Austin grabbed her hand and tugged her into a bedroom. He left the door open a crack so they could still see the kids. His bedroom, she realized. She shivered, her pulse hammering. He pushed her against the wall with his body.

"Stop teasing me," he growled.

"Or what?" She arched against him, heat pulsing between her legs.

His mouth landed against hers, rough and open. She wrapped her arms around his neck, stretching up on tiptoe to reach, her heartbeat thudding in her ears, goose bumps tingling all over her skin. Her head was as light as if she'd just finished five cocktails. Kissing Austin turned her stomach inside out—she'd never been so out of her head and out of control. She bit his lip, grinding against him.

He pulled away, panting, then took a few quick steps back. "Ellie, wait." He crossed his arms, turning away from her to face the window. "You're driving me crazy, woman. Hold on a minute. I need to talk to you."

Ellie squeezed her thighs together. She kept her back against the wall with an effort. Reality trickled in through the lust fog clouding her brain—the kids were awake. She peeked through the door opening to check on them and saw Kinley lying on her back, chewing on her favorite rubber giraffe. Ryder appeared totally absorbed in his show. She turned back to Austin.

"Okay," she said.

"I'm still married."

"I know." She shifted from foot to foot. "But you're getting a divorce."

"I'm fucked up. Not in a good place. You're a sweet girl and I don't want another thing to carry guilt for."

She squinted at him. "A sweet girl? I haven't been a child for a long time, Austin."

"You don't know shit about me."

They stared at each other. Suddenly, she wasn't willing to put up with him pushing her away. "I like everything I have seen. A lot. And the way you kiss me…I've never wanted anyone more in my life."

He covered his face with his hands. "Not helping."

"I don't care!" She threw her hands up and paced around in a tight circle. "I can't figure out what direction I should go most of the time. But I know I want you. I want to meet you in the backyard, on the blanket I've set up out there, after the kids are sleeping."

He looked up at the ceiling. She waited, her fists clenched. He opened his mouth, then closed it. She turned around and walked out of the room.

"Goodnight, Ryder," she said, and she bent over to scoop up Kinley. "See you tomorrow, buddy."

"Night, Ellie."

She marched out without glancing back. Back in her duplex, she blew out her breath in long exhalations, walking in a circle around the living room. Kinley nudged her chest, gazing up at her face with wide expectant eyes. Ellie kissed her forehead. Then she sat down on the couch to feed her and begin the pre-bed ritual.

On her phone was a missed text message from Kinley's aunt, Nora.

Nora: I miss Kinley and hate you so much.

Ellie sighed.

Ellie: Well, I love you and miss you very much. Kinley is rolling over like a champ. Maybe you can visit us soon?

There was no reply. She sent a few photos of Kinley that Nora hadn't seen yet. Nora still wasn't talking to her. She'd followed through on her promise to hold a grudge about Ellie moving away from the row house in New Jersey. So, Ellie mostly had one-sided text conversations with her, dutifully sending photos and updates about the baby. But she missed actually talking to Nora, who had become her closest friend during the hellish time after Mitch died.

Ellie tapped her phone case. Then she texted.

Ellie: I had some big news: the student daycare offered me a spot. I could go back to school and finish my degree starting this fall. I have to decide in the next four days. If I do it, I'll be crazy busy for the next year or two and living poor. I'll stay in touch and visit as soon as I can. I'll let you know what happens.

She closed her phone. The looming elephant in the room-sized problem was that her degree would be basically useless. She'd been working on a Bachelor of Fine Arts, with an emphasis on painting. A BFA did not translate into a job that would pay off your student loans, let alone cover your rent. She hadn't been able to decide what she should do, so she'd just kept doing what she loved. Tentatively, she'd planned on staying in school for a graduate degree in art therapy—which would create even more debt and not compete, salary-wise, with a server working a part-time breakfast shift.

Ah, reality, it kicked her in the rear every chance it got. She leaned her head back against the sofa and stared up at the ceiling. Being a poor artist had seemed romantic to her: a life open to road trips during the summer and traveling for a job in the southern hemisphere during the winter. She'd planned on setting up a booth in the fair circuit, not settling on any troubled relationship, and creatively living however she could.

She kissed Kinley's head. Her fantasies about life had begun to burst before her baby had come along, ground down by the sobering absolute necessity of money. Becoming accidentally pregnant at twenty-two had shattered her, for a time. She'd understood why women decided a baby didn't fit into their lives. Then she'd told Mitch and he'd completely surprised her with his offer to start a family together.

Yet, here she was again, her road map at a dead end. *One day at a time.*

Kinley finished breastfeeding, her little belly full and rounded. Ellie walked around the living room with the baby facedown on her shoulder, gently patting her back. Austin was at least ten years older than her. She thought he was thirty-three. At a restaurant, she'd caught sight of his driver's license one time, but too briefly to be sure. In any case, he had trouble seeing her as another autonomous adult.

A burp rippled out of Kinley. Her belches were more like high-pitched squeaks. Ellie walked into the bathroom to fill up the little baby bath inside the larger bathtub. She rinsed, applied lotions, and diapered Kinley before putting her in her pajamas and sleep sack. "She's the sweetest, easiest, baby," her mother had said. "You have no idea how lucky you are." Ellie kissed and hugged Kinley one last time before setting her in her crib. It didn't seem easy to her, but what did she know.

She wandered back into the bathroom to splash water on her face. Her reflection looked drawn, with blue-tinged puffiness under her eyes. Austin might not realize it, but he was the one forcing them to confront what they were doing —instead of obliviously enjoying it. There was a good chance she'd go out into the backyard, glass of wine in hand, and sit there by herself. Again.

CHAPTER NINE

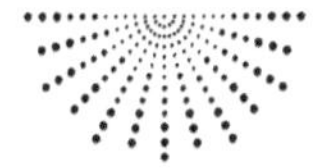

Ellie opened the back door and saw him crouched down by the fire, sparks flying up into the darkening sky above his head. She stepped outside. The screen door closed quietly behind her. A board creaked as she knelt down to leave the baby monitor propped up on the edge of the deck.

His head turned toward her slightly, putting his face in profile, backlit by the warm flames behind him. She walked across the grass, barefoot, breathing in short gasps. He stood up and tossed his stick into the fire. Frogs chirped in the forest surrounding the little yard. Ellie pressed her front against his rigid back, reaching around him to run her hands up his stomach. His muscles twitched as she pulled up his shirt.

She kissed his back, inhaling the smoky pine musk of him. Her fingers ran over firm abs and smooth skin. "Austin," she said, letting her hands wander lower, her fingers skimming the waist of his jeans.

He blew out his breath. Fabric slid through her fingers as he turned around. He bent over and scooped her up into his arms. *Yes.* She ran a hand over his flexed shoulders as he carried her a few steps to the blanket laid out on the grass. His eyes were focused ahead of them, his face hard.

He sank to his knees, still cradling her against his chest, and opened his mouth. "Ellie, I—"

She leaned forward and pressed her lips against his, wrapping her arms around his neck. If he rejected her now, she'd shatter. He groaned, dropping his hold under her knees to slide his hand up her thighs. She wrapped her legs around his hips, her short skirt bunched against his stomach. Kissing him harder, she shivered when his hands grasped her behind, kneading her closer against him. His fingers slid closer to the slit between her legs.

Heat pulsed right where she wanted it. She was desperate, on fire, the delicious, coiled thrumming frightening in its intensity. Their mouths separated, both of them panting.

"I want you," she gasped out. "No, I *need* you. Now."

His hands slid up her sides, bunching up her camisole top. "We're both going to suffer for this," he said.

She swallowed. He was right. In the months to come, as a struggling single parent, the idea of him would stick with her like a game of roulette when she'd gone all in and come so close.

"Worth it." She pulled her top off over her head, the night air cold on her tight nipples. His hands cupped her breasts, gently, his eyes glinting at her through narrowed lids. She put her hands down behind her and tipped back her head.

He slid down the blanket. One of his hands yanked the front of her thong to the side and his hot mouth landed on her throbbing cleft. "Oh," she moaned, shivers climbing up her spine and neck. The nub of her clitoris ached, and her stomach clenched, then she was spasming, falling all the way back on the blanket.

In a haze, she felt his mouth leave her. Clothing rustled and a zipper slid open. His big male body stretched out beside her, his long cock rigid against his stomach. He ripped open the condom she'd left on the blanket and slid the rubber sleeve over his shaft. Ellie leaned forward and stroked him, cupping and circling with her hand. He exhaled, nostrils flaring like a bull, then he grabbed her hands and pinned them above her head.

Her mouth opened. His weight settled over her, his shaft gliding over her rhythmically without sliding in. He kissed her, hard, his tongue stroking into her. Electric arousal pounded between her legs. She spread her knees wider, trying to catch him inside of her, as she rubbed shamelessly against him.

He let go of her hands to grip her hips, forcing her to be still as he, finally, slid in. The slow glide rippled into her. As he drew deeper, a little pain twinged in her pelvis. She tensed, suddenly remembering it wouldn't be the same after having a baby. He stopped moving and paused, still and panting above her.

His hands shifted her hips, his shaft pulling out of her a couple of inches then sliding forward again in a shallow thrust that slid against her swollen nub. A breath shuddered out of her and her hips began nudging against him, as pleasure spiraled up again. He pushed further in, her slight tenderness overcome by urgent building pleasure.

She opened her eyes and stared up into his dark narrow eyes. He pumped against her, and she fell over the edge, crying out, grinding up against him.

He shuddered, his back arching, as his hips drove into her. She pulsed around him as he collapsed down onto his elbows, his face landing between her breasts.

Ellie stared up at the indigo sky, the first visible stars glimmering above her. Her chest rose and fell under Austin's head in shallow pants, her heart still pounding in her chest. *Hold on to this.*

Austin pulled out of her then turned away to remove the condom. Rubber snapped as he tied it closed. He tossed it into the fire. She laughed.

"I wouldn't have thought to do that," she said, rolling onto her side and propping herself up on one elbow.

He peered at her over his shoulder. "We burn a lot out on the ranch."

"Huh. Makes sense, now that I'm thinking about it."

"Put your clothes on."

"Why?"

He stood up and stepped into his shorts and jeans, the clothing still layered together. "First time for you, since the baby."

She sniffed and made a halfhearted raspberry sound. "I'm fine. Give me five minutes, a few sips of wine, and I'll be chasing you around for round two."

He dropped her clothes on top of her. "Nope. You were barely ready for round one."

She let the clothes slide off her chest and land on the blanket. "It was amazing. I want more."

He stared down at her, his hard expression raising the hairs on the back of her neck. "You'll get more, just not tonight."

"Shouldn't this be the other way around?"

"Somebody has to think about tomorrow."

She sighed, rolling onto her back to stare up at the sky. "That should make me angry. But you know what, I don't want to think about tomorrow. Those problems will be here soon enough."

His shirt landed on top of her. "Put that on."

"Fine. But I might not give it back."

She slid her arms inside the cotton button-up shirt, bending forward to breathe in his scent on the collar. She buttoned one button.

"I noticed you're wearing your fish necklace," she said, smirking at him.

"It's hideous."

She laughed. "If I'd known you'd wear the things I gave you, there would be a tie-dyed hat on your head right now."

He sighed. "This doesn't feel right. Not casual enough."

Did he have to kill the buzz? She drew her knees up to her chest. "I'm not going to pretend for you, it isn't my style. I'm a zero to a hundred kind of gal."

He rubbed the top of his head, his hair still smashed from wearing his cowboy hat earlier. "I keep telling you I'm leaving in a week and it's like you're not hearing me."

Ellie grabbed her clothes then stood up. He couldn't wait to get away from her, she thought. "I don't look a gift cowboy in the mouth. I'd rather kiss him. Goodnight, Austin."

AUSTIN STARED at the fire until the burning log had crumbled into coals. Images of Ellie below him, arching into him, coiled through his mind, tensing and hardening his body. She'd said she'd never wanted anyone more in her life.

He forced himself to stand up and kick apart the embers in the firepit. How could she possibly know what the hell she wanted at twenty-three? He was just the first man to float by her in a lifeboat while she flailed about in deep water, trying to find firm ground for her baby.

The door to her duplex was closed. He blew out a breath. At least she'd remembered that much. She was the type that didn't think to lock her doors. Or put her car keys in the same spot. And struggled with any kind of schedule. He let himself into his own dark and silent living room.

After a quick shower, he got himself into bed. Then he stared at the ceiling. On the bright side, Ellie had shoved

Becky to the far back corner of his mind. It was a change to not be brooding over that failure.

Dating was the answer. There were a couple of women he could call not too far from home, unlike Ellie who would be a seven-hour drive away. Suddenly, he was more than ready to try—and to share his bed. Austin punched his pillow and forced his eyes closed.

His phone ringing woke him up before five. "Yeah?"

"Austin," his mother said, her voice cracking. He sat up and threw the covers off. "Your father's in the hospital. It's his heart."

He switched on the bedroom light. "You in Boise?"

"We are. I used that device you bought for him. It got us through."

"The defibrillator."

"Yes."

Austin walked out to the kitchen, headed for the coffee maker. "Is he conscious?"

She sobbed, then took in a shuddering breath. "No. We should have gotten that oxygen tank. I did some CPR, but he was so hard to move…"

"It's okay. You kept him alive." He rubbed his head. "Have you found out anything yet from the doctors?"

"Not much. We haven't been here long. After I used that device on him, his heart started beating again and then he could breathe on his own. I hope…I'm not sure…" She gasped, her voice trailing away.

"You did good and got him to a major hospital. I bet they'll want to do surgery real soon." Austin leaned on the kitchen counter. "How many cowboys on the ranch?"

"I sent Billy back this morning after he drove us to the hospital. Diego is there."

"Good, they'll handle everything for a few days. I'll be to

the hospital as soon as I can. Hang on Ma, and update me as soon as you can."

They hung up and Austin stood there staring at the wall while the coffee machine hissed and spluttered. He had to leave, right away.

~

ELLIE HEARD a car door shut in the driveway. She tweaked the curtain aside and glanced out the window behind the couch. Austin stood by his truck, swinging a bag into the back.

As soon as Kinley was done breastfeeding, she wrapped her up in a blanket. She walked out the front door. At just after six in the morning, the sun had barely risen, and the crisp sea air was chilly. Birds sang in the trees all around them. Austin walked out of his duplex with a big cardboard box in his arms, the open top showing packages of pastry, bags of chips, and bread. All the food from his kitchen island.

He met her gaze and his face tightened. Kinley squealed at him, managing to work an arm out of her blanket and wave it around. Austin put the box inside his truck.

"Bad news this morning," he said, his solemn eyes remote. "My father's in the hospital. Heart attack."

Ellie's mouth dropped open. "Oh no—Austin, I'm so sorry." She wanted to put her arms around him but settled for resting a hand on his shoulder. He flinched under her touch. She pulled away.

"Old man's known he needed surgery for a while but kept puttin it off. Hopefully they'll do the bypass surgery, or get a stent in, before too much damage is done." He rubbed his head, bare of the cowboy hat. "Ryder's not going to be happy about leavin, but we have to go as soon as he's up and fed."

Ellie stared at him, her eyes darting over every inch of his tight, withdrawn face. "Ryder will be sad," she said, slowly, "but you're not. Maybe you're even a little relieved?"

He took a deep breath, closing his eyes. "My head is eight hundred miles away, wondering how the hell I'm going to get the ranch through the summer, and fall, without my father. I have to go—it's not what I want."

She didn't believe him. "I understand."

"Hey." He reached out a hand, then let it drop. "Don't cry. Can you text me those photos you took? I want to stay in touch. Know how you and Kinley are doing and where you end up."

She looked away. Kinley kicked her legs and reached toward Austin. Ellie turned and walked a few steps in the direction of her duplex, her vision blurred.

"Dad," Ryder yelled from their front door. "Where are my toys?"

"Son, your grandpa's in the hospital and Grandma Dolly needs us. We've got to go this mornin and see how we can help."

Ellie wiped her eyes. In a way, it was better to do this now rather than in a week when she'd be even more crazy about him. She drew in a deep breath.

"What?" Ryder stumbled further into the driveway. "I don't want to leave, Dad."

"I know. We've got to do it."

Her bare foot banged on the step as she went toward her front door. Pain shot up her leg from the stubbed toe. She opened her door and went inside. She stared at the kitchen. Austin had been right. Starting something with him had hurt her, badly.

She put Kinley in her high chair. Happy baby babbling filled the room. Ellie arranged small chunks of banana and cooked sweet potato out on the tray, along with a baby spoon. After a minute of effort, Kinley picked up the spoon and chewed on it.

At the sink, Ellie let cool water run over her hands, a void opening in her chest. Her eyes closed. What had she expected? She was such an idiot and way too careless. Okay, in her defense, the coincidence of them being thrown together, side by side in the duplex, had seemed like a gift from fate. Two lonely single parents that were actually attracted to each other. Although, perhaps on his end, she'd merely been a body.

The front door flew open and Ryder came stomping inside, wiping his nose with one hand, his face red and splotchy and dripping tears. "Ellie, Dad says we have to go. I don't want to."

She turned around and opened her arms to him. He came stumbling over, hiccuping sobs, and pressed his face into her stomach.

"I know, buddy, me too."

They stayed that way for a few minutes. Ryder took a breath. "We're supposed to stay until Friday, that's six more days."

Ellie sniffed, wiping her sleeve across her cheeks and chin. She grabbed a tissue and dabbed at Ryder's face. "I don't think I'm going to stay here either. Won't be any fun without you guys." She stood up straighter. Actually, going back to her mother's wasn't a bad idea.

"Wait, where are you going to go?"

"Well, I want to check on my family now and make sure everybody's okay. Your grandpa's heart attack is scary. I'm glad you're going see him. Kinley's grandpa is okay, but I want to be with him and her grandma too." Well, he was Kinley's step-grandpa, but her mother's husband, Bart, was more of a grandfather to Kinley than Ellie's father ever would be.

Ellie held out a cookie to Ryder. He picked it up out of her hand and took a bite, his eyes unfocused. "Is my grandpa going to die?"

"That's what everyone is worried about. It's good you're going to the hospital to visit him. Your grandpa is going to be happy you went to see him when he was sick."

Ryder's bottom lip stuck out. Ellie handed him a glass of milk. He drank a few sips then set it on the counter. "But, Ellie, I want you to come with us. You and Kinley."

Ellie put her hand on her chest, closing her eyes again. "Thank you, that means the world to me. I can't do it though, buddy."

"Why not? Just come with us."

Austin walked into the room. She glanced up at his shoulder, then away.

"Ryder," said Austin, "Ellie can't come with us. Let's go, son, we need to get ready for the road."

Ellie squeezed Ryder around the shoulders, hugging him tight. "Bye, Ryder, I'm really going to miss you, buddy. Go on now, this is making my heart hurt."

Ryder shouted at his dad then stormed out. Ellie kept her back turned to Austin, aware of Kinley throwing things on the floor in her peripheral vision.

"Ellie, I…" Austin cleared his throat.

"Goodbye, Austin," she said.

Something crashed in the driveway and Austin ran out. Ellie started packing. The truck backed down the driveway about thirty minutes later.

Having something to do sent a burst of intense feverish energy into her. With a seven-hour drive ahead of them, she had to get on the road by Kinley's morning nap. Actually, it would take at least eight hours with stops for breastfeeding, diaper changes, and food.

With the car haphazardly packed, and Kinley lying on a

blanket on the floor, Ellie dashed into the bathroom with her phone. Her bladder was now the size of a pea, apparently. She went to sit down, punching in a text message to her mother before her butt had hit the plastic toilet seat cover. Next, she called Grace and had to leave a voice mail. When she rang the property management company, someone answered and gave noncommittal responses about any kind of refund. Ellie wasn't above pleading—now that school looked like a possibility, she was seriously regretting spending any money on a vacation.

Last, she sent Austin a couple of photos she had taken of Ryder, and one of himself. She typed out a text message.

Ellie: Austin, the best thing for me is to not stay in touch. I need the space in my mind and heart to move on. Wishing you the best, and Ryder too, Ellie.

She stared at the words on her screen, biting her lip. Her finger descended on the send button and pressed. Cold shot up her spine and her limbs ached.

Kinley wailed in the next room, a desperate scared cry that had Ellie up off the toilet in a second. She yanked up her pants one-handed, turning to flush with the other hand. Her phone slipped from her fingers. It plopped into the toilet with a splash.

Ellie stared for a moment, stunned. The screen went dark. She lurched forward and yanked it out with one hand, gaped at the disgusting mess and set it on the floor. Kinley was still yelling. Ellie washed her hands then ran over to find Kinley with a corner of the blanket flopped over her face.

She scooped up her baby, cuddled, breastfed, and changed her, then at last loaded her into the car. Before leaving, she managed to wipe down her phone and stick it in a plastic bag, but all signs pointed toward a dead electronic. That second Saturday in July was one for the books. How in the world was she going to find the right highway, and generally survive, without her phone?

～

AUSTIN GLANCED in the rearview mirror at his son. Ryder stared out of his window, his mouth turned down.

"We're coming up on Eugene," Austin said. "What do you feel like for lunch, son?"

Ryder shrugged and didn't say anything.

Austin felt the nerve twitching in his face. He hated the way they had left. Ryder had been enraged, in full meltdown mode, and there hadn't been the space to try and talk with Ellie. She was mad at him. Ryder was mad at him. He wasn't too happy with himself either.

Ellie grinning at him, her big green eyes sparking with laughter, throughout his short week on the coast flashed through his mind. She'd seen something in him, despite the fact that he was at his grumpiest. His hand found the ugly necklace around his neck.

He missed her. *We had something right, the four of us.* When they'd been out with the kids, everything had clicked, like when he had enough people for a job on the ranch and everyone knew what to do. With Ellie, simple daily tasks became full of laughter, fun, and silliness. No wonder Ryder loved her. Austin rubbed the top of his head—she wouldn't even look at him when he'd said goodbye.

A drive-up place with milkshakes caught his attention and he managed to pull off the highway in time to catch the exit. "Burgers and ice cream," he called back to Ryder.

"I want a sundae, Dad, with chocolate sauce."

"If they have it, you're gonna get it."

Ryder sniffed. "I miss Ellie."

"Me too, son."

"When are we going to see her again?"

Austin took a deep breath. "I'm not sure. But, I think, once Grandpa's better, we can try to check up on Ellie and Kinley."

He found an open spot for the drive-in service and stepped out onto the concrete next to the ordering terminal, his legs cramping. Ryder jumped out behind him, moving freely despite being in his booster seat for so many hours. They put in their orders, then Ryder stood beside the picnic table, digging through the toy box he'd hauled out.

Austin opened his phone, his mouth twitching up when he saw a few pictures from Ellie. Still nothing from his mother. He'd have to give her a call. He opened the messages from Ellie first, smiling at the shots of Ryder at the beach and at the hippie fair.

Then he saw her message. She "needed space…to move on." His hand dropped down to his side. He stared at the truck.

"Dad, are you okay? Is your heart hurting?"

"I'm fine." He was hollowed out. She didn't want to even talk to him. Could he blame her? "I'm gonna call Grandma and check on how Grandpa's holding up."

His mother answered, distracted and exhausted. They were hoping for an emergency surgery. After hanging up, he texted his brothers to make sure they were clued in. The food arrived and Austin hustled them along, anxious to get back on the road.

Ryder, at least, seemed to be feeling better. He played games on his tablet for a while then watched *Willy Wonka and the Chocolate Factory* as the miles burned by under their wheels. Ellie had been hurt—she thought, he suspected, that he didn't care about her. He'd made it pretty clear he wasn't available for any kind of relationship. Was he now? He needed more time, but maybe…

His ma texted that his dad was stable and awake, complaining about being stuck in the hospital. Austin could breathe again. In Bend, he pulled into a pizza place with a kid arcade. Ryder needed time on his feet and Austin could use a spell out of the truck as well. He loaded Ryder up with tokens for the games then ordered food.

At the table, he read Ellie's text again. On impulse he hit the call button and put the phone to his ear. His call went straight to voice mail.

"Hey, it's Austin. Ellie, I'm real sorry about—a lot of things. Everything happened too fast for me, and it's only now that I've left that I'm realizin I…want to see you again as soon as I can. Will you give me another chance? Please, call me."

CHAPTER TEN

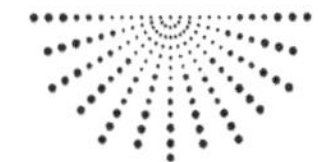

After three weeks of living with her mother, Ellie found the courage to move to Riverside. She dropped her bags in a tiny room at Mari's house and blew out a long breath. Kinley kicked her legs in the baby carrier on her chest.

"Kinley will sleep in here," Mari said briskly, hauling in the pack and play portable crib. She set it down on the floor to lean against the locked accordion desk that took up half the room. The twin bed took up the other half.

Ellie chewed on her lip. Where would she change diapers? Maybe she could squeeze a table under the window—which would leave about two feet of floor space.

Mari dusted her hands off. "We'll set up a bed for you in my room. I have the large bedroom next door. You'll only have to sleep in here when I bring one of my fboys over—so, like, Friday and Saturday. Don't worry. This is temporary because we're going to find you somewhere better, I know we will. Also, Sarah wants this room back in September. And she made me sign a contract promising I wouldn't kick her out."

"Thank you, this is great." Ellie put her hands in her hair. "What's the matter?"

"I'm…stressing a little. No, a lot. Kinley won't take a bottle and she starts daycare tomorrow. My mother spent the last three weeks implying I've screwed up her babyhood, because I should have started bottles months ago and now it's too late so I'm doomed."

Mari slung an arm around her shoulders. "Hey, where there's a will there's a way. Those daycare pros are going to know what to do." Mari tickled Kinley's feet, making her squawk and squirm. "You're the sweetest baby girl, I know you're going to figure out those bottle waddles-dingle-dongles." Kinley made a spit bubble, her wide eyes locked on Mari's glittering earrings.

"Who lives in the basement?"

"Oh, that's Greg. Engineer." Mari's face scrunched up derisively. "He has his own kitchenette down there. We won't see him much. Gets out to play indoor soccer with his nerdy friends a few times a week, and that's it. I told him you and your baby were moving in for a little while and he stared at me like I'd said alien baby."

Ellie rested against the doorframe, her back aching. Driving long distances to move every few weeks was getting old. "Well, at least she's a cute alien. Maybe Kinley will win him over?"

"Who cares what Greg thinks. Come on, we have plans. I'll make us lunch while you set up your gear. Later, I'm taking us out to dinner—nope, don't argue or make faces at me, it's my treat."

Ellie squeezed her in for a side hug. "You're the best. The very best."

"Your hair looks better—I mean really nice. Okay, look, that haircut you gave yourself was a disturbed mullet. This layered shag with bangs, in a softer pink, is aces. You're my new favorite anime character."

"Wow, such faint praise."

Mari marched out of the room and Ellie stared down at the pack and play, which refused to set itself up. Austin crept into her mind, like he did at least five times a day. Men were the aliens, but darn useful ones. They did amazing feats like lug heavy bags around and not throw out their backs. Her back was still recovering from twisting around a baby lump.

She sighed and set Kinley on the little twin bed and surrounded her with pillows. She'd asked Austin not to contact her and that's what he'd done, probably with relief. Most days, she regretted it. She missed Ryder. After tripping into that sinkhole, she eventually talked herself back into the sensible, responsible outlook that a cowboy hook-up on the other side of the state would distract her from some kind of more stable future. All for the best. Of course, it was.

The portable crib snapped into position. Ellie pushed herself up off the floor, then reloaded Kinley into her carrier. She trudged out to her car, which she saw she'd left wide open, exposing her pile of clothing stuffed in garbage bags to any passerby.

"Hi," said a low voice from the side of the house. She jumped. Kinley started crying. "Sorry, I didn't mean to startle you. I'm Greg—I live downstairs."

"Hi," Ellie called over Kinley's screaming, fumbling with the baby carriers' straps and flashing the tall dark-haired man a smile. She pulled Kinley out and turned her, tummy down, onto her shoulder. "She's a little cranky from all the travel today." She thought about apologizing to him but stopped herself—if she started, there would be no end. Would he try to kick her out of the house? Putting all her eggs in Mari's basket had been a little shortsighted...

"Can I help you with those bags?" Greg walked forward with his hands in his pockets.

"Um, yes please." She beamed at him. Greg's good looks and short curls brought to mind the actor Jesse Eisenberg, except with darker brown hair. His long face ended in a pointy chin, with deep-set, slightly asymmetrical eyes and a larger nose. He appeared to be someone that could fix a computer and didn't spend much time in the sun. One of his cheeks twitched a little as he passed, his eyes meeting hers then darting away.

Kinley sucked her thumb, a new habit that looked like it was going to stick, and laid her head against Ellie's neck, doing her best to communicate how little she appreciated being kept from her afternoon nap. Ellie managed to grab her pillow and followed Greg inside, who was hauling six of her garbage sacks.

He dumped everything on the bed in Kinley's room. "Anything else?" Greg glanced at her with his eyebrows up, valiantly ignoring a bra that had spilled out of one of the white plastic sacks.

"Yes, actually, if you don't mind, would you haul in the roll-away bed crammed into my back seat and put it in Mari's room?"

"Sure." He flashed a tight smile at her.

"Wow—thank you so much. Really, you're saving my bacon here."

"Yeah, no problem. And, um, nice to meet you. Actually, I didn't catch your name?"

"I'm Ellie, short for Eleanor—which only my mother calls me, when she's angry, because she has the power. Call me Ellie. And this is Kinley, who spontaneously turns from princess to pumpkin when I mess up her routine."

He sniffed, his mouth twitching, and gave her a little wave, then wandered out to flex his masculine strength. Ellie closed the door after him. She plopped down on the bed, collapsing against the soft clothing-filled plastic bags, and began breastfeeding.

The rest of the day blurred by for her in an exhausted haze. She had to take a rain check on going out to dinner because of her desperation to get to the grocery store before Kinley went to bed. Then Mari was even more disgusted with her when she crashed at nine.

Her next day began at five. The three hours before getting to the daycare were not enough to organize herself. She had a checklist of things to pack for Kinley's bag. The daycare policy was supportive of her stopping by to breastfeed, which she planned on doing, and they also provided formula as part of the student service. At a bit over eight hundred dollars for three months of daycare, it was an amazing deal, but still a painful stretch for her budget. Plus, the on-campus daycares closed from noon to one-thirty, inexplicably, so she had to be available to pick up Kinley during that time. Between the breastfeeding and lunch hiatus, her original plan of seeing about lunch-hour food-service work crashed and burned.

At the daycare, Ellie handed over Kinley to a middle-aged woman with tidy short brown hair. "What a pretty baby," she said. Kinley startled and stared with her mouth open. Ellie turned away, biting hard on her bottom lip.

Dropping off Kinley wrenched open a gaping hole in her chest. *I'm doing this for her.* She had to get a career going—Kinley was depending on her.

Not wanting to spend money, she went back to Mari's house to search online for some kind of job. Mari bustled in around nine, dressed in a suit for her day at the business school. She poured coffee into a portable canteen.

"What's the matter, Ellie? You okay?"

"I'm...not, actually." She pinched the bridge of her nose.

"Go on, talk."

Ellie's mouth twitched up in a wobble. "The daycare seems fine, I guess, but I feel guilty sitting here without my baby. I don't know, it's hard to explain. I miss her."

"I'm sorry, that sounds really hard. Hey, don't start crying—here, eat this cookie, and drink a cup of tea, or whatever. What's your job plan?"

Ellie wiped her face, then blew her nose into a tissue. "Impossible. I'm breastfeeding, and the daycare closes for lunch—how did I miss that before today? School starts in like six weeks…"

Mari nodded, tapping a finger on the counter. "Gig work," she said, decisively. "Like senior care, and childcare, and housekeeping. Feed cats. Water houseplants. There's also driving and delivery." She paced back and forth in the kitchen. "If you develop in-home clients you can work around your schedule. Aim high with pay—this town can afford it. At least research what the going rate is out there."

Ellie sat up straight. "Okay, where…"

Mari rattled off a bunch of websites, glanced at her watch, then charged out. Ellie started creating accounts. She paused, an hour later, to call the daycare. Kinley had taken a few ounces from a bottle and went down for a nap. Ellie put her head down on the table and cried.

Austin walked into the diner and saw her right away. Blonde hair pinned up on her head, showing off a pretty neck, Gina the real estate agent turned and flashed a predator's grin at him. She sat up straighter, pushing out her chest.

"Mornin," Austin said as he stopped by her booth. "I'm glad you had time to meet with me today."

"Hello, Austin." Gina cocked her head at him coquettishly.

"Let's just skip to first names. I've been hoping for a call from you for ages."

Austin slid onto the bench across from her, hanging his hat on the hook the diner provided on the wall next to its tables. Gina's hungry eyes were a little intense at eleven in the morning. Another man might throw money on the table, grab her hand, and find somewhere to lie her flat. Or a dark alley. The possibility of it stirred him up.

The corner of his mouth twitched. He'd never been that guy. Becky had been a wild girl who he'd slept with off and on for years after they'd met in college. He'd been loyal through it all. She'd been more than enough for him to handle.

"You asked about investment properties, and boy do I have some zingers to show you." Gina leaned forward, displaying very plumped-up cleavage. "Here's a file with a stack of printouts." She pushed a manila envelope across the table, her long red nails grazing his hand. "I've also arranged a couple of private showings. We'll have them all to ourselves."

Her skin had that perfect look, like one of those fashion dolls that girls played with, eyelashes unnaturally long. She was sexy as hell and obviously interested. He knew she had at least five years on him. Old enough to know what she was doing. Austin took the file and rested back against his seat. He flipped through the printouts, stalling.

"Thank you, Gina."

"Oh, hun, you bet. How much time do you have today?"

His phone rang. He glanced down and saw his mother's name on the screen. "Gina, excuse me a minute. I need to take this call."

"No problem. I'll wait right here."

Austin grabbed his hat and slid out of the booth. "Ma," he said, walking down the aisle and out the front door.

"Austin, your father is behaving like a crazy man. I can't talk a lick of sense into that idiot."

His father bellowed, "I can hear you!" in the background.

"He's saddling up?"

"You bet he is. Huffin and puffin and clutching his chest. Says the cowboys don't know shit about fixing a fence. Ha."

His father's bypass surgery had been successful and had made a big difference, fast. But the chunk of his father's heart that was damaged during the blockage would be slow to heal, if it ever did. Now the old man was as cranky as a pinned bull at the rodeo. Austin sighed.

"He's left the house and slammed the door." His mother sounded ready to murder Austin's father herself.

"Well, if he kills himself, you'll know you did your best to stop him. Billy and Diego will have that fence half fixed before he gets there. Then they'll let him boss 'em around from up on his horse."

His mother sighed. "He won't stay in his bed."

"I'm gonna finish up the shopping and head home right away."

They hung up. Austin went inside the diner to apologize to Gina and tell her he had to get back to the ranch. She pouted a little, then put extra happy into her goodbye. He grabbed his manila folder and escaped out the door.

On the drive home, he tried to work through why he hadn't gone for it. Gina had been signaling she was up for a quick screw, or at least ready to lead him in that direction. He'd set up a meeting to test the waters, see if she was interested in dating. His answer was a resounding *come and get me*. When the hell had he become such an upstanding citizen? He didn't feel any pride, only resignation. Even Ellie had barely convinced him to enjoy what the universe dished up to him like ice cream on a hot day.

He rubbed his head. Ellie was what he craved. Not even a

delicious dessert like Gina did more than bring home what he was missing. The real problem was, Gina wasn't right for him. Ryder wouldn't like her. A woman like that was tied to her career in the city and all its luxuries. She wouldn't last two weeks on a ranch. Him and her could try for a while and stir up all kinds of gossip.

Still, he was a little tempted. He tapped the steering wheel. She'd moved too fast for him, and he needed time to think.

The next day, his mother had warned him, ladies from the church were coming out for a luncheon and she expected him to make an appearance with Ryder. That meant the teacher she'd been telling him about for the last six months would be there. So, late Saturday morning, he made sure to have on a clean shirt and corralled Ryder out of the converted barn loft they lived in, and over to his parent's big house.

Austin often didn't make it to church because there was too much work to do. And he didn't care for it. Ryder, however, loved getting into town and went with his grandmother every Sunday to play with the other kids. Presumably, Ryder knew the teacher.

"Son," he said as they crossed the big back lawn. "Your grandma wants me to meet a teacher from church. Her name is Winnie, I think."

Ryder stopped walking and pivoted to face him. "Miss Winnie?"

"Yep, that's the one. Grandma says she's nice." He cleared his throat. "And pretty."

Ryder stared up at him, his eyebrows crammed together. "She's with the babies. I don't go in that room anymore."

"Okay. Well, we're gonna drag out our good manners for this lunch party. You ready?"

"Dad," Ryder said, shoving his hands in his pockets, "when are you going to call Ellie again?"

Austin took a deep breath. "Well, I'm not gonna. I tried callin her and she didn't call me back. That's her choice."

Ryder was shaking his head. "No. It's not right. What if Hulk attacked her in the street and broke her phone. Smash."

"That might happen in a video game or a movie, but not in real life."

"Call her, Dad. One more time."

They glared at each other. The mulish set to Ryder's mouth implied noncompliance for the afternoon party if Austin didn't give in. The boy was a mean negotiator.

"I'll think about it. Now hustle in there and say hello to all the ladies."

Miss Winnie the teacher was a pretty, very chatty brunette who looked to be fresh out of teaching college. She crouched down in front of Ryder, nearly as soon as they'd walked through the door, and said, "Hello, Ryder. Remember me? I'm Miss Winnie."

"Hi, Miss Winnie," Ryder said in a robotic voice, glancing sideways toward the family room where he had his Nintendo. Austin nudged him. "Nice to see you."

Winnie stood up, beaming at Austin. "Wow, I just love his manners. Hello, Austin. How are you?"

Ryder took the opportunity to run off. Austin followed him with his eyes. "I'm fine. How are you?"

"Really well. You know, I want to pepper you with like a million questions, but I know you need to say hello to everybody. Can we chat later? There's a horse question I'm dying to ask you."

"Yep. Can I get a drink for you?"

She turned the smile up a notch, like he'd really impressed her. "Thank you, yes. I'd love a sweet coffee."

He nodded to her then walked further into the room to

be hugged and shake hands. Maybe he needed more time. He wasn't divorced yet. Becky was dragging her feet, mostly too caught up in finally winning her barrel races. His mother gave him the stink eye, like she knew what he was thinking.

He brought Winnie her coffee, dutifully enough, and sat down on the open loveseat with her, the eyes of the entire room keeping tabs on them. She chattered and asked him a lot of questions, then appeared disappointed at his laconic answers.

Much later that night, he glared at the stupid fish necklace hanging next to his bed. Maybe something had happened to Ellie—the thought had occurred to him about a hundred times. It seemed out of character for her not to respond in any way to his message.

He picked up Gina's business card instead. And stared at her personal cell phone number, handwritten on the back.

ELLIE WALKED BRISKLY UP Tenth Street toward Sasha's house for her third call back as a babysitter. Parking was always tight, as students moved back into every available space, overpopulating the small town now that fall term was about to begin.

Sasha did nude modeling for art students. They'd recognized each other from Ellie's days as one of those art students, and they'd struck up a tentative friendship. Sasha's two little boys were high-energy, rambunctious and, according to Sasha, didn't like any of their babysitters but Ellie. She waved at them as she hustled closer, not surprised to see the boys already immersed in the "mud pie" factory in their backyard. Sasha's sons were sweet boys that entertained themselves for hours in their outdoor play yard. Ellie suspected it was Sasha that didn't like any of the babysitters.

"Okay," called Sasha, standing next to her car with keys in hand, her black dreadlocks beautifully tied up in a colorful scarf. "I'm off. The savages didn't want to eat the lunch I made them so they can starve, or you can feed them whatever. No, Marcus, we already hugged and now you're covered in mud pie and soaking wet. We're gonna hug, baby, when I get home. If you're clean. Goodbye, Marcus. Goodbye, Amari. See you in three hours, Ellie."

Ellie distracted little Marcus with more water in the mud pit as his mom drove off. Their father had built them an elaborate "outdoor experimentation lab," complete with a hand-cranked pump in a tall rubber trash can. The pump cranked water onto a slide that then spilled it into a sandpit. Battered wooden shelves around the pump-slide contraption contained old aluminum pans and plastic dinosaurs. Various other plastic toys littered the yard, covering the struggling grass. The boys loved it.

After helping to dig a "dinosaur river," she had a chance to collapse in one of the lawn chairs and check her phone. In the last two weeks, she'd found a fair number of gigs. The problem was, most of them didn't pay well, some people cheated her out of paying at all, and she spent more time driving than working. She'd had to get a little tough and set boundaries with otherwise nice-seeming well-to-do people.

She scanned for any new rental notices. There was one but it was out of her price range—like everything else. Rents had skyrocketed. She wasn't going to be able to attend school at this rate.

Thirty minutes later, they all began Sasha's strict cleanup routine that was designed to limit how much mud tracked into the house. Ellie eyed the big garage at the end of the driveway. A staircase led up to a second-story door on the side of the detached building.

"Sasha," Ellie said to her at the end of her shift, "is that an apartment above your garage? Any chance you're looking for a new tenant?"

Sasha eyed her sharply. "You still don't have a place to live, do you?"

Ellie sighed. "No, I don't. Single moms with infants aren't the vibe your average college student wants to live with. I don't blame them."

"Hmph." Sasha tapped her foot, face turned toward the door to the apartment. "Well, I don't like your average college student. Drunken brats, most of them. Hang on." She disappeared into her house for a moment. "Let's go take a tour," she said, reemerging with a key. "The boys are glued to that movie. I have at least five minutes before they set fire to something."

"Really?" Ellie bounced on the balls of her feet.

"Come on, girl. Having my favorite babysitter next door is worth a lot to me."

Ellie tried to tamp down her surging hope—most likely, Sasha would want more than she could afford to pay. "I wasn't sure if somebody lived up there or not."

"They do. My niece, who's never here anymore because she has a bread-baking internship up in Portland. She dropped out of accounting to become a baker." Sasha huffed. "Her last girlfriend dragged her through a whole lot of crazy, and next thing I knew she was sleeping on somebody's floor in the city so she could bake bread all night."

Sasha unlocked the door, and they walked into a bright room with cute furniture and a very nice small kitchen, complete with a kitchen island and a countertop made of sparkling white stone. "This is adorable," Ellie said.

"Yeah, Pippa has a knack for decorating."

"Is that one of your paintings, Sasha? Oh, my goodness, it makes the room."

"It is." Sasha sighed. "I thought for a while I'd be able to paint in here, but it's just too much with the boys. So, I'm messing around with fabric on that screened-in back porch."

"I saw your sewing machine and a pile of beautiful projects. What a workspace on that covered back deck, I love it."

"I'd let you in there while I'm sewing after the kids go to bed. I might even get motivated enough to clear out a corner for you to work in, as long as you don't leave any paint out. The boys would poison themselves."

"I'm thinking to switch over to the design school, if they'll take me." She'd gotten her preliminary application in the night before, along with sending out emails begging them to add her to the program late. She put a hand on her chest. "This is too amazing to be true. But I know you could be charging the moon for this place. I don't think I can afford it."

Sasha crossed her arms. "I'll charge you what my niece is supposed to be paying, except I actually expect you to pay me on time every month. Five hundred."

Her mouth hung open. "Really?"

"Come on, I'll show you the second bedroom. George will move Pippa's desk down to the garage—you know what? I have a crib you can use. He'll be excited to get it out of his basement. You can sleep on Pippa's bed when she's not here. Don't start crying, it's all going to work out."

"You are the most amazing and generous person ever. But shouldn't I talk to Pippa first? Don't you think she'd like to meet me?"

Sasha waved her hand around. "Leave Pippa to me. You'll be good for her."

"Oh…"

Something crashed in the yard below them and Marcus yelled for his mom. "Gotta go," Sasha said, trotting to the door. "Lock up when you leave. Move in here as soon as you can. George and I need a date night." She disappeared out the door.

Ellie stared around her in a daze. The apartment was immaculately clean—how would she keep spit-up off the couch and thrown banana mush off the white shag carpet? She had a feeling Sasha and Pippa would be on opposite sides of letting Ellie move in.

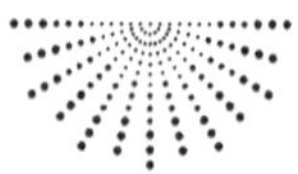

CHAPTER ELEVEN

Ellie threw another too-small onesie in the donate pile. Kinley needed new clothes again. The bottle feeding at the daycare had her putting on weight fast.

"You've only been here two weeks," Mari said, grabbing another garbage bag to haul out to Ellie's car. "I like our hangs in the evening watching shitty television, drinking cheap wine, throwing up a little as Greg drools over you. Did he give you a teddy bear last night?"

"He gave Kinley a teddy bear. It was sweet. Stop talking about him when he might walk through that door at any minute."

Mari put her finger in her mouth and gagged. Ellie rolled her eyes. Greg was nice—but she wanted to see him drunk, or something, so she could get a handle on who he was. He was definitely cute. And a little terrified of babies.

"I need to be settled before school starts. The best part is, I'll have a babysitter I can afford—which is free. We're going to trade weekend nights. A babysitter. Sasha took dibs on this coming Saturday, but how about Friday? Let's go to

Squirrels Tavern and split a big greasy woodcutter burger with tots."

"Okay," Mari said, morosely.

Ellie smiled, shaking Mari's shoulders. "This is good. I'm staying in Riverside."

"Yeah, yeah. But how long until you can come out dancing with me and get drunk again? Little Miss Responsible is a drag."

Ellie snorted and turned her back on her friend. She shoved more clothing into a garbage bag. "Wow, salty."

"I'm sorry, okay? I'm really sorry. It's freaking lonely without you around here. Give me that ugly garbage sack—get some better bags, girl. Shit." Mari stomped out.

Kinley burbled in her crib, doing tummy time and chewing on her rubber giraffe. She whacked her feet against the thin mattress. Ellie put her forehead against the doorframe, blinking her eyes, trying to ignore the stinging in her nose. Life was hard, every which way she turned. Kinley sleeping in Sasha's old crib, with an actual mattress, would be a big step up for them. One baby step forward.

Austin, where are you now? He was haunting her. She needed to move on, sign up for a few dating apps, and try to find a family man. In the overall scheme of the universe, losing her ability to be a careless twenty-year-old didn't even count as a tragedy. But she hated being lonely too.

Ellie survived another move, mostly because Sasha and her husband, George, swooped in to save her. The crib was already set up for her when she arrived, along with two empty dressers in the little room she would share with Kinley. She'd found a thrift store rice paper screen that kept Kinley from realizing she was on the other side—for now. George hauled up her little twin roll-away bed and put it in the room for her. She doubted Sasha was correct in thinking Pippa wouldn't mind if Ellie slept in her bedroom.

The week sped by, and on Friday Ellie walked downtown to meet Mari with a bounce in her step. "Did you order the burger?" Ellie slid onto the wooden bench across the table from her friend. "My stomach sounds like it has a steel drum in there."

"You know I did. And I bought you a pint of weak-ass beer."

"You're an angel from heaven."

"Ha—oh, great, there he is. Guess who followed me down here."

Ellie turned around and waved at Greg, who was sidling through the other tables in the outdoor seating area. "Hey," she said, "how are you?"

"Hey," Greg said. "Nice to see you. How's your new place?"

"Um, hello," Mari said, leaning around Greg. "You're standing right in front of me, dude. Sit down next to Ellie for a minute."

"Sorry. Do you mind?"

Ellie scooted over and patted the wooden bench next to her. "My new place is nice for Kinley and me. The backyard is set up for kids. The couple that owns the property, and lives in the house next to my apartment, cook every night and seem like they want to feed me. I think it's so I'll sit with their kids while they work in the kitchen. It's a sweet deal for me. I feel a little bad about it actually. Like I should be bringing a dish with me to put on the table—but I don't have any time to cook before I go over there. I managed to bring some berries the other night. Maybe I should pitch in for the food."

"Relax," said Mari. "Pick up a few toys or whatever, but watching their kids is a fair trade."

"What do you think, Greg?" Ellie smiled at him, bumping his shoulder with hers.

Greg's mouth hung open. "I'm not sure."

Ellie watched Greg, wondering what was rattling around up there, underneath all of that nice hair. "Oh?"

His face wrinkled. "You should ask them, your landlords, about it."

Mari rolled her eyes. Ellie slapped her hand down on the table, making Greg jump. "That's it."

Greg swallowed, appearing a little lost and suspicious. "Um, I wanted to ask you something. I'm having some friends over tomorrow for a barbecue at one. Can you come by, Ellie? There'll be plenty of food."

"Wait, what?" said Mari. "You're having a party and I'm not invited?"

"No, you're invited," said Greg, his eyebrows pinching together.

"Oh, there's our dinner," said Mari, ruthlessly. "Ellie, I forgot to grab that hot sauce you like. I think they have it inside."

Ellie shook her head at Mari, feeling guilty for teasing Greg. He gave her one of his mouth twitch smiles and slid off the bench. The server leaned around him to slide their burger basket on the table. "See you," he said and wandered off toward the door leading inside.

"What just happened? I used to be a sweet person. I think I'm going bitter."

"Nah," said Mari. "That's not it. You're just not interested in him. You're still stuck on that hot cowboy."

Ellie checked an invisible mark in the air. "What I need is a power-word pep talk. Shoot some of that sexy business-speak my way."

Mari squinted at her, chewing on her bite of burger. She swallowed. "Integrated synchronization. Boosted collaboration."

"Damn, that's good."

"Maximized development."

"Spearhead my heart."

"You're mad crazy."

"Um, you missed the mark on that one."

"Forget about that hick dude. One, he's married. Two, he didn't call you. Three, he lives too freaking far away. What are you gonna do with a guy that lives with a bunch of cows? Go be *Little House on the Prairie*?"

"I like cows. They're cute."

"He's a rancher. He fattens them up then drives them to a slaughterhouse."

Ellie put down her burger. "Hey, it's me, Ellie, not your ten-year-old cousin."

Mari huffed. "I'd be so pissed if you disappeared out into the boonies."

Ellie pretended to throw a tater-tot at her. Mari's eyes widened then lit up with murderous intensity.

"Relax, fire-cat," said Ellie. "Let's go catch some of that live music at The Dirty Bird. I have one more hour before I turn back into Cinder-mommy."

ELLIE TOOK Kinley to the barbecue the next day at Greg and Mari's house, then had to leave after an hour to get Kinley down for her nap. Greg didn't really talk to her. *Oh well.*

She began to viscerally understand the expression, "the days are long, and the years are short." Getting laundry done became a herculean task. Baby care was all-encompassing, a tidal wave of endless tasks devoted to the little person's care. Sasha was her anchor, normalizing everything from diarrhea to diaper rash with practical advice and no-nonsense baby care.

By the time the following Saturday arrived, Ellie's night

to go out with Mari, she collapsed on a chair in Sasha's screened-in back porch and put her head in her hands.

"Okay, what is it?" Sasha looked her over, then went back to arranging bright squares of fabric on a table. "You have on a cute red dress so something good is going on."

"Mari wants to take me to a red dress party. I went to three thrift stores before I found this. But I'm exhausted. I don't know, Sasha. Kinley's barely over the diarrhea…"

"Nope. Go. I'm here, I'll call you if baby's sick again. Even if you only stay for twenty minutes, it's worth having something new to think about."

"Fine." Ellie pushed to her feet. "But I'm bringing you back a Jell-O shot if I spot any."

"You do that, sugar. Have fun."

Twenty minutes later, she walked into a respectable-seeming ranch-style home on an otherwise quiet street and found herself transported into a disco with strobe lights. There was a fireman's pole in the living room, and mirrors lined the walls. They were early enough that nothing was really happening on the dance floor yet. Mari pulled her through a kitchen packed with people and out into a large backyard landscaped around a central firepit.

"That living room was giving me BDSM-club vibes," Ellie said. "Remember, pineapple is a safe word."

Mari grinned, a wild sparkle in her eyes. "Don't get my hopes up. Look, I brought this." She held up a thin joint. "Come on, let's go over to those chairs."

Ellie rolled her eyes when Mari had her back turned and followed her. A little second-hand smoke buzz wouldn't be too bad. When Mari held out the smoking joint, Ellie shook her head.

A guy Mari knew sat down beside her and they sunk into stoner talk about the weed, and after a few minutes, started giggling. Ellie pulled her phone out. Being a mom was changing her ideas about ideal entertainment. The party was interesting but—now that she'd been forced into sober living —mostly tedious.

A new friend request popped up in one of her social media accounts. 'Friend request from Austin Montgomery.' Ellie stared at her phone. She clicked on his name and went to a social media page that was empty. His profile picture was the photo she had taken of him at the Oregon Country Fair, scowling next to a parade of mostly naked people dressed as rainbow zebras. He had zero friends linked to his account.

Her hand covered her mouth. Had he joined just for her? All signals pointed to yes. She looked over at Mari, but she was deep in flirt zone with the guy. Ellie swallowed—did she need to be thinking about Austin any more than she already was? Her finger hit accept almost despite herself. She messaged him.

Ellie: Is that really you, or an impostor who's actually friendly?

The typing icon went up on his side. Her heart leaped into her throat.

Austin: It's me. Unfriendly as ever. How the hell do you have over a thousand friends? Never mind. Hello. Thanks for friending me or whatever.

She chuckled, then bit her lip.

Ellie: I guess you meet your friends outside of a screen? I thought your tribe was extinct.

Austin: Not dead, just stubborn. Don't tell anyone I'm

on here.

Ellie: So, I guess you lowered your standards to talk to me.

Austin: I've missed you. A lot.

Her breath caught.

Ellie: Really?

Austin: Yeah.

Ellie: Me too.

Austin: My face hurts because of this thing my mouth is doing.

Ellie: Don't worry, it will pass. How's your dad?

Austin: Good. Surgery made a big difference. He's slowed down but is better every day.

Ellie: I'm so glad for you. I really miss Ryder. Does he still remember me?

Austin: Oh yeah. Wears his wings every night. I convinced him to keep them in the house, so they don't rip like the damn tutu, which finally fell off him about three weeks ago.

Ellie: Wow, you really talk a lot when you're not using your mouth.

Austin: Yeah, I'm sorry I was such a grump at the coast. How's baby girl?

Ellie: Getting bottle-fed at daycare and becoming adorably chunky. Like a cherub out of a renaissance painting. Picked up an intestinal bug last week but is better now.

Austin: Hang on a minute. I'll be right back.

Ellie: Okay.

She looked up from her phone and realized the party was crowded with people. Mari had her face pressed against the guy's. Their lips were locked together. Ellie stood up and walked out of the side gate. She crossed the front yard in the direction of her car. Before starting the ignition, she texted Mari.

She sent another message to Austin.

Ellie: Driving home now from a party.

She tapped the steering wheel, trying to think of a way to say she really wanted to talk to him more that night, but it all came across as desperate.

Back at the house, she popped into Sasha's workroom, where the sewing machine whirred away, to say thank you and grab the baby monitor. She hustled up to her apartment. The door was open.

Ellie froze, her chest constricting around her heart, then rushed inside. She'd just seen Kinley on the baby monitor, asleep in her crib. Inside, all the lights were on. A tall, pretty young woman with a fro of black curls, wearing overalls and a shocked expression, stepped out of the main bedroom. They stared at each other.

"You must be Pippa," Ellie croaked, then put her hand over her heart and sat on the floor. "That," she panted, "almost killed me. I saw the door open and thought my baby was in danger."

"Um, what are you doing in my apartment?"

"You're staring at me like maybe Sasha never talked to you?"

"No, she didn't."

"Can we go downstairs and see her? My baby's asleep in the bedroom."

"Baby?"

"Yeah. I'm so sorry, Pippa. I should have gotten your number and called you, but Sasha wanted to take care of it. I knew better, but I was desperate. I'm really sorry. My name's Ellie, by the way."

AUSTIN STARED AT HIS PHONE. Where the hell was she? She hadn't responded to his last message asking if she'd made it home.

He put his phone down on the side table next to his sofa. She was about four hundred miles away and going to parties to meet men. He stood up to grab another beer out of the fridge. She'd also said she'd missed him.

He caught sight of the real estate agent's business card stuck to the side of the fridge. He hadn't called her. Maybe he would, when Ellie inevitably told him she was seeing someone.

Ryder was sound asleep, so he grabbed his book, beer, and—grudgingly—his phone then stomped down the wooden steps to the main floor of the barn. Out of the side door was his deck. Life seemed alright when he settled into his chair and gazed out over a thick blanket of stars above the mountains. He put his feet up on the matching chair to his, in use these days only as his ottoman.

His phone buzzed with a message.

Ellie: Yes, I made it back safely to find a disaster at my new apartment. It turned out that my new friend Sasha, who owns this apartment over her garage and lives next to it, never told her niece I was moving in. The niece, Pippa, has been in Portland all summer and came back unexpectedly tonight—and found me, and a baby, living in her office. Pippa is in a state of shock. Not yelling or ranting, thankfully, but pacing around. Sasha said Pippa doesn't return phone calls. Or pay her rent. I'm sitting on the outside staircase feeling horrible about it. In my desperation to find a place to live before school started, I went along with Sasha even though I knew I should've talked to Pippa first. Also, I'm busting my butt to pay rent for a tiny room I share with Kinley. Argh.

Austin: Is it that hard to find somewhere to live over there? Sounds rough.

Ellie: Yeah. Pippa just walked past me without saying a word. Oh dear.

Austin: Stick with Sasha, she's got the right of it.

Ellie: What are you doing?

Austin: I'm wondering if you still have that shirt you

stole from me. And sitting on my deck looking at the stars.

Ellie: Per aspera ad astra? I have the shirt. I might be sleeping in it most nights.

Austin: Through difficulties to the stars. A man can hope. I'm wearing my necklace.

Ellie: You're making me smile. And blush.

Austin: Are you still single?

Ellie: I'll tell you if you tell me.

Austin: I figured it would work that way.

Ellie: Yes.

Austin: Yes. Now I'm smiling too. What happened at the party?

Ellie: Well, there was a stripper pole in the living room and the walls were covered in mirrors. The disco ball reflections were amazing.

Austin: Damn. Tell me more.

Ellie: I left after twenty minutes. Being the only sober person is kind of…lame. Boring. Creepy at times. I wasn't in the mood, I guess.

Austin: I'm glad.

Ellie: You're different in text. Flirty. Are you sure you're Austin?

Austin: It's me.

Ellie: If you say so.

Austin: I think about you every day. About us, on that blanket.

Ellie: Mari says I should get over you.

Austin: That's not what I want.

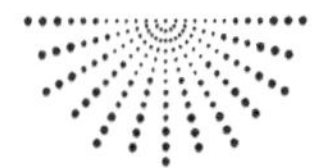

CHAPTER TWELVE

"What the everlasting f—yeah, yeah, freak—did you say?" Mari glared at her.

Ellie smiled. "He's really sweet on messenger, like a different man. I'm still not sure it's him."

Mari flopped down on Pippa's pretty white sofa. "Long distance relationships stink." She looked around. "This place is so cute. It smells like fresh bread. Where's the new girl?"

"She leaves whenever I'm home." Ellie bit her lip, glancing down at the monitor. Kinley was fast asleep in her crib. "It's awkward. I'm not sure what to do about it."

"Tequila shots are my go-to. Can we eat some of that bread? There's a pile of it sitting there—she can't eat all that before it goes stale. I know, let's get her to come to the toga party tomorrow. And ask about the bread. You have anything good to put on it?"

They left the apartment and went down the steps toward Sasha's backyard. The boys were busy in their play zone while Sasha and Pippa sat on the covered deck with the door open.

Ellie popped her head inside. "Hi Sasha. Hi Pippa. I want you to meet my bestie, Mari. Can we come in?"

"Come on in, ladies," Sasha called out, "just watch out for the fabric on the floor. I'm laying out one of my quilts over here and crossing my fingers the boys will give me five more minutes. Hello, Mari, I've heard about you. Business, right? That's cool."

"Hi, Sasha. Yeah, MBA program. Thank you for helping Ellie—I thought she was gonna be homeless there for a minute."

"It's working out." Sasha glanced over at Pippa, who had hunched over her phone, staring down.

"Mari keeps asking me about your bread, Pippa," Ellie said, mock grunting when Mari pretended to elbow her. "Can we buy some from you?"

"Uh, no," said Pippa, eyes flicking up before landing back down on her phone. "I mean, go ahead and eat some. You don't have to pay me."

"Can I at least buy you some flour or something?" Ellie said.

Pippa's face took on a strained expression. "I special order my flour."

"I can't wait to eat that bread." Mari sniffed.

"Pippa's a baking artisan," said Sasha. "But even Gordon Ramsey gets out, once in a while." Sasha stared meaningfully at Pippa, who cocked an eyebrow at her then looked back down at her screen.

"Hey, speaking of getting out," said Ellie, doing her best to sound bright and cheerful. "Pippa, want to come out with us tomorrow night? Mari is having a toga party at her house."

"Yes, she would," Sasha said, enthusiastically. Pippa's mouth dropped open and she stared at her aunt in open disgust. "Okay, see you later, Ellie—I can help with the toga sheets, if you need it."

"See you." Ellie smiled, then walked over to the boys to help them with the water hose and to unclog their pump—which had a tiny car stuck in the bottom. Mari scrunched up her face as she examined the pile of mud dinosaur food that had been shoveled onto a lawn chair. Ellie was forcing herself not to check her phone while Mari was over. Austin had sent her a "good morning, beautiful" at six a.m. Then he'd started cajoling her for a picture of her and Kinley.

"You think she's gonna go?" Mari glanced over her shoulder as they walked up the stairs.

"My bet's on Sasha."

Mari stayed for the afternoon, fussing with how her toga draped and playing with Kinley after she woke up. They sat in the backyard on the remaining clean lawn chairs and then went for a long walk around the neighborhood to shop at garage sales.

Ellie crammed in a few moments to work on her drawings for the design school application and started compiling a portfolio of her work to submit to the program. She had been in the fine arts program, focused on painting. However, a design degree would create more opportunities, even though it would be harder and take longer to finish. She was still sending emails to everyone she could think of at the university, begging them for a chance to join the program late.

After Mari left, Sasha waved her and Kinley inside for dinner as usual. Ellie presented her offerings from the garage sales: random cheap toys for the boys, some cotton quilting fabric for Sasha, and a set of olive oil dipping dishes for Pippa.

Pippa pushed up her chunky, black-framed glasses, her mouth twitching in a smile. "Thanks. I didn't have any of these."

"You're welcome." Ellie ignored the boys pulling on her

and smiled at Pippa. "You might peek in at the estate sale tomorrow, it's four blocks south on Twelfth Street. Somebody over there was a baker."

"Really? Yeah, I'll do that." Pippa took a deep breath. "Hey, it takes me a little while to process things. I'm a pretty extreme introvert. But, um, I think we'll do okay as roommates."

"Thanks, Pippa. I'm sorry to have surprised you and totally understand you needed a minute."

The boys dragged Ellie back to the half of the family room where the kids had their toys. The big space was open to the kitchen and dining room. Kinley was pulling toys out of a bin, propped up into a sitting position with a pile of pillows. She blinked up at Ellie and a wide smile spread across her face. Ellie exhaled, grinning back, her throat tight. *This is love.*

When the boys were busy setting up a train track around Kinley, Ellie pulled out her phone. She swiped through the photos Mari had taken earlier. In the pictures, she'd been holding Kinley outside in warm soft light. Ellie had even managed a little makeup and a cute jumper. *Stop obsessing about the man.* He was affecting her like an addiction. She sent him one of the photos and wrote, "Thinking about you xoxo."

Later that night, as she started Kinley's before-bed feeding, she stared at her phone, which had five missed text messages from Austin. Suddenly, she was in some kind of situation with him. She'd never had a partner that was so openly affectionate, and it seemed at odds with the withdrawn man she remembered from Siletz.

Austin: Ellie, I can't stop staring at that photo. You look so good.

Austin: I want to see you. Can I come and take
you out?

Her breath caught and her heart started racing in her
chest. Kinley looked up at her. Ellie took a deep breath.

Austin: Hey, my soon-to-be sister-in-law has family
that lives in Riverside. She's driving over there
tomorrow in her little commuter hybrid car and has
an empty seat. I'm going to talk to my mother now
about watching Ryder for me this weekend. Ellie, will
you see me?

Austin: My mother can do it. Just need to hear back
from you.

Austin: Hey, I'm going to get Ryder into bed. I'll be
back soon.

The last message had been sent about ten minutes ago.
Ellie stared across the room at the empty kitchen. After a
minute, Kinley reached up and patted her chin. Ellie took her
little hand and kissed it.

Ellie: Yes? Yes. I really want to see you too. But I'm
nervous about it—I don't know, it was very hard to
say goodbye last time.

Well, there, her heart laid bare in a text message. She
sniffed and tried to ignore the prickling in her eyes, shifting
Kinley upright to start patting her back.

Thirty minutes later, Kinley was in her crib and Ellie
went back out to the living room to face her phone and see
how Austin had responded.

Austin: How we said goodbye last time was wrong. It's going to be better. I'm going to be better. There isn't another woman I want to be with. You took me by surprise in Siletz and I'm a slow man sometimes. The time apart showed me I've started falling for you.

Ellie put the phone against her forehead and exhaled. It still didn't feel real.

Ellie: I'm overwhelmed. You know I was falling for you in Siletz. I still feel that way but now I have my guard up a bit. I want to see you so much. My heart is beating too fast in my chest.

Austin: Ellie. I can't wait.

Ellie: How long can you stay? My place is tiny—I'm actually sleeping on a cot in the same room as Kinley.

Austin: I figured I'd check in somewhere downtown, by the river. I'll only be there two nights then I have to get back to the ranch. How much of your time can I get?

Ellie: Do you have a toga?

⁓

ELLIE ADJUSTED the knot of her toga dress below her left shoulder. She stepped up onto a stool in the little bathroom and then held out a hand mirror to see the back. The white cotton sheet was folded in half lengthwise then wrapped snuggly around her body, the ends of the sheet crossing behind one shoulder and tied together high on her chest. Gold cording around her waist cinched in the middle.

"Can you help me with mine?" Pippa whispered, popping her head in the door.

"Yes." Ellie stepped down off the stool then slid it out of the way. "Switch places with me." They wiggled around in the small space until Ellie could grab the ends of Pippa's sheet and get them wrapped behind her back. "They're surprisingly cute dresses, don't you think?"

"Yeah, I guess." Pippa frowned at herself in the mirror. Ellie handed her a piece of gold cording for her waist.

"What's the matter?"

"My aunt pressured me into doing this, but I hate being social."

"Oh no. Are you going to stay home?"

Pippa smiled a little. "No, I'll go. I know I need to get out more. Just don't leave without me, okay?"

"Of course." Ellie slipped her feet into the sandals she'd snagged at a thrift store last week then spray-painted gold. "I don't plan on staying long and I'll for sure give you a ride home. But I'm actually meeting someone there. His name is Austin."

"Are you bringing him back here?" Pippa's face wrinkled up and her mouth hung open.

"No. I'll be back a little late though."

"Oh." Pippa did one of her fluttery quick smiles. "Hey, if you can, would you come to a party with me next weekend? I just want to drop in, but I think my ex-girlfriend is going to be there and I don't want to go alone..."

"Sure. As long as Sasha is willing to keep an eye on Kinley."

Pippa's shoulders sagged. "Thanks."

"Come on, let's boogie. I heard a rumor there would be dolmas there and I don't want to miss them."

Ellie slung a little bag over her shoulder, peeking inside one more time. Goose bumps were popping out on her arms and there was an empty feeling in the pit of her stomach. Austin was less than two hours away.

"Pippa." Ellie turned toward her. "Hey, I have a really big favor to ask. Would you be willing to take the baby monitor from Sasha when you get home? I don't want her to worry about me if I'm a little late…"

"Yeah. But, I mean, I don't know anything about babies—what do I do if she wakes up?"

"Call me if you're worried. She usually goes back to sleep after a few minutes. Of course, you could call Sasha too—she always knows what to do with babies. It's amazing. When I get home, you can turn off the monitor, so you don't have to get out of bed. I'll get it back from you in the morning."

"Um, okay, I guess."

"You're wonderful—thank you, and I owe you one."

The party at Mari's house was already packed with people when they arrived at eight. It was fun navigating through the crowd with Pippa, who stuck to her side and made wry faces at overly loud or debauched people. Mari flitted around, sloshing wine from the side of her glass, a happy grin on her face. She pulled Ellie out onto the dance floor, which was the living room rearranged with dim red lighting. That early it was only a few brave women being goofy and one guy that did an impressive robot. Pippa adamantly refused to dance. Ellie convinced Mari to show Pippa the backyard.

Greg, she discovered when he picked her up for a hug, was many drinks into the evening. "Oh," Ellie said, grabbing his shoulder for balance. He slipped an arm under her knees and held her cradled against his chest. "Wow, Greg. But, um, I'm heavier than I look—"

He hauled her across the yard. "You're the perfect flavor for my grapes. Come and stomp for me."

"That kiddie pool is filled with grapes?"

Greg grabbed her shoes and threw them off toward the bushes. "Ready, my dear?"

"No. Who are you and what have you done with Greg? Ahh—oh my goodness, it's very slippery in here."

AUSTIN DECIDED to skip going into the crowded party house and tried the backyard first. The gate was wide open. Groups of people were clustered all over the front and backyard, many of them dressed up in toga sheets, everyone drinking heavily.

He sidestepped having wine spilled on his shirt. He'd briefly gone through a heavy drinking phase in his early twenties, the same time he'd met his soon-to-be ex-wife. Now he didn't have time.

A woman screamed as he walked into the backyard. His gaze jerked to Ellie, cradled in another man's arms, being hauled toward a blow-up swimming pool sized for toddlers.

Every muscle in his body tensed. He stopped, not sure if he wanted to go forward or turn around and leave. The man dumped Ellie in the pool then stood back laughing. She said something, slipped, and fell backward into a pile of grape mush.

In the next moment, he was shoving his way past the jackass that had dumped her in there and reaching out a hand to help her up. She smiled, but it seemed forced to him, and her body was stiff.

"Hi, Austin," she said a little breathlessly. "I don't think grape stomping is my thing." She stepped out of the tub, holding his hand, juice and grape sludge dripping from the ends of her hair. "Hey, do you want to get out of here?"

He exhaled, a reluctant smile pulling up one edge of his

mouth. She wasn't looking at the jackass. "Where are your shoes?"

"Don't care. Come on." She kept hold of his hand and pulled him toward the big back deck. She ignored the jackass when he called out her name. A muscle in Austin's face was twitching. He wanted to hit the guy.

A tall girl stood on the deck watching them. She had light brown skin, black curls, and a shocked expression on her face. Ellie called to her, "Hey, Pippa, ready to go? I'll text Mari in the car." They all trotted back out the gate he'd just walked through, Ellie still holding his hand. His chest expanded with a full breath.

"I'm so sorry, Ellie," said Pippa. "I didn't know what to do when that tall guy grabbed you."

"I didn't either," said Ellie, limping on her bare feet down the sidewalk toward her car. "I hope I have a pair of shorts in my trunk, or something. At least my cell phone made it out okay—I sacrificed myself to hold my purse above the sludge. Two drowned phones in one summer is too many."

"Two?"

She pulled away from him to open the trunk of her car. Austin's heart rate picked up as he realized she was taking off the toga right there. He caught a glimpse of a strapless bra before he turned his back.

"Yeah. Shortly after you left the duplex in Siletz, I dropped my phone in the toilet. Not my best moment."

So, something *had* happened to her phone.

"Ellie," said Pippa, "here's a baby blanket. At least you can wrap it around your, um, waist."

Ellie gave a soft laugh. "Okay, I'm ready. If a cop pulls me over, hopefully they have a sense of humor."

Austin turned around and saw Ellie holding a scanty pink-and-yellow blanket up over her hips. It covered about half of her thighs. He did his best to keep his smile flat.

She shook her head at him. "Come on." She closed the trunk of the car. A passing idiot honked his horn and whistled at her. Austin glared after the SUV. Ellie ignored them and strode over to the driver's side door of her little car and got in.

He put himself into the passenger seat and Ellie pulled out onto the road. "How was your drive?" she asked him. As he studied her face, he realized she was flushed. He wanted to reach out and trace the curve of her shoulder with his finger. Instead, he turned his gaze forward.

"It was long. My soon-to-be sister-in-law records yoga videos. She warned me she had a few places she wanted to stop to do some filming. But we made pretty good time overall, and it was nice to do a little hiking."

"Yoga videos, like for YouTube?"

"Yep."

"I'm on YouTube all the time," said Pippa from the back of the car.

"My brother's gung-ho on it now too. Started his own channel and the whole thing." The other day, Buck had been talking about making a video about putting a fence in the ground, rattling off a bunch of marketing nonsense. Austin had suggested that they make another video on watching paint dry.

"Here we are," said Ellie, pulling into a long driveway at the back of a large two-story home with a big garage in the side yard.

"I'll go get that monitor from Sasha," said Pippa. "Goodnight. Nice to meet you, Austin." She opened her door and hopped out.

"Night," said Austin. He turned to Ellie, then froze when he realized that she had tears on her face.

CHAPTER THIRTEEN

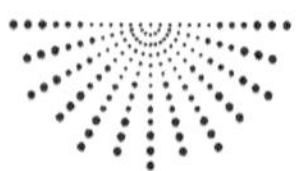

"Ignore them." Ellie wiped at her face with the backs of her hands and forced a smile. "I've always cried really easily, and these days it's even worse. I'm, um, overwhelmed I think…getting thrown in the grape pool didn't do anything for my confidence. Now, you're here, and I can hardly believe it. I'm happy and I don't know…"

"Hey," Austin said, leaning over and pulling her toward him. He wrapped an arm around her shoulders and kissed the top of her head. "I don't mind if you cry. As long as you want me here, I'm staying. There are some things I'd like to talk about tonight, if you're up to it."

She put her face on his shoulder, breathing him in. The tension in his body was enticing; his hand cupping her shoulder and running across her back made tingles shimmy down her spine. They were both breathing heavily, and slowly. She turned her head and kissed him.

Their lips met softly and then their mouths both opened at the same time. She'd kissed a fair number of people in her lifetime, everything from drunken and sloppy mouth-mashing to awkward shy pecks. With a few people, it was like the kissing was creating its own intoxicating electrical charge, winding you up instantly. Kissing Austin made her want to press her body against his. And when he took a shuddering breath, pulling away to press his forehead against hers, she didn't have a doubt of what she wanted to do next. He squeezed her hand, breathing raggedly.

"Okay," she said. "I'll be right back. I have some clothes in the laundry room in the garage."

She forced herself to open the car door and limp across the bumpy driveway to the garage. Since her room upstairs in the little apartment was so small, she kept boxes of her and Kinley's things next to the washing machine and dryer. She pulled on a pair of shorts and a T-shirt and managed to scrounge up flip-flops to wear. Moving fast helped her to not think—she was doing this, and it only made sense when she was kissing him.

Within minutes, she was back in the car. His mouth quirked up at her in that lopsided half smile he did. She grinned back at him and turned on the car. "Where's your hotel?"

She heard him blow out his breath as she was backing the car out of the driveway. "It's the Marriott, downtown on First."

"Let's go." She accelerated down the street.

"Yeah?"

"Yes."

He leaned toward her across the center console, his big shoulder next to hers. He smelled like pine, and leather, and a bit of sweat. Her lips parted, the tingling warmth between her legs almost an ache.

"You're all I think about," Austin rumbled next to her. "When I want, I want you."

She groaned, her legs opening wider on the seat. His hand

touched her thigh and she jerked, swerving the car sideways. "Whoops," she said as he pulled his hand back.

He chuckled. "Yeah. Are we there yet?"

She snorted. "Hold your horses, cowboy."

His head cocked toward her. "Come out to the ranch and I'll teach you to ride my horses."

She glanced sideways at him, her shoulders tensing. That had sounded like he was thinking past this weekend. This new Austin was baffling—openly interested and warm in a way that was missing from the dating they'd done in the past. It made her nervous.

"I called you," Austin said, "that day we left Siletz. Your phone must have already been broken. Asked you to give me another chance."

"Oh, I didn't know—I would have called you back. When I changed phone carriers, I lost all of my messages." She blinked, a sensation like losing her balance was in her stomach.

"Yeah, I figured." He took a deep breath. "I'm not here to hook-up, Ellie. I want to see you again."

Her breath left her chest in a whoosh. She pulled into the hotel's parking lot, found a spot, then turned off the engine. One of her hands kept a grip on the wheel. "Austin…" She paused and took a deep breath. "You're so different—I don't know what to think sometimes."

He picked up her free hand. His thumb stroked the inside of her wrist, raising goose bumps on her arms. "My ex signed the divorce papers. I still have some hoops to jump through, but it untied a knot inside me. You caught me at my worst in Siletz. I'm gonna show you my best from now on." He kissed her fingers. "You're somethin special, Ellie. I like everything about you."

She turned to face him. "Even the pink hair?"

"Yep." His eyes crinkled at her. "It's grown on me." His hand cupped her face. "Every part of you is beautiful."

They both leaned forward, and their mouths met in a velvety glide. The chemistry with Austin was so easy—had been palpable for her from the beginning. Him suddenly openly caring about her was harder. She didn't want to think about feelings or get her hopes up.

One of his hands landed on her thigh, his fingers skimming under her shorts. She shivered, pressing harder against his mouth. Then he cupped the throbbing folds between her legs, the heel of his hand pressing against her. "Oh," she gasped, pulling her mouth away from his to pant, their foreheads pressed together.

He unbuckled her seat belt. "Come on, woman. Your car's too small for this."

She grinned a little, reaching up to put her hands on both sides of his face. "I'm ready." She pecked him on the mouth then pulled away.

He took ahold of her hand as they walked across the parking lot. Her heart beating in her chest was loud and fast. He opened a door on the ground floor and pulled her into a dim room.

She inhaled, her eyes landing on a large bed in the middle of the room, then he was on her. He gripped her butt checks and hauled her up hard against him, his fingers sliding forward to press into her swollen folds. She wrapped her legs around his waist and her arms behind his neck. Their mouths came together in a hungry press, his tongue stroking over hers.

He walked forward, his fingertips kneading and massaging between her legs, and an almost feral excitement gripped her. She wanted him, quick, rough, she didn't care as long as he was inside her. He put a knee on the bed then pulled away to tear her shirt off over her head.

"Ellie." He was breathing hard, a focused look on his face. Her shorts were yanked off. He groaned, gazing down at her in the lacy thong and sheer bra set she'd found in the garage. Her mouth opened to beg but his landed on her first, pushing the underwear aside and lashing her with his tongue. Her back arched off the bed.

She cried out. Everything between her legs clenched tight and pulsed with waves of pleasure that surged up in her stomach. He pulled his mouth away and blew on her, sending her into another tingling shudder, her hips rising off the bed. "I can't wait," he growled as a zipper was yanked down and then clothing fell on the floor.

With an effort, she managed to raise her head, eyes squinted open to see his strong muscled body, his erection long and rigid against his stomach. He ripped open a condom packet and slid one on.

"Good job," she said, hoarsely, reaching up a foot to touch his leg.

"I'm prepared this time."

He stalked back onto the bed, intent, the expression on his face almost angry. She shivered again as he took hold of her leg, pushing her knee up and her legs wide open. The tip of him slid inside her, hot and hard. As he surged forward, the intoxicating sensation of stretching around him had her pressing her head back against the pillow and jerking her hips. He gasped and thrust all the way in, triggering a spasm of deep intense pleasure inside her.

"Yes," she panted. The slight discomfort of the last time was gone, her insides clenching and pulsing around him greedily. His hips pumped into her, pushing her higher, a great mindless climax building until it burst open. She gasped, flooded with sparkly showers that thrilled along her skin. Austin let go of her knee and pushed hard into her, his broad torso flexing. He collapsed down, braced on his elbows, his cheek resting on the top of her head.

Her phone rang. "Oh, crap," she croaked out. "I bet Kinley is having a bad night."

Ellie managed to be home in under fifteen minutes. She ran up the steps, listening to her baby cry, then flung open the door. Pippa's eyes were round saucers in her head.

"She howled for ten minutes straight," Pippa said as soon as Ellie walked through the door. "Kind of calmed down for a minute, then started crying in this like horrible desperate way. I went in there to try and talk to her, but she only started screaming again, louder, like I was going to murder her or something."

"It's okay, Pippa. Babies are ruthless like that. Thank you."

Ellie went into the room where Kinley was whimpering and scooped her up. Kinley clung to her, pressing her head into the crook of Ellie's neck. "It's okay, Mommy's here." The sleep sack was soaking wet from a leaked diaper.

It took thirty minutes, but eventually Ellie had Kinley back in her crib, cleaned up with new sheets, pajamas, diaper, and sleep sack. Pippa had gone back to bed. Ellie grabbed her phone and stepped outside onto the steps.

"Hey," she said when Austin answered. "Leaked diaper. Pippa and Kinley are both rescued. Thanks for offering to come with me but I'm glad I didn't drag you over. Everything's fine."

"Good. Scared me when you ran out of here."

She smiled. "You looked pretty relaxed. I'd like to see you scared, I think."

"Woman, you've got a mean streak hidden under all that cuteness."

"Who, me?"

"Yeah, you. What happened is a perfect example of what I want to talk to you about."

Wariness crept over her. "Right, the talking. Lay it on me."

"Calm down, it's a good thing. I hope." He shuffled around something on his end. She resisted the urge to tell him to just say it already. "Well, as soon as I realized I was coming over here to see you, it got me to thinkin about what it would be like, trying to have time with you while not stayin at your place. At the same time, I didn't want to presume that you'd be ready to stay the night with me—or even sleep in the same house as me. But, maybe, now I can say you wouldn't mind traveling a little way to stay in a vacation rental with me. You, Kinley, and me. Am I right?"

"Are you asking if I want to sleep with you again?"

"Yeah, I guess I am. But sex is not a requirement for me."

"Austin. Yes. Yes, I want to sleep with you. To have sex."

"Well, I thought that's what you might say."

She bent over her knees, chortling. "I had to work very hard to convince you to start sleeping with me. I deserve my reward."

"You do. So, because these rentals need some advance notice, I went ahead and booked one in case this all worked out. They all want at least two nights to be rented, and after pulling in a few favors on the ranch, I arranged it so I can stay tomorrow and the next night. If you want me to."

"You know I do. You're telling me you rented a vacation house for us to stay in together?"

"Yes. In Lebanon, forty-five minutes east. Right next to a river."

"Wow. I thought you were about to tell me we were going back to the duplex."

"Not yet. We'll bring Ryder on that trip."

Her heart turned over. He was thinking about the future. She wasn't sure she was ready for it. "Okay, but I have a few jobs to do tomorrow morning. Did I tell you I do gig work now?"

"I'll help. How 'bout I show up tomorrow morning to help pack and take you out to breakfast?"

Why did it seem like the ground was unsteady? "You're too good to be true. See you in the morning." They hung up.

Ellie stayed out on the steps, staring down at her hands in the dim light. Everything with Austin was changing too quickly and she didn't think she was ready. She'd kept wearing the wedding ring Mitch had given her after he'd died, a simple gold band because they had been saving money. She'd taken it off that morning and stored it carefully in her jewelry box. Her bare fingers seemed empty.

Austin walked up to Ellie's early the next morning, just after sunup. Warm golden light speckled the sidewalks, filtered through a canopy of oak and maple leaves, figs, and ginkgoes —the place was green everywhere he looked.

A big orange tabby cat lay sprawled out on the path up to Ellie's apartment. Austin slowed down so he could step carefully over the long feline, who turned on his back and batted his paws. Austin smiled. He couldn't remember the last time he'd had a bounce in his step—like a gawky Fred Astaire, ready to jump up and click his heels.

When Ellie opened the door, wearing minuscule shorts and a tank top, she smiled up at him in that flirty way, cocking her head sideways and putting one hand on her hip. "Good morning, handsome," she said. "Come over to borrow a cup of sugar?"

He grabbed her, hardening even more at her excited giggle, and hauled her up for a searing kiss against the doorframe, her legs squeezed around his hips. "I'll take all the sugar," he grumbled against her neck.

A throat cleared inside the apartment. He put Ellie back

on the ground, her face flushed a pretty pink. "Morning, Pippa," Ellie said. "I didn't realize you were up. Come in, Austin. Would you like some coffee?"

Pippa muttered something he didn't catch. Kinley babbled from a blanket on top of the pretty area rug in the center of the room. He took off his hat.

"No, thanks. I'll wait till we eat." Austin noticed the pile of shoes by the door, so he bent over and pulled off his boots.

"Hey, babe," Ellie said, and his eyes jerked up to stare at her while a smile broke out on his face. The cute dimple on her left cheek peeked out at him when she grinned back. "Would you keep Kinley company while I shower? And I have a little more packing to do." She glanced at Pippa, who was in the kitchen with her back to them. "Kinley loves a walk if you feel like taking her out—oh and the portable crib is in the garage, if you get a chance to grab it. Right next to my pile of things by the washing machine. Here's the car keys."

He took the keys out of her hand. "Alright, honey, I'm on it."

She leaned in and pecked him on the mouth. "I'll be as quick as a cricket. Kinley has a sweater on the hook in my room, if it's still chilly out there."

He gave her a soft swat on the rear. "We'll be fine. Get a wiggle on, woman."

Ellie scampered off, pausing to grab her mug of tea. Austin crouched down beside Kinley. She stared up at him with wide blue eyes, the swirls of red hair on her head longer and curlier. "Hey, little chicklet. How did you get even cuter?" She grinned up at him, leaning forward from her pillow prop then pushing herself back up again. He reached out a finger and she grabbed hold of it. A tender warmth spread in his chest—he'd missed this baby, and had worried about her a little.

He scooped Kinley up, taking the blanket with him to keep her warm. She held her arms out, her face stretched in alarm. He paused, waiting to see if she'd holler. After a moment, she reached out to pat the shiny metal buttons on his shirt. "Okay?"

She stuck her thumb in her mouth.

"Let's go get the packing started."

An hour later, they sat down to lunch in a big local place that had artwork of famous athletes plastered all over the walls. "Are you a football guy?" Ellie opened her menu and glanced over it. "College and Pros or just one or the other? What teams do you follow?"

"A football guy? Nah, not really. I do watch the Olympics." He used to watch football with his brothers. His father watched but he blew up and yelled at the television half the time, arguing with the refs and criticizing the coaching. Made Ryder upset. "What about you?"

"I root for either the Seahawks or the Forty-Niners, depending on who's more fun to watch. Fair weather fan all the way. I'm with you on the Olympics. Winter or summer?"

"Well," he said, leaning back and closing his menu, "they're both good. But I have to admit, snow sports are my favorite."

"What about the figure skating?"

He sighed. "I'm a completist, all in. So, I suffer through those too."

The server came by and took their order. The food came quick, or at least it seemed that way to him, chatting with Ellie while Kinley babbled in her high chair. At one point, Ellie leaned against his side in the bench seat, and he put his arm around her. He swallowed, already dreading leaving, and then what would have to be a long separation. She would be starting school and there was always more work than he could handle at the ranch.

Kinley's nap time was quickly approaching so they hustled off to do the couple of jobs Ellie had lined up for that morning. "I have the cat lady and the plant lady," she said, jumping out into traffic in a way that made his heart race. Somebody behind them honked. "The cat I feed, clean up after, scoop his litter box, then spend about twenty minutes hanging out with, combing him if he'll let me. He's all fur, like a walking puff ball with a mean streak. I usually drag Kinley's bouncy seat in there with me. Would you mind hanging around outside—the little bugger tries to dart out the door. Oh, and her hanging flower pots and garden containers need to be watered all over the yard. Divide and conquer?"

"I'm on it."

Kinley rode around in the crook of his elbow, watching him water plants with interest. Particularly when she could stick her hand in anything wet or grab a flower. He managed to keep her from putting sticky petals in her mouth, but she was sneaky. At the next house, they all worked together to spritz the hundred and fifty plants tucked into every possible space of the medium-sized house. Ellie refilled some humidifiers and picked up mail, then they were done.

The drive to the vacation house was quiet, especially after Kinley passed out for her morning nap. He'd offered to drive, and Ellie seemed happy enough to relax in the passenger seat. She pulled a sketch pad out of her bag and worked on a series of complicated designs that involved animals surrounded by radiating lines and shapes. He only caught glimpses but thought she looked really talented.

The two-bedroom cabin, made out of big logs in the A-frame style, was rustic with a deck facing out onto the river. He parked under a towering fir tree. They got out, leaving their doors open while Kinley still slept. "I love it," Ellie whispered at him. He grinned, then grabbed her for the kiss he'd been wanting all morning.

They unloaded the car. Kinley slept through it all and Austin eventually carried her inside the cabin, asleep in her car seat. She woke up, fussy and hungry, not happy with anyone. Ellie got to work calming her down and feeding her up. He left them there to take the car out to grab groceries for lunch and dinner.

Lunch on the deck, a walk by the river, then it was time for Kinley's afternoon nap. Ellie emerged from Kinley's bedroom, grinning at him. "Come here," she said, "I want to show you something." She put an extra wiggle in her hips as she sauntered over to their bedroom, pausing to glance at him over her shoulder and bat her eyelashes.

"Are you sure it's worth puttin my book down?" He was already rock-hard.

"I'm sure. But if you want, you could bring it along so I can swat you with it."

"Alright, honey, I'm coming," he said in a mock put-upon voice.

"You might be."

He walked slowly over, his eyes on her leaning against the bedroom's doorframe, still wearing her bikini under a loose tank top and shorts that showed off her round bottom and curvy legs. He pounced on her, making her squeal, then picked her up to carry her to the bed. She tussled with him, trying to take control, which he wouldn't mind, but he decided they both needed it hard and fast.

She landed on the bed with a bounce then he pinned her against the mattress with his body, trapping her arms over her head with one hand and cupping her between the legs with his other. "Like this," he growled in her ear.

"Yes." She arched against him.

It was so easy with her. His mouth landed on hers with a

possessive demand. He wanted her. All of her. Them staying together was a long shot. Part of him knew the end was looming and it made him angry—determined to show her what she'd be missing.

He let go of her to strip their clothes off and then he put his mouth between her legs until she was shuddering underneath him and running her fingernails through his short hair. He kissed her stomach, cupping her pink-nippled breasts. "I'm going to turn you over."

She hummed at him then helped him flip her over to lie on her stomach. He pulled her hips up, feverish and desperate to plunge into her wet folds, his rod stiff as a marble tower and aching. He yanked on a condom then took a moment to mold and swat her luscious bottom before plunging forward. She cried out, burying her face in a pillow, pushing up higher for him as he pumped.

He went to a place made of pleasure, keeping his eyes open to watch her, knowing he would think about this for the next year. "Ellie," he groaned, and she clenched around him. His head rolled back as he held out a little longer, sliding in and out of her slick grasping center. He let go, shuddering, reaching a hand around to rub her swollen clit. She cried out, grinding up and down against him, wet and hot.

They collapsed sideways onto the bed, spooning together, drifting off into a light doze. Austin tried to stay there, in the moment, on vacation with his girl. *You're happy. Stop borrowing trouble.* But half of him was already wondering how the hell he'd make it through another long, lonely winter.

CHAPTER FOURTEEN

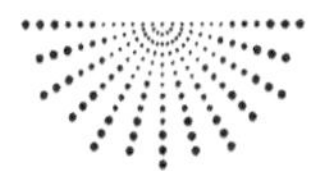

The next afternoon, Ellie sunbathed in her bikini on the wide deck overlooking the river and watched Austin walk around the yard with Kinley. He spoke to the baby in a low gentle voice that had Kinley waving her arms around and bobbing up and down in his large, confident hands. When she watched them together, the inside of her chest melted.

Austin was exactly what she wanted right now. Everything was so easy with him, and they seemed to get each other on a level she'd never experienced before. He glanced up at her, that crooked smile cocking up half of his mouth.

She grinned back at him. Every inch of her sun-cooked skin was relaxed, and all of the parts underneath. She and Austin were like a couple of horny rabbits, jumping on each other whenever they were left alone. She'd never been with someone where they just got right to it—usually there was a lot of alcohol involved, or a movie, to break the ice. He had insisted on feeding her ice cream in bed last night, between rounds…She blushed, remembering him licking dribbles off her stomach.

She sighed, staring down at the empty sketch book page. School started in a week. Life was going to be intense, a daily endurance marathon. Her mouth went dry. She grabbed her phone to check her emails, wondering if anyone from the graphic design program had emailed her.

They had.

She sat up, hunching over her phone to see the screen more clearly. She was in, on a trial basis, with a review of her work at the end of the term. Her breath whooshed out.

Austin stepped up onto the deck. "Is it time for chicklet here to get fed up before her nap?"

Ellie held out her arms and Kinley smiled, bouncing and reaching back toward her. "Yes, right you are, Mr. Cowboy. Hello, Kinley—Mama is so happy to see you too. Come here for some snuggles."

Austin pulled out a book and sat down on the chair next to hers as she stood up to head inside. She wanted to lie on the bed while nursing. Kinley needed the dim quiet to wind down and she wanted to close her eyes and think about design school.

Almost an hour later, Kinley was down for her nap. Ellie stepped back out on the deck, a slip dress pulled on over her bikini. Austin glanced up from his book. "Clothes. Well, they come in handy sometimes."

She huffed. "You're always wearing them. Your tan lines look like clay meeting a cut sheet of marble."

"I'm a modest cowboy. I only show my marble to my woman."

A goofy grin spread over her face. She sauntered toward him. "Wow, dirty talk in the afternoon. And here I was thinking you were decent."

He swatted her with his book. She yelped in mock outrage and stepped away from sitting on his lap. "Rein it in for a moment, woman. I want to talk to you."

She plopped down in her own chair. "Okay," she said, leaning forward and putting her head in her hands. "But I'm warning you, my mind is a muddled mess. I'm not a great decision maker during the best of times and lately…well, everything's crashing down on me."

He put a hand on her shoulder. "Hey, you're doin fine. More than fine. You're makin it work, and it's damn impressive."

His words settled a bit of the whirlwind inside her. "The design school let me in. I had an email today. It's going to be crazy hard."

"You can do it. You'll hit your stride."

She took hold of his hand. "You're pretty wonderful, did you know?"

He squinted at her. "Ellie, I want to take the next step with you, whatever that is." He squeezed her fingers. "At least make some plans to see each other over your winter break. I'd like to get you and Kinley out to the ranch, if the weather isn't too bad."

She closed her eyes. Three months of not seeing him— she'd been trying not to think about it. "This has happened so fast. You were right, back in Siletz when you said I didn't know anything about you. I knew, and know, that I like the man. That I'm insanely attracted to you. That everything about you when we're together makes me happy. But what your life is like on the ranch, what it really means to live in rural eastern Oregon—I have no idea about that."

He nodded. "That's true. Out there, you're stuck in with your person and your family, more so than most places. It's a two-hour drive to the nearest town with a real store."

She swallowed, staring back at him. "I don't know, Austin. I don't know if it's right for me."

He sighed, turning his head away from her toward the

river. "I'm not trying to put pressure on you to decide now. We'll see how it goes this fall."

She crawled onto his lap and hugged him, holding on tight.

❧

AUSTIN WOKE UP EARLY. Ellie was asleep beside him, the sheet mostly kicked off her naked body. He rolled onto his side and propped his head up on one hand. She swallowed in her sleep, moving her head on the pillow.

He rubbed his face. In a few hours, he'd have to say goodbye and start for home, where an empty bed waited for him. Ryder would be disappointed. The kid's hopes were sky-high, and he assumed that Austin would be bringing Ellie home with him after one weekend. Austin had tried to explain that's not how things worked. When he'd left the ranch, he hadn't been ready to bring her home. Now…a tight knot sat in his stomach because she wasn't sure she even wanted to visit him. He shook his head at himself.

"Hey," Ellie said, groggily, "why are you awake?"

"Just admiring you, honey. You can go back to sleep."

"Ha," she croaked, then slipped out of bed to scamper off to the bathroom.

Austin rolled over onto his back. Ellie was exactly the person he'd like to be snowed in with over the winter. There was more than chemistry. She had a temperament that would hold up with him, the kids, the dogs, the homeschooling, because they were miles away from anything…

He loved ranching. Even though he felt all of the privilege and fortune of being born into a ranching life, he recognized that the hard labor, long hours, and isolation of rural life weren't for everyone. His ex-wife could outride and out-cowboy most people. She understood every aspect of running a ranch. But the truth was, she was too brittle to settle down. Becky had needed a lot more excitement than day-to-day life on a working ranch could provide—or him.

Ellie crawled back into bed. "I almost feel chilly, even though it's still at least seventy in here."

He rolled on top of her. She chortled. "Challenge accepted," he said.

"To warm me up?"

"I'm aiming for hot and sticky. Then you'll take a shower with me." He kissed her neck. She wound her legs around him.

"I can't wrap my mind around you being gone in a few hours." She sniffed. "I'm kind of freaking out. This has been too good."

He cupped her face in his hands. "Ellie, I'm falling for you. I'd say more but I don't think you're ready. I'll be patient, for you."

They made love. A few tears leaked out of Ellie's eyes, and she clutched onto him. She wasn't ready to name what she felt, he thought. For him, *I love you* rang in his mind, the words sweet.

~

ELLIE PRESSED her hands against her eyes. They were meeting Austin's ride, his almost sister-in-law, at a gas station next to the freeway going south. She swiped at her face. Austin was driving because she couldn't get ahold of herself.

"Get all those tears out now," Austin said. "Don't cry and drive. Next time, I'll make sure you're home." He glanced at her, his face tight and worried.

She fanned her face, blowing out a long breath. "I'll grab something sugary and wait it out. Don't worry. Really. I think I'm drying out now. Besides, Kinley keeps me on a schedule, and I need to get back for her morning nap…"

"Text me when you're parked at the apartment. I'll probably be driving but I'll get back to you as soon as I can."

"Yeah, that would be nice." She bit on her trembling lower lip, wondering when he would get back to Riverside to see her again. *Get ahold of yourself.* He'd wanted to make plans and she'd said she wasn't ready—now she was acting unhinged because he had to go home.

Committing to a serious relationship, with feelings acknowledged and talked about, had always made her freeze up like a department-store mannequin. Ever since her father had left…But that box could stay closed. At the moment, she needed to focus on moving forward with her goals. *Finish college.*

"Alright, here we are." Austin took a deep breath. He pulled into a large gas station parking lot. "I'll write more about what I'm feeling later, because the mushy stuff would set you off again." He parked her car next to a white Prius with a young woman sitting inside who looked up and waved at them. Ellie waved back.

Austin twisted around to face Kinley. "See you, little chicklet." He reached back and squeezed Kinley's foot. She flapped her elbows and made ba-ba sounds.

"Okay, safe travels. Tell Ryder I miss him." Ellie kept her face turned away, staring out her window. "You should get going—I really hate goodbyes."

He pulled on her hand. "I'm not leaving till I have my goodbye kiss."

She turned to him, her nose stinging, a fist-sized knot in her throat. He kissed her lightly, then leaned his forehead against hers. "Talk to you soon. Now get home so you can relax. Don't forget to text me."

She closed her eyes as he opened his door and left. By the time she opened them, the Prius was gone.

Kinley kept her going. She blew her nose, then forced herself to move and drive them back to the apartment at Sasha's house. Going through the motions like a robot that never stopped moving, she got Kinley down for her nap, the car unloaded, laundry started, and food put away in the fridge. Finally, she stopped and lay down on the rug in the living room.

Her chest rose and fell, despite the deep hollow ache inside it. The lingering throbbing pain in her head and stuffiness in her nose were a constant reminder that she'd spent the morning crying. Of course, she could look in a mirror as well.

I have feelings for him. There, she'd admitted it to herself. He'd gone from basically rejecting her to super affectionate, and she still couldn't wrap her mind around what was happening. What did taking the next step with him even mean? She'd said something about not knowing if living on a ranch was right for her—which had been unbelievably arrogant of her to think that was what he was considering.

Pippa came home, loaded cloth grocery totes hanging off her arms. Ellie forced herself to get off the floor.

"Whoa," Pippa said. "What happened to you?"

"My guy went home." Ellie took a shuddery breath. Pippa kept staring at her. "Which is really far away, and I'm not sure when I'll see him again. I'm…a mess. Needy. It's awful and I really hate what's happening to me here."

"Oh no. Well, um, sit down. I think you should eat something. Oh—I have an idea. Give me a minute…"

Ellie put her head down on the counter. Some minutes later, a plate of bread, cheese, and jam materialized in front of her. She took a bite. "Is this fig spread? Wow, I didn't know jam and cheese together was heaven."

Pippa smiled. She chewed on her own bread heaven, a meditative expression on her face. "I like him. Your cowboy."

"Yeah?"

"He's solid. The way he looks at you—like he doesn't want to miss a moment." Pippa shook her head. "I'm a hopeless romantic. You probably shouldn't listen to me."

"Nope, I'm always going to listen to you. There's Kinley waking up. Thank you, Pippa, I'll take care of the dishes in a few minutes."

The day settled into the usual rhythms, except everyone was giving Ellie sharp second glances. She spent the evening sitting with the kids in Sasha's house and trying not to think.

After Kinley was in her crib for the night, Ellie's phone dinged with a new text message. She stared down at Austin's name, a fresh flood of liquid burning behind her eyes. Having him, then losing him, each time it gouged out another piece of her. She wasn't sure it was worth that much pain.

Austin: Hey, I wish I was with you. I miss you. Nobody has ever made me so happy, Ellie. The drive was long. We pretty much drove straight through. Now I'm sitting out on my deck and I want to show you the stars lighting up the night sky over the jagged line of the mountains. The coyote calls are forlorn and musical. The air smells of sage and hay. I'm lonely without you.

CHAPTER FIFTEEN

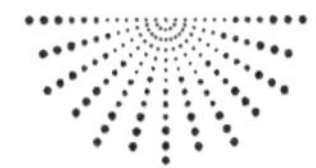

"Just tell me," Mari said, glaring at her.

Ellie took a sip of the fancy soda she'd brought to drink at the party. It was a clear and warm evening for a backyard barbecue, but her thoughts were about four hundred miles away. She sighed. "I miss alcohol. Maybe I'll ween Kinley off breastfeeding soon—except she still doesn't want to take a bottle from me. It's crazy how stubborn babies are sometimes."

Mari slammed her beer bottle down on the little outdoor table they were standing next to. "You took off with that damn cowboy last weekend—and didn't even say goodbye to me at my own freaking party…"

"Because I was dumped in grape mush. My toga was dripping slime."

"Then you disappear for three days, to bone non-stop at some shack in the woods. Now you're a giant sad sack who mopes around and won't talk about it. What's going on with you?"

"Don't you think shag is a better euphemism? You say 'to

bone' and all I can think about are picked-over chicken carcasses."

"Ellie!" Mari threw a grape at her.

Pippa walked over to them, a strained smile on her face. "Hey," said Ellie, "I like your friends, Pippa."

"Thanks." Pippa glanced over her shoulder. "My ex showed up. It's the first time I've seen her since...This is really awkward."

"You should break the ice," said Mari. "Say hi to her, or whatever, but for like a minute. Then go flirt with somebody else."

Pippa's eyebrows went up and her gaze shifted over to Ellie. "You've got this." Ellie clinked her bottle against Pippa's.

"I think I need gelato," said Pippa. "Let's grab some on the way home. I'll be right back."

Ellie took a bite of the lemon bar she'd been carrying around for the last twenty minutes. Pippa knew some serious foodie types, judging by the potluck tables. Too bad she didn't have much of an appetite.

"Come on, I'm your best friend. Talk."

"What about you? This is supposed to go both ways."

Mari scoffed. "My shriveled up little heart is not in charge. The guys I know are boys, not men. I'm not settling for nothing. But you're acting all crazy. What's going on with you?"

Ellie gazed at a pear tree in the center of the yard, so loaded with fruit its branches were sagging. "I'm...embarrassed, I think. There are a bunch of unanswered text messages from him on my phone."

"You're ghosting him?"

"No. I start crying when I think about him too much. So, I'm trying not to."

Mari's jaw dropped. "Shit, that's bad."

"Yep."

"You gonna go see him?"

Ellie rubbed her face. "That's a long drive with a baby. And my car needs a truckload of money dumped into it. Also, I don't know what I'm doing. What if I go out there and I hate it? Or I don't want to leave? Somehow, I made it back to school—I don't even know if I'm going to be able to pass the smallest credit load they'll give me as a full-time student, which I have to for aid and loans. Then there's my baby, who I miss all the time when she's not with me. And working to pay for daycare—it's a lot to handle with classes. But he's the one wringing me out the most. I don't know what I want, but he says all the right things to light up my neediness like a forest fire." Ellie sniffed and pinched the bridge of her nose.

"Shit," Mari said. "You've got it bad."

Ellie closed her eyes and shook her head.

"Oh, my gawd, come here and give me a hug. Okay, okay, look, undergrad classes start on Monday. That's in like three days. You just need to hang in there, girl. Eat that disgusting lemon thing in your hand. If I'm gonna eat sugar, it's chocolate." They stood leaning against one another, arms around each other's backs. "Greg asked me today, 'is Ellie mad at me?' I just looked at him."

"Drunk Greg is another person that takes over sober Greg's mind and body. It's a little creepy."

"Greg's a dweeb." They stood together, watching people jump in a hot tub on the other side of the lawn. "Hey, you're gonna figure it out. With the cow dude."

Ellie huffed. "I didn't mean to start something like this. The anniversary of Mitch's death is coming up in a couple weeks...It was too soon. For him too, he's barely divorced. I just wanted to feel good. Like desperately needed an all-natural dopamine drop after the toughest year of my life—I even went on a date with Todd."

"He's got the best hair."

"Yeah, he does." Ellie shook her head. "It was awful. Then I get back, cowboy grabs me, and it's fireworks from one kiss." They both sighed.

"I want fireworks." Mari stuck out her bottom lip. "The best I can find is a Pop-It. Throw me on the ground for a quick bang."

"You'll find your fireworks. Come on, there's Pippa. Let's get ice cream."

They went downtown and ate their small bowls of ice cream while walking along the sidewalk next to the river, which was festooned with giant hanging flower baskets. They lingered next to open doors with live music playing inside and Mari veered off to join a friend of hers for a drink. Ellie and Pippa headed back to Sasha's house, both of them yawning even though it was barely ten.

Sasha was waiting on her back porch, still up. "Have fun?" She peered at them over the top of the reading spectacles she wore for hand sewing.

"Yes," said Pippa, flopping down into one of the open chairs.

"Pippa's friends can cook," said Ellie. "That was an impressive potluck spread."

"Well," said Sasha, "I'm afraid your baby might be coming down with something. She isn't sleeping well. Better take her temperature."

Ellie sat up straighter and took the baby monitor from Sasha's outstretched hand. "Oh, no." Dread settled into her stomach like a stone.

"Don't panic. Babies get viruses like everybody else, especially in daycare. They do tend to get more feverish. What do you have in your medicine cabinet?"

They talked over medications Ellie could use to bring

down the fever. "Thanks, Sasha." Ellie's throat constricted. "I'm going up now, goodnight."

Kinley was a little warm, but not alarmingly so. Ellie followed all of Sasha's advice to cool her off—less clothing and a lighter sleep sack—changed her diaper, and then put her back to bed.

She got into her pajamas, trying not to panic at the grim premonition that the next few days were going to be tough. She glanced at her phone, plugged into the wall, full of unanswered text messages from Austin. *Why am I ignoring him?*

Sighing, she settled herself on the floor and read over his string of messages. They were all along the lines of "how are you," then "are you okay?" She leaned her head back against the wall, tempted to bang on it with her hard, stubborn skull.

Ellie: Hi. I'm sorry. I'm not dealing with this well…
Everything's okay, except Kinley is getting feverish
and I have a bad feeling about it. I miss you a lot. I'm
going to bed now and I have to leave my phone
plugged in to charge out here in the living room. I'm
going to be better about messaging you back—I'll
prove it.

She forced herself to get up and then go lie down on her narrow little cot of a bed. Life as a single mom of an infant, with very little money, was shockingly tough. And she knew she had it better than many people. Was her longing for Austin simple desperation?

KINLEY WOKE her up at three in the morning, the poor baby burning with fever and covered in blister-like red spots. Ellie stared down at her scrunched-up, screaming face, the sound of her own heartbeat thudding in her ears.

Forcing herself to breathe through the sick dread clogging her throat, she grabbed her go-bag, the diaper bag she now religiously restocked every evening, and then loaded a whimpering Kinley into her car seat. She drove to the emergency room.

The following two hours mostly consisted of her pacing back and forth in a series of waiting rooms, holding Kinley's hot body against her chest, while other patients kept as far away as possible from her and her painfully rash-covered baby.

She was staring at her phone, with Kinley dozing against her chest, when a soundless incoming call lit up the screen with Austin's name. They hadn't talked much on the phone before. She blinked, her mind blanked out and dazed.

"Hello?" she answered on autopilot.

"Hey, how's Kinley?"

Ellie sighed. His voice was an ice-cold drink of water on her parched nerves. "Covered in a rash. We're at the hospital —I panicked. I'm hearing hand, foot and mouth disease, which sounds and looks horrible, but I guess about every kid goes through, especially in daycare. They gave her Tylenol and now want me to hang out. I feel like an idiot."

"Fevers are tough. Got a good thermometer?"

"They're giving me one."

"You're a good mom. Better to be safe. Ryder never had that one, but I read a little about it. Takes about a week for those spots to clear up."

She closed her eyes. "I'm going to miss the first week of classes."

He grunted.

"Thanks for calling, to check on us."

"Wish I could do more."

The corners of her mouth turned up. "You're pretty wonderful. Have I told you that?" She leaned into her phone, wishing it was him, waiting for him to speak. Ready or not, he was now in her life, calling her.

"Ellie, I miss you. The ranch gets busy this time of year and I'm low on hands. It's gonna be a spell before I get out to visit again. Can you be patient with me?"

She huffed. "You're the patient one. Whoops, here's the doctor. Talk to you later?"

"Yeah," he said. "I'll be thinking about you all day."

Ellie arrived back at the apartment two hours later. The clock had barely ticked past seven in the morning. It seemed as though she'd been through a full day.

"Oh no," said Pippa when she walked through the door. "What happened? I heard screaming and saw that you left last night…"

"I took Kinley to the ER. She has a super contagious kid disease; adults are mostly okay—although there was some different confusing info about that—and now we're going to have to quarantine here for the next week. Sorry."

"What—oh god, hang on, I'm a pretty serious germaphobe. Ellie, I'm really sorry, but could you stay off my furniture until the rash clears up? And out of the kitchen? I'll make your meals for you. First, I need to go buy some gloves for handling your dirty dishes—just leave them by your door for now. Do you want to go in your room? I'll leave you a breakfast tray soon…"

Ellie shut the door of her tiny room. She stared for a moment at her tiny bed, separated from Kinley's crib by curtains tacked to the ceiling. Her sketches were taped to the wall. It could have been a prison cell.

〜

ELLIE SURVIVED THE NEXT WEEK. She and Kinley spent time in the garage to get out of the bedroom, doing laundry then stepping outside to walk laps around the neighborhood. Kinley clung to her, and fussed, and had to wear mittens so she wouldn't scratch herself. Ellie started jogging during nap times to keep herself sane, quick fifteen-minute sprints if Pippa was home. But after two days she became ill as well, with what felt like a bad cold, although mercifully not with red spots.

Her professors were supportive, for the most part. After reading over the design coursework, the costs of the books and supplies she needed to buy settled on her like a lead weight.

Austin called every day, early in the morning. They texted at night. The Saturday after the sick week, Kinley was nearly better, but Ellie stayed home. So far, Sasha's boys had managed to not catch the virus, and they were all staying far apart until the rash was totally gone. Austin asked her on a phone date.

"I'm here for my date," Ellie said into her cell phone Saturday evening, settling into a chair in front of the garage. "Kinley is sleeping, the bumps are almost gone, and she hasn't had a fever for three days. I'm drinking bubbly apple juice to celebrate."

"Cheers," said Austin. "I like that picture you sent today, of you and Kinley. She's got a new tooth."

"Yep. She's munching down more of her mushy solids every day. How's Ryder?"

"Irritating his Grandma Dolly lately. He wants to ride out with me on his horse. He could do it. The kid's great on horseback. But I can't run him home after two hours when he's tired and hungry. I keep telling him he's only six and is gonna have to wait a few more years to start workin." Austin chuckled. "He can't wait."

"You two have such a great relationship. I love it."

He grunted. "Will you tell me about your father? You've never mentioned him and I'm curious."

The easy simple way he asked didn't trigger her usual anxiety at the mention of her dad. "Yes. I mean, I'll tell you a bit, but I don't want to get too dumpy." She tapped her fingers against her chair. When would the distance come? The whole thing still felt like yesterday.

"He left my mom when I was a toddler. Just moved in with another woman across town. My mom had to take him to court to force him to pay child support. We spent some weekends with him, and parts of school breaks—but mostly it was his girlfriend reluctantly watching us while he worked. Then, when I was starting high school, he married a woman from China and moved there. He didn't have to pay child support anymore after that."

"I'm sorry."

"Yeah, me too. He isn't in my life now. My mom remarried and my stepdad, Bart, is a good person." Bart had wanted to adopt her and her brother. Her brother Zack had taken him up on it, he'd even changed his name. They were very close. Ellie, well, she hadn't wanted to get too close. She'd wondered the whole time when Bart would disappear too.

"I wouldn't leave my family." Austin sniffed. "My ex-wife had a hard time getting rid of me and we haven't lived together for the last three years."

Ellie leaned back in her chair and gazed up at the stars. "Why is that, do you think?"

"Well, I still don't understand it totally. Mostly for my son's sake. I cared about her too. For myself, I wanted a family. I thought she'd grow out of her short temper, learn how to manage it better at least. Part of me kept hoping her and Ryder would become close if I tried hard enough—that they both needed that. Showed my arrogance."

"Did she win at rodeo this summer?"

"She won some prizes, made a little money. Ryder told me he doesn't want to talk about her right now so we're not keeping close track."

"He's an unusual kid. Smart, like you."

"That sounds like flirting. Want to take your dessert to-go and come to bed with me?"

Ellie's smile wobbled. "You don't have to ask twice."

Austin swallowed on his side of the cell phone connection, the swish and crinkle of what was probably a beer can passing by the mouthpiece of his phone. "Tell me this," he said, "if you came out here for winter break—never mind about the transportation for a minute—would you miss seein your mother, stepfather, and brother for the holiday?"

"Um, no, not really. My mom and I…well, I love her but she's a bit controlling. I keep hoping she'll start respecting me, but it hasn't happened yet. Maybe we'll be closer in another decade or two. Bart and my brother are both engineers—it's hard to explain."

"Okay. I'm not asking you to make a decision now but I'm going to look into options."

"How do you know about my decision problems?"

"Boyfriends always know."

"Boyfriend?"

"Yep."

"Okay."

"Glad that's settled." He sounded like he was smiling.

"Anyone ever tell you that you have odd taste? A pink-haired single mother with a rancher family man—wait, are we like Blake and Gwen?"

"Who's that?"

"You don't watch television, do you?"

"No."

"Whoa, that's heavy."

"Hold on, I like movies. Sometimes."

"What was the last movie you watched?"

"Huh, give me a second." He took another swallow. "I rewatched The Godfather movies. Last month."

"Wow."

"You're yawning. Go catch up on some sleep. Your boyfriend will be distracting himself with an ancient artifact, called a book, before I hit the sack as well."

"Goodnight, boyfriend."

"Night, Ellie. I miss you."

Ellie hung up. She leaned back and stared at the bright sliver of moon, sitting like an ornament above the line of trees in her sight. Little giddy butterflies swirled around in her chest. The word *boyfriend* was inane, like a whispered secret between twelve-year-olds. Even so.

A cool breeze raised goose bumps on her arms. She forced herself up to start making her way to bed. Part of her didn't believe any of it would last. What had happened to the brooding, sullen cowboy she'd first met at the duplex? Would he reappear when she was least expecting it?

Kinley was back in daycare on Monday. Schoolwork swelled up around her like an ocean wave lifting her off her feet. She spent every moment Kinley was in daycare feverishly working on school projects, then she stayed up late and woke up early to try and keep her nose above water. Of course, she had to make money as well, and the weight of all the things she wasn't paying for was as heavy as a sunken ship.

~

"Hey, son," Austin shouted toward Ryder's bedroom, "your ma's calling."

Austin took a deep breath, staring down at Becky's name on his phone. He'd rather be doing anything else.

"Hello," he answered.

"Austin," said Becky's gravelly voice, tough to make out over the din of what sounded like an auction in the background. He turned up the volume on his phone.

"Hey, I can't hear you too well. You riding today?"

"Barrels tonight," she said, exultantly. "Where's Ryder? I want to talk to my baby."

"Hold on a minute." Austin put the phone against his chest and walked over to Ryder's room. Ryder was sitting on the floor, with his back to the door, banging two action figure guys together. "Your ma wants to say hi."

"No thanks, Daddy."

Austin stared down at his dark hair, the same color as Becky's. "Okay, I'll tell her."

"Good," said Ryder.

Austin walked out, shaking his head. Forcing Ryder wasn't in him and would backfire all over their lives, probably with bed-wetting. So far, talking wasn't making a dent. "Becky, he said no. He needs more time."

"Jesus," she muttered, something slamming on her side. "What the hell are you saying to him?"

Austin swallowed, forcing himself to stay calm. "Hold on, you know me better than that. I don't talk badly about you. He's a big kid now, and stubborn."

"I miss him."

He rubbed his head. "Yeah, I know."

"I'm having second thoughts about your parental plan, or whatever the hell they call it in all those papers. When am I going to see my boy?"

Eyes closed, he clenched his teeth together. They'd been

over this so many times. "You'll see him as soon as Ryder's ready." He hesitated—giving Becky advice went about as well as petting a cat backward. "Listen, try a new approach. Send him letters, some toys, pictures of you and what you're doing."

She sniffed. "You think a bunch of junk is going to win him over—damn kids these days. Don't spoil him, Austin."

He grunted. Kids were always spoiled, according to Becky.

"I want to come for a visit, after rodeo wraps up. This divorce feels right—I've never been a good wife to you. But that don't mean we can't still see each other. Hell, it'll be easy again, when we're not married. We've got a good thing between us, you and I. I miss it."

He rolled his eyes. She thought he'd wait around? "That's not gonna work for me. I'm seeing someone now. And I want Ryder to be ready."

She hung up on him. He sighed and put his head down in his hands. At least she'd already signed the papers—he'd had the impression she'd barely read them. Still trusted him, apparently. And she was happy about keeping the car he'd paid for, plus rent on the apartment for another six months. The "no fault" divorce, or marriage dissolution, made it all fairly simple—cheap and fast too, which they'd both wanted. The hold-up was waiting for their paperwork to shuffle its way to the front of the line. He'd say this for Becky, she was honorable in her own way. Wringing more money out of him hadn't ever been her goal.

"Dad," Ryder said, stomping out of his room. "I ain't stubborn."

Austin's mouth quirked up a little. "It's okay with me. I like stubborn people."

"Oh."

"You'll see her when you're ready."

"Do you think she'll send me somethin?" Ryder's bottom lip quivered. Austin's chest tightened.

"I don't know. It was my idea. Maybe she'll have her own ideas about it one day." Austin held an arm open, and Ryder walked over to lean against his side.

"I miss Ellie, Dad. When is she going to come see us?"

He missed Ellie too. "Not sure, but I'm workin on it."

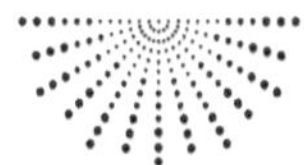

"Ellie," Mari said, her face pinched up, "take a breather, girl. Come out to Octoberfest with me tonight and live a little." Kinley clapped her hands while Mari bounced her up and down on her lap.

Ellie dropped her head back against Pippa's sofa. "I closed my phone in my car door this morning and broke it."

"What, how?"

"My ex-favorite long cardigan has big pockets that hang low. I put that sweater in a box to teach it a lesson." Ellie rubbed her face. "Why didn't I pay for a warranty?"

"Dang, that stinks. No wonder you didn't call me back. Or return my texts all day. I was a little pissed, rode my bike over here to chew you out. Now I think I'll take us out for greasy sausages and German beer. It's fun down there, there's even like polka music or whatever." Mari tickled Kinley's tummy, making her squeal with giggles. "Give Sasha my number and borrow a bike if you can. Then put this little gordita to bed. What are you feeding her? I can barely lift her up."

Ellie snorted. "Hush, she's perfect. I'll go check with Sasha and see if she plans on being home."

"Where's Pippa?"

"In Portland, doing an internship for the next week. Austin was thinking about traveling over—he was going to let me know today and then I broke my phone. He hasn't thought to look on socials yet."

"There's a bunch of ways to call from a computer."

"Yeah, I was too busy today to figure it out. That was my big Friday night plan, until you showed up."

"Get a move on. I'm thirsty."

Ellie sent another message to Austin via her laptop before she left, letting him know she was headed downtown with Mari and would try and call him if it wasn't too late. Sasha took the baby monitor with a smile and made swooshing go away hand gestures. "Go have some fun. You need it."

As brisk autumn air whipped the hair away from her face while she sped down the bike lane behind Mari, Ellie had to admit life was less grim while on two wheels. Bicycle images bloomed in her mind as the focus of her next design project.

The Octoberfest downtown was set up on one street, blocked off from traffic, with a giant building-sized tent housing the beer garden and long wooden bench tables. Mari locked up their bikes to the pile of tangled wheels in front. Inside the tent, walls amplified the jaunty German music and clatter of voices laughing and talking. They walked in, arms around each other's waists, to queue up for beer and brats.

When Ellie ordered a pint, Mari stared at her open-mouthed. They carried their trays over to a table and sat down. "What about your angel?" Mari glared at her while squirting a pile of mustard on her paper basket.

"She'll take a bottle from me in the morning now, if she feeds herself. I kept trying out of pure desperation because there isn't enough time to breastfeed most days. I think she's really proud of herself, because she can aim the nipple for her mouth and get it there after a few cheek squashes. Then she smiles and bounces around, like, yeah jackpot. So, tonight is my inaugural return to drinking—well, two beers instead of one. Cheers."

A few of Mari's friends joined them and they drank and shouted conversation at each other to be heard above the din. Ellie smiled, convinced for a moment that she was where she should be, out with other adults on a beautiful fall night. School was intense, and also mediocre at the same time. She was paying so much money for it while a constant litany ran through her mind that she didn't need a degree to learn any of it. It was a stepping stone, she'd tell herself. More and more it settled on her shoulders like a dangerous gamble.

One of the guys at their table kept leaning into her to bump shoulders, his eyes heavy-lidded and focused on her mouth. Ellie stood up to go wait in the long line for the toilet. She wanted to go home and figure out how to call Austin. He'd declared himself her boyfriend, in his no-pressure and charming way, and yet she'd hesitated to announce her own commitment in any sort of tangible way. Not that he'd demanded to know. She didn't want anyone else—and yet found herself holding back, unable to decide.

After stepping out of the toilet stall, while washing her hands, her eye snagged on a tall man wearing a tan cowboy hat. He turned and she saw his profile, a long straight nose with a slight hump in the middle, thin-lipped mouth, and a strong jawline.

"Austin," Ellie shouted, vaulting forward, pushing through the crowd to get to him. He turned, a grin cocking up one corner of his mouth. She launched herself up onto his chest and wrapped her legs around his waist.

A low laugh rumbled out of him. "There you are."

She pecked him on the mouth then slid back down to the ground, keeping ahold of his waist. "And there you are. Wow."

"Glad I found you."

"I broke my phone. Again."

"Figured. Took me a while to think to check that online stuff. Glad you told me where you'd be."

"Can we go—or do you want a drink first? Or some dinner?"

"Nah, let's go."

She smiled up at him and took his hand. They grabbed her bike and loaded it up into his truck. "Ellie, should I get a motel room? I have no problem doin that. I did bring a camping mattress. Thought I could sleep in your living room, if you're comfortable."

"You won't fit on my tiny cot. It's smaller than a twin. Yes, stay with me. I hope your mattress is big enough for two."

He caught her around the waist and yanked her in close, bending his head to press his mouth hard against hers. She wrapped her arms around his neck and leaned into him.

"I missed you," he mumbled when they both came up for air.

"How long can you stay?"

"Gonna have to drive back on Sunday."

Two nights. She closed her eyes. "Come on then, we don't have much time."

THEY BOTH WOKE up early the next morning. Ellie's warm naked body was tucked in close against his chest. She hummed, wriggling backward against him, until he growled and nipped at her neck.

In another minute he slid inside her, hot and wet, already clenching around him. He lost himself in her sweetness.

Ellie rolled over to lie with her cheek on his shoulder, her head rising and falling as he panted. Tingles of pleasure washed over his body. "Ellie, I love you."

She startled, glancing up to peer at his face. "Are you sure? I've been doing my best to fry your brain with sex."

He put his hands behind his head and took a deep breath. "I know you're not ready to hear this and that's okay. You don't have to say anything. It took me a while to figure it out. We met each other when neither of us was really ready, but maybe that's what we needed. Hey, relax. I don't need you to make any kind of decision right now." He kept his hands to himself with an effort.

She bit her lip. "I've never felt so much for a partner before—everything is too good. But I worry because most days I'm so desperate and overwhelmed by surviving and parenting and just being alone." She rolled away from him to lie on her back. "I used to be pretty wild, ready to travel the world however I could, and not planning on ever settling down. I don't want to be that person anymore, but I'm still…lost."

After what she'd been through she seemed older, but Ellie was only twenty-three. "I'm real impressed by what you're doing here, to get through school."

"Thanks." Kinley let out a soft cry in the other room. Ellie leaned over and kissed him, a brief peck. "I love you too, I know I do. I'm just not sure what I'm doing."

She jumped up to scamper off into the bathroom. Kinley had quieted down so he stayed where he was, staring up at the dim ceiling. Turned out, he wasn't always a patient man. Pushing her might have been the wrong move but he was tired of hanging around in limbo. And wouldn't it be a damn fine thing if someone chose him, for a change.

~

ELLIE WENT about that Saturday sometimes floating and mostly wound up tight by what would happen next. Austin might not have admitted it to himself, but he wasn't going to wait around. She tried to smile as much as usual but found herself startled by him wrapping his hand around hers when she'd been staring off into space.

The L-word wasn't mentioned again. During the day, he helped her with her various housesitting jobs, Kinley giggling and babbling in his arms. They picked a brewery to try for lunch. At night they ordered in pizza. She turned on the television, which they largely ignored to make out, have sex, then both pass out.

Sunday morning, he left. "See you next month," he said against her cheek. He kissed her and Kinley before leaving them at the door still in their pajamas. Kinley mimicked her waving as his gray truck drove down the street.

Ellie shut the door, her eyes stinging, but kept moving all the same. He loved her. Knowing it was like spraying Bactine on a bleeding scrape—the shock of pain jolted into you and then the pain-killing stuff kicked in. She huffed at herself.

The end of October settled into the same frantic rhythm as the beginning, except perhaps she was a hair more organized by the end. Halloween fell on a Tuesday. She regretfully refused to go out with Mari and spent it instead with Sasha's family, managing to keep kitty ears on Kinley's head long enough to take a picture.

Austin became intensely busy on the ranch, working long hours to herd up and sort all of the cattle scattered around the ranch lands and take some of them to auction. They didn't talk as much, both of them too busy and exhausted, but every day he sent her a message of some kind. Austin and Ryder lived in a converted barn, she learned, filled with beautiful woodwork he'd crafted himself. He started sending her photos from his days. Views of high desert, and mountain peaks, the animals, and occasional gems of himself and Ryder stacked up in her inbox. She loved them.

November brought a long stretch of freezing weather—a polar vortex, apparently. Ellie battled exhaustion. The relentless pace of each day ground on her, especially after she tweaked something in her back while bending over to pick up grocery bags.

Austin was starting to plan a visit, with Ryder this time, during the long weekend she'd have for Thanksgiving. She wanted to see him, desperately, and relied on his daily texts or phone calls, and yet part of her didn't want the distraction from her precarious juggling act. The plan went forward all the same. Austin rented half of the duplex in Siletz—they were going back to where they'd started, except they'd be together.

A week before Thanksgiving, Ellie skipped lunch to race back to her apartment and find clean baby clothes. She gripped the steering wheel with white-knuckled hands, keeping her bleary eyes intent on the road.

"Hold on, kiddo," she called back to Kinley, who was sitting in her car seat with just a jacket on, kicking her bare legs. A bad diaper followed by a water spill had blown through all of the spare clothing she'd packed, and the daycare was wiped out of their lenders.

The temperature was still barely above freezing. She pulled in carefully on the slick driveway, giving Pippa's car as much room as she could manage. A cat darted out in front of her. Ellie slammed on the brakes and her back wheels fishtailed on the icy pavement. Kinley let out a howl and started crying. Ellie swallowed, hand on her chest. Her heart hammered against her ribs.

She opened her door to go find the cat. Nothing had

bumped against her tire, but she hadn't seen the cat run away either. She swung one leg out of the cab then turned back to grab her purse, halfway standing on the driveway. The cat howled under her car. She jerked toward the sound but her purse strap caught on the emergency brake, yanking her off balance. Her foot slipped. The world went sideways until her head cracked against the doorframe on the way down. She groaned, twitching from a blinding rip of agony in her ankle, the one still in the car that had somehow become wedged under her seat.

Kinley's scared cries kept her from really passing out, although she thought she'd lost a few seconds. How could she do this to herself? It was bad, really stinking horrible.

"Ellie?" Pippa appeared by her. "Oh no, you're hurt."

"Is Sasha here?" Ellie croaked out. "Kinley needs to go inside."

"No—her car's gone. Just me. Oh crap. Ellie, there's blood on your forehead."

Ellie blinked and pressed against her roiling stomach. The throbbing in her head vibrated in time to Kinley's wails. "Hand me my phone. Then please take Kinley inside to her crib. Put warm clothes on her if she calms down."

"Um, okay. What about you?"

"I can't think while Kinley is screaming. Maybe pull my foot out. It's stuck under this piece of crap seat."

Pippa moved her foot and Ellie screamed. She kept her head down, pressing her face into the puffy sleeve of her jacket. After a minute of breathing, Ellie realized Pippa was still crouched next to her, hands frozen in midair.

"Hey, will you bring me some painkiller?"

"What kind?"

"All of them."

Pippa stood up. She put her hands on her cheeks, big

brown eyes round in her face. "I think I should call an ambulance," she shouted over Kinley's increasing volume.

"No. I can't afford it. I'm going to see if Mari can take me to the student health center."

"Oh my gosh," Pippa muttered, but finally started toward the back of the car to get Kinley.

Things began happening around her, and all she could do was lie back in the driver's seat of her car, stiff ankle awkwardly propped up on the dash, and try not to move while stabbing pain lashed at her. Pippa reappeared with frozen peas, one package for her ankle and the other for her head, and bottles of pills.

The poor cat had the end of his tail stuck under a tire and they managed to set him free. Sasha arrived back from the grocery store and carried off Kinley, relieving Pippa, who hadn't been able to take off Kinley's jacket but had done her best to keep an eye on her. Mari rushed over. She hauled Ellie off to the health center on campus.

"YOU HAVE A GRADE TWO ANKLE SPRAIN," said Doctor Martinez, her sharp brown eyes scanning over Ellie's legs. "Our x-ray didn't show a fracture. Also, while I don't think you completely tore a ligament or tendon during your fall, a partial tear would account for this level of pain and swelling. The peroneal tendons and the ligament tear need careful treatment and time to heal."

Ellie stared at her, mouth hanging open. "But I can walk on it soon, right?"

Doctor Martinez leaned forward. "I'm sorry, I know this is hard to hear, but no, you can't walk on it soon. I'm prescribing crutches for when you absolutely have to move, like to go to the bathroom, and a boot to stabilize and protect the ankle. You came close to a grade three sprain, which is a complete tear. Without proper treatment you could very well have ankle pain for the rest of your life and suffer from repeat injuries."

Her nose stung. She blinked hard, covering her face with a hand. "I have a baby, and finals, and a second-story apartment…"

"Rest, ice, compression, and elevation." The doctor patted her shoulder. "You need to stay in bed for the next week. Once the swelling is gone, I have some exercises for you to work on as you slowly strengthen the ankle. This is a serious injury. You are going to have to make changes to get the help you need. Most professors are set up to help students online now and I believe they will work with you. I'll include a doctor's note to show them, explaining your injury."

A tissue box was set down next to Ellie on the examining table. "Okay."

"Right," said Doctor Martinez, standing up briskly. "I'm going to print out various things for you and see about getting a boot on that ankle. Rest here until your friend returns to pick you up."

Ellie blew her nose, staring down at the leggings they'd cut off her rather than trying to remove them over her foot. *Call Mom.* She had to do it, and her good mother would swoop in and take over everything. Ellie fiercely loved the formidable matriarch of the family, who had a striking resemblance to Jane Fonda. She also suffocated after five minutes in the same room as her.

Her phone rang. She squinted at it suspiciously, then swooped it up and answered.

"Ellie," said Austin's deep rumble. "Honey, what did the doctor say?"

She'd texted him during one of the endless waiting

periods between exams. "Bad sprain—torn but not ripped, I guess. No breaks." She sniffed. "The swelling is really bad."

"Damn, woman." Cows mooed close by him.

"Yeah." She closed her eyes. The paper-covered table crinkled as she turned her head.

"You should come out here."

"What?"

"Hold on." He covered the phone to shout something. "I'm going to look into empty legs from Riverside over to Boise. With that big football game yesterday there might be something—I'll call you back." He hung up.

She stared at the wall for a minute, blinking. The painkiller was slowing her down to slug speed. Then she googled "empty leg" and realized he was talking about private chartered flights, particularly when there was an empty plane that had to fly back to its home airport.

Go out to the ranch? Her head felt like a traffic accident. She wanted Austin, she wanted to stay in bed even more. Except she couldn't ask Sasha and Pippa to take care of her, or Mari. Her phone rang.

"There's a flight today," said Austin.

Ellie gasped. "Today?"

"The airport is sixteen miles from Sasha's house. Empty leg flights on private jets get canceled all the time if they find somebody to pay full price, or for a handful of other reasons. Point is, if it don't work out, we'll figure something else out tomorrow."

"But today?"

"Somebody can drive you right up to the plane. Pack as much as you can fit in the car. If you make it on the flight, I can be there to pick you up in Boise. I'll park on the tarmac, close to where you land, and help you down the jet steps. Can Pippa and Mari load you up?"

"I think so. I mean, I'll ask them."

Austin blew out his breath. "What do you think? Want to try and get here tonight?"

Ellie bit her bottom lip. Her mother's voice was shouting inside her head.

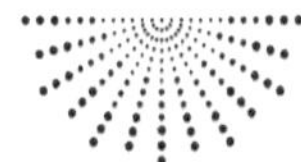

CHAPTER SEVENTEEN

Kinley took to flying like an excited sparrow. She vigorously chewed on her binky during the altitude shifts and banged on the window with her hand. They shot into the air during sunset, Oregon's coastal range mountains dropping away behind them as they flew east toward the high peaks of the Cascades.

Ellie groaned as Kinley bounced up and down on her chest. Even distracted with pain, the leather upholstered recliner, with a massage button, was the most comfortable chair she'd sat in—probably in her entire life. She opened the plastic bag next to her to break off a chunk of the dry bread Pippa had hastily packed for her. The bowl of cereal at breakfast had been a long time ago.

"Babes," she said to Kinley, "we're doing this. Is mama cray cray?"

Kinley spit out her binky, luckily attached to a cord that was clipped to her jacket, and grabbed the bread out of Ellie's hands. Drool dripped from the side of her mouth as she gnawed on it.

Ellie managed to snag a few photos of Kinley grinning

toothily in the luxurious jet. Austin had promised the fare was a fraction of the normal cost of booking a private chartered jet. She was willing to bet it was still outrageous. She hadn't really given Austin's financial situation a ton of thought, other than to assume he did fairly well, since he had a new truck.

One of the pilots stuck his head into the main cabin. "Doing alright back here?"

"Very comfortable," said Ellie. "But I don't need this whole space to myself."

He smiled at her. "Well, best I keep our captain on course in the flight deck. I'll make sure he doesn't hatch any cock-eyed chickens up there in his roost."

"I heard that," yelled back another voice.

The co-pilot smirked, then disappeared back through the curtained door. Ellie had taken the max dose of both Tylenol and ibuprofen, which made her vision fuzzy and also gave the entire day the ambience of an out-of-body experience. She held on tighter to Kinley.

The flight was barely over an hour long. Before she knew it, they were touching down, landing easily after a few bumps. The co-pilot opened the door and minutes later Austin stepped into the cab. Kinley bounced up and down in her lap.

He cupped Ellie's cheek with one hand while she tried to smile up at him. "Hey," she said. "Cool ride."

"Hold on for a sec while I load up your gear." He picked up Kinley's car seat then disappeared back through the door.

Kinley needed a new diaper, and Ellie needed the lav before either of them left the jet. Austin managed all of it with a gentle confidence that had her moving where he pointed before she thought about it twice. *It's the drugs.* But she found herself a little grumpy at becoming another piece of baggage to manage. Even so, she kissed his cheek when he carried her down the steps of the plane and into his truck that was parked very close with a clean Kinley drinking a bottle inside her car seat.

"It's about a three-hour drive to the ranch. We'll hit a drive-through, and I better run in a store on the way. Text me a list of everything you want."

He arranged her in the passenger seat so the big stabilizer ankle boot was propped up in the middle of the cab between them, then broke open another one of her chemical ice packs to lay on top. "You are too good to me," she said. "How in the world did I talk you into this?"

His mouth quirked up at her. "I reckon I'm finally going to see your peppery side. Your stomach's growling at me already."

She managed to eat something, enough to take another dose of pain meds, then dozed during the drive once Kinley was sleeping. At last, they slowed down and turned off the main highway.

"We're here," Austin said softly.

Ellie blinked open her heavy eyes. She leaned forward and covered her mouth with a hand. At the end of the long drive was a mansion.

AUSTIN OPENED THE PASSENGER DOOR. Ellie sat hunched over in the passenger seat with her eyes closed. A little makeup was smeared down her face. He'd never seen her in physical pain before, worn down and ragged. He blinked with his chest tight.

"Almost there, honey," he said, reaching out to rub her shoulder. "I'm gonna help you out first so I can get the baby."

"That manor house back there belongs in a magazine photo shoot." Ellie winced as he guided her onto the ground.

Behind Ellie he saw his parents walking over. He sighed. "Time to meet my folks. Sorry, I'd hoped they'd give us a little space."

"What?" Ellie whipped around, banging her elbow on the truck door. "Crap." She bent over wincing and Kinley jolted to screaming wakefulness.

"Austin," his ma called out, "we thought we'd lend a hand. Oh…" Her eyes stuck on Ellie, who was holding her elbow and grimacing.

He wanted to roll his eyes. Except, to be fair, it had taken him a spell to get used to the hair. After a while that pink was so Ellie you forgot to notice it. But Ellie was staring back at his ma with one eyebrow up. He had a bad feeling about the lack of smiles on either face.

"Nice to meet you, Ellie," said his father in the gruff and skeptical way he always met strangers.

"Hi," Ellie croaked. "Sorry, Austin, I know I need to move so you can get Kinley. Those pills made me so dizzy." She stumbled sideways.

He picked her up and hauled her into the barn. He sat her down on the bench next to the stairs up to his loft. She plopped over onto the pile of saddle blankets stacked up next to her. "Hold on, Ellie." He jogged back out to his truck.

His ma had managed to calm down Kinley a bit and get her mostly unstrapped. His father was hauling Ellie's gear from the bed of the truck. Austin blew out a breath.

"Look at this baby," his ma cooed. "What a pretty girl. Don't you worry, little darlin, here he is." She backed out of the cab of his truck.

Austin extracted Kinley from her car seat. She stuck her bottom lip out and wrapped her arms tight around his neck, still sniffling. His ma draped a blanket around Kinley's back.

"Austin," his ma whispered at him. "Is that girl a drug addict? Are you sure you know what she's really into?"

He tipped his head back and stared up at the stars, counting to five.

The next morning, Austin watched Ellie for a minute, still sleeping next to him in his bed. She'd lost weight and had dark circles under her eyes. The pink hair was partially grown out. Looked like she had brown hair when she didn't mess with it.

He rolled out of bed carefully. His mother meeting Ellie could have gone better. *It is what it is.* His mother wasn't going to approve of someone that didn't resemble herself, at least a little. Ellie was surprisingly pugnacious at times—she didn't ignore snubs.

Convincing Ellie to stay with him would either be the disaster that ended things, or keep them on course. He buttoned up his shirt. Did he really want to try with another woman that wouldn't commit to him? He shoved the thought aside. Maybe she'd see how much he needed her.

The coffee machine woke her up. "Austin?"

"Mornin." He walked over to the bed from the kitchen. His barn loft, with his bed next to the living room, could use the addition of another bedroom. "Kinley's still sleepin."

"Where's Ryder?"

He put down a glass of juice for her then sat down on the edge of the bed. "At the big house for now. My loft here only has the one small bedroom, Ryder's room, where we put Kinley. You're gonna get at least a few days of quiet in here. I found a babysitter, Ms. Peggy, who can come over during the day while I'm out working. She's a crotchety old biddy but she'll keep the kids fed and watered. Helps out my ma so it's not all on her hands."

"Everything's so high-end. I didn't realize you lived like this—doesn't feel like I belong out here."

He leaned over and kissed her. "I want you here. There are some perks to living in the middle of rangeland, two hours from the closest town. And my barn loft's not that fancy. Suppose I'll have to give in soon and move back to the big house. I cook over there most nights anyway. Helps out my folks." He smoothed hair away from her face on the side without the bruise. "You took a beating yesterday. Everything you need is here so you can stay in bed and rest. Even decent satellite internet. I'll tell Ryder he can come make you lunch but the little varmint will probably sneak over here sooner."

She smiled a little. "I brought him a few things—some old action figure guys I found that still have all of their limbs. And a Strawberry Shortcake figurine. Will you grab the orange tote bag for me?"

With her directing him, they arranged all of the things she wanted around the bed. He helped her get out of bed and grab her crutches so she could use the toilet. Kinley woke up not long after and fussed until she saw her mama and spent a little time on the bed with her. The other cowboys had started an hour ago. He tried not to show how impatient he was to get out there.

"Alright, chicklet," he said, "let's get you going on your day. Everybody's gonna love ya." He picked Kinley up off the bed. Ellie collapsed back, probably that bump on her head making her dizzy.

"Thank you," said Ellie. "Sorry I'm not myself—but really, thank you."

He put down a plate of pastries on the table next to her. "Try not to worry. Just rest."

ELLIE TRIED DOZING for a couple hours and thought she dropped off again briefly. Her swollen ankle and tender head ached, making it too hard to get comfortable. She needed to save the painkillers for later.

Austin's barn loft, as he called it, had the kind of understated elegance that belonged in a magazine spread. There was a massive modern chandelier dangling down from the high ceilings. A floor-to-ceiling black leaded window and balcony door filled one wall of the large loft space, spilling light onto exposed wooden beams that were stained a warm teak, some mid-century modern blue velvet chairs, and a beige, textured couch. The farmhouse-style fireplace was topped by a large painting of a car in primary colors hanging on the wall. A long wooden table sat in the middle of the open floor, a beautiful hardwood, in front of a white tiled kitchen. The space had been created by a talented designer.

She covered her face with her hands. His family was very wealthy. She'd grown up comfortably middle class, after her mother had remarried and finished her nursing education. They'd lived in suburbia, gone out for pizza once a week, and vacationed every other year. Her mother, though, had grown up hungry and didn't let any of them forget how easy it was to slip into poverty. "You're too much like your father," her mother used to say when Ellie refused to put her nose to the grindstone. Austin's ma, as he called her, was like her mother. Dolly had taken one look at Ellie the night before and seemed to know she didn't belong.

Her phone had a handful of missed text messages asking how she was. *Austin is taking good care of me*, she copied and pasted into the reply box for Mari, Sasha, and Pippa. Her mother she couldn't face yet.

She'd just sent emails to all her professors when the door to the loft burst open and Ryder ran through. "Ellie, you're here!"

"Ryder," she said, opening her arms. "I missed you."

He ran toward her and launched himself on the bed, then

smothered her with a tight hug. It hurt, but the boot protected her ankle very well. "I thought you was never gonna be here," he mumbled against her shoulder.

She sniffed, squeezing him back. "I came." She wiped her cheeks.

"Are you gonna stay now?"

"I'm here for a visit." She meant to say it firmly and didn't quite get there. His big brown eyes studied her face. "Hurt myself trying to help a cat." An embellishment of the truth but redirection sometimes came at a cost. She pointed at her ankle.

"Oh." He cocked his head. "But, Ellie, I want you to stay and be my new mommy."

She took a deep breath. "That's a big step for all of us. I'm going to college right now, and I have a place where I live close to that school. Your dad and I haven't been together long enough for me to be your stepmom." She patted his back, struggling through the pain-tinged fog in her brain to find the right words.

"But I've been waiting forever."

"You're the best boy in the world. Thank you for being patient. Whatever happens, you'll always be my friend." And now for the big guns. "Hey, do you want to see what I brought for you?"

He rubbed his nose. "Yeah."

The tote bag of action figure guys completely distracted him. Ellie collapsed back against the pillows. She couldn't put off taking the painkillers any longer.

Austin's mother, Dolly, walked in holding a plate with a tall sandwich and chips. "Good morning, Ellie. I thought I'd bring this over and stick it in the fridge for you, once I realized where that rascal had run off to. Ryder, time to go. We have to let Ellie rest, so she gets better."

"Thank you for lunch, Mrs. Montgomery. And thank you so much for helping with Kinley."

"Call me Dolly." She stood very straight, her chin up, shoulder-length blonde hair blown out and styled above her collared, white button-up blouse.

"I wish I was in better shape for my visit here," Ellie tried. "This country is stunning."

Dolly glanced at her sharply. "We certainly love it."

"How's Kinley doing?"

Smiling, Dolly's face softened. "That's about the sweetest baby I've ever met. She's won over Ms. Peggy—I haven't seen her smile like that in years. Kinley had her bottle and tried cooked squash from my garden. Come on, Ryder, time to go."

Ellie waved as they left. She blew out her breath when the door closed. Dolly didn't like her, and they both knew it.

FOR THE FIRST TWO DAYS, Ellie didn't leave the loft. She was incredibly grateful and also a little lonely. The kids stayed at the big house with Dolly and Ms. Peggy, for the most part, until it was time for Kinley to go to bed.

The first full night she was there, Austin showered, walked out in plaid pajama pants and a T-shirt, then collapsed facedown in the bed next to her. "Hey," he mumbled into the pillow.

"Wow, you're pretty faded." It was only eight o'clock.

"Roll over."

Her pulse picked up. She raised an eyebrow at him. "Do I get a treat?"

He huffed. "Yes."

She rearranged the pile of pillows propping her up and shifted her sore body around to lie facedown. "Ruff."

He patted her bottom then pulled up the back of her shirt.

Oil dripped onto her skin. His strong hands pressed firmly down into her back next to her spine. She groaned.

"This is the sexiest thing you've ever done to me," she said.

"Uh huh." He efficiently worked over her back, arms, and legs, only carefully chaffing the calf above her swollen ankle in the boot.

"Your secret's out now. I didn't know you could do that."

He fell back onto the bed, landing on his back this time. "Yep, but now I'm gassed. A tumble-down worn-out shell of a man. Wanna put on a movie so I can fall asleep?"

She cuddled up against his side. "Sure."

The next night, Wednesday, followed the same pattern. Except, after two days in bed she was starting to become seriously restless. She'd always been on the high-energy side of the spectrum and liked to stay moving.

"Wait," she said, "what's going on? I mean, you used to call me after nine some nights."

"It's the end of roundin up, cleanin out the winter corrals, and checkin over the animals. And gettin ready for winter in general before the first big storm hits. Too many long days in a row right before you got here. Things'll mellow out by Thanksgiving."

The next day, Austin promised to bring her over to the big house in the afternoon. Ellie managed to shower herself, although the experience set back the healing on her ankle sprain. Disgruntled with the lack of options, she had to settle for a clean pair of sweatpants because they were easy to get on. Her throbbing, stiff ankle had had enough for one day.

Sweaty and splattered with mud, Austin walked into the loft and grinned at her. "You look cute."

She huffed. "I'm a hot mess. I wish I had something to give your mother—a bouquet of flowers, chocolates…This has been an odd way to introduce myself."

"Don't fret. There's nothing you can do about being injured. All the rest of it will hold for another day."

He carried her down the stairs to the main floor of the barn then plopped her down on the seat of a four-wheeler. After strapping the crutches to the rack on the back, he straddled the seat behind her and squeezed her in close. "You smell like my soap," he said, nuzzling into her neck and making her giggle. "Works for me."

They rode down a graveled drive toward the main house. On second glance, it probably didn't qualify as a mansion exactly, although it appeared very big to her. Maybe in the four thousand square feet category—way larger than anything she'd lived in. The architecture could be described as modern farmhouse, with wide double gables full of windows and a steep high roof. They crossed a wide lawn, passed a stone firepit surrounded by chairs, and then Austin parked on a beautiful concrete patio that flowed around the exterior of the house. Ellie bit her lip, an empty pit opening up in her stomach.

Austin helped her off the four-wheeler. She squeezed his hand hard. He chuckled. "I don't think I've ever seen you nervous."

She raised her chin. "I'll get you back when you meet my mother."

He pulled her in and kissed her. "Can't wait."

She wiped lipstick off his mouth. "That reminds me, I still haven't called her about all this. Whoops."

"I'll give you privacy for that conversation. Come on."

They walked into the big house, and she found herself in an expansive foyer with a wide wooden staircase. Warm wooden floors creaked slightly under her crutches as she swung herself slowly after Austin, who led the way toward the family room and kitchen, passing a formal dining and sitting room.

"Mommy's here," shouted Ryder, popping up in front of her to wrap his arms around her waist.

"Whoa, careful, son." Austin put a hand on Ellie's back.

Dolly appeared in front of them, her mouth hanging open. "Ryder," she said sharply, "that is not your mommy."

"Mommy." Ryder pushed his face harder against her stomach.

"Oh, boy," said Ellie, managing to pat Ryder's back with one hand. "We have a special relationship, Dolly, it's hard to explain. But, Ryder, we talked about this. Remember?"

"Austin," Dolly hissed, "what the heck is goin on here?"

CHAPTER EIGHTEEN

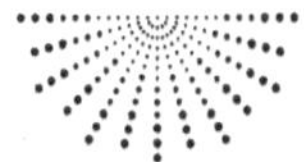

Austin pulled his son off Ellie. "Come on now, let's all calm down and get Ellie in a chair before that ankle swells up. Ma?" He glared at her and tried to swallow down the edge in his voice. "Would you please grab Ellie an ice pack?"

He led Ellie past the big family room his mother kept in pristine condition. "Through that door is the den. It houses the monster television, ugly recliners, and piles of toys that Ma hates seeing anywhere else." He walked ahead of her and opened the door wider.

Kinley looked up and grinned as Ellie swung into the room. "Hi, pumpkin," Ellie said. Kinley squealed and held out her arms. "Thank you so much, Ms. Peggy, for taking care of the kids. I'm glad to finally meet you."

Ms. Peggy gave Ellie a hard stare and only nodded her head once.

Austin pointed Ellie toward the largest recliner then got her settled in it. Kinley started whimpering and scooting across the carpet. "I've got ya," he told the baby and picked her up to plunk her down on her mom. Ryder bounced around the room, ready to pull every toy he owned off the shelves to show Ellie.

"Thank you, Ms. Peggy, for getting us through these couple of days." He pulled out a check from his back pocket and handed it over. Ms. Peggy jerked it a little sharply out of his hands, her eyes squinting as she stared at Ellie. "We'd like to have you keep coming, if you're available. And you're welcome to stay for dinner too."

"Well, Austin, I can keep coming. But I'll be headed back to my place now to check on my cats. Your mother's sending me with a Tupperware of her stew, bless her."

Ms. Peggy stomped out of the room, sniffing and not saying a word to Ellie. Austin rubbed his head. Women were vicious sometimes.

"Dad, I'm tired of old mean-head Ms. Peggy. She won't let me play with my toys."

"Ryder, don't you talk like that about our neighbor. She wants you to keep things tidy so nobody trips and falls. Pick out your books and we'll do your schoolwork when I get back with a drink for Ellie."

"Ahh, Dad, come on. I already did worksheets."

"Pick your books. Be back soon, Ellie."

She nodded at him, her mouth quirking up, while Kinley patted her cheeks.

He found his mother wiping down her clean kitchen counters. Polishing them was a better description for her vigorous buffing. Crossing his arms, he stood and waited.

"Did you know Ryder's carryin around some pink-haired doll she gave him? Keeps it in his pocket everywhere he goes." She huffed. "The wings, the tutu skirt. He's a rancher, Austin. And what the hell is his mother going to say?"

"Nothin, if she can't control her temper. Becky has hurt him enough. And as far as I'm concerned, Ryder can wear whatever makes him happy. I won't put up with anyone bullying my son." Ellie had taught him that much at least.

"You're not even divorced yet."

"Becky signed, as you know. I have full custody. Was emailed today that our paperwork hit the front of the line. I'll be clear next week."

"What's your father going to say?"

"Not much, I imagine. He always was pretty opened-minded, 'bout people at any rate. Ma, you're tryin to blame Ellie for what Ryder is going through. Not her fault. She just happens to be sweet-tempered and good with kids."

She threw her rag down in the sink and gripped the edge of the counter. "It's a small world out here, Austin. We've all got to be able to work together."

"That's right," he said, coldly. "And I pick who I'm with."

OVERALL, Ellie's dinner with Austin's parents could have gone worse, but not by much. The kids were grumpy, Dolly stiff and formal, and Chip, Austin's dad, arrived back from an auction very late and exhausted, worrying everyone. Ellie sat in a recliner with her ankle throbbing.

The following days fell into a kind of pattern. Ellie spent the morning feverishly trying to keep up with her college classes. There was no telling when Ms. Peggy would stop coming to nanny—the woman didn't talk to Ellie at all.

Mid-afternoon, she limped her way down the stairs with one crutch, starting to gingerly put weight on her sprained ankle again with the boot on. At the bottom of the stairs, she picked up the other crutch she'd tossed down. Then she made her way to the big house.

The first time she did it, Austin gave her a hard stare and grumbled something under his breath. That night he started making love to her again, so at least she'd accomplished something.

On the fifth day of her visit, the Saturday before Thanksgiving, her phone rang as she reached the bottom of the barn loft stairs. She limped over to the wooden bench against the wall and sat down.

"Nora?" Ellie wasn't sure if she wanted to smile or chew Nora out. "Are you finally talking to me again?"

"I want to see my niece," Nora said briskly. "I'm only talking to you because I have to."

Ellie leaned her head back against the wall and smiled. "Got it."

"Don't laugh at me. It's been a week since you've sent any pictures. What the hell is going on?"

"Has it been a week? I didn't realize. Well, Kinley has a new tooth. She says mama. And ba-ba, for bottle. She's crawling on her tummy, commando style, but only when she's really motivated."

"Oh my god, baby girl is growing up so fast," Nora said, her voice cracking. She sniffed and blew her nose.

"Also, I sprained my ankle and now we're staying with my boyfriend at his ranch. It's close to Boise. Sort of."

The silence stretched out. Ellie turned sideways and put her ankle up on the bench. She stared at the massive American flag tacked up on the wood-plank wall.

"You're dating a rancher? Like a cowboy?"

"His name's Austin."

"I don't talk to you for six months and all sorts of crazy shit happens."

"Seven months."

"Wow. Okay, so should I fly into Boise?"

"When?"

"Next week. Dad and I have time off for Thanksgiving."

Ellie jerked. "Yeah, fly into Boise. I have to think about

where we're going to be—maybe an Airbnb in Boise. How long do you have to visit?"

"Dad has to get back after the weekend. Me, well, I'm tired of asshole fans taking the piss out of me at the stadium because some shithead notices my tits. I commissioned a cake with the words 'I quit, see you in hell' written in frosting on top."

"So, you're doing well. Not much happening."

"Shut the fuck up. I'm hanging up so I can look at plane tickets. See you next week." The line went dead. Ellie sighed. *East coasters.*

Ellie put her phone against her chest and lay back on a pile of saddle blankets behind her on the bench. She'd been at the Montgomery ranch for less than a week and her mind was split about it. There was so much beauty, and she loved Austin and Ryder, and yet living in close proximity with Dolly, another woman like her mother, made her head ache.

She lifted her sprained ankle up higher and rested it against the top of the bench. There wouldn't be another day in her life that she took her ankles for granted. Being injured had flipped a switch inside her, revealing a thin ballast at her core. What was she doing on a ranch? She had no idea how to contribute or even what was happening most days. Inevitably, things would change with Austin, turn sour, or cold, or withdrawn, or just missing—and then what?

That night, Ryder announced he was going back to the loft with them, and Austin agreed to try. The kids took an extra hour falling asleep in the little bedroom they were sharing. After, she and Austin collapsed next to each other on the sofa. He picked up her booted foot and put it on his lap.

"Hey," he said in a low voice, "thank you for doing some of the homeschooling with Ryder these last couple of days. It's a big help."

"Of course. My coursework has been too intense for me

to help out much. I feel like deadweight out here. Where's the closest school?"

"Jordan Valley, two hours away. You're not deadweight."

"Were you homeschooled?"

"I was. Did some high school stuff in town. Then went to college, only two years cause the ranch needed me. Got my pilot's license."

"Really? Wow."

"Now all I need is a plane. Dad's against the idea but it sure as hell would save us time findin cattle. Anyway, someday I'll make it happen."

She took a deep breath. "Nora called me today."

"Your sister-in-law? I thought she wasn't talking to you."

"That was the first call I've had from her since I left New Jersey. She wants to fly into Boise next week for Thanksgiving. I'm thinking of spending the holiday with her and Brody, my father-in-law. At an Airbnb."

He stared at her, his mouth parted. "You're leaving me?"

She covered her face. "No. I don't know. I'm a little uncomfortable out here—not with the housing, it's beautiful. You and Ryder are great. But I miss my friends, and having a direction in my life that makes sense to me. Out here I'm another chore for everyone to deal with, the city girl that doesn't know what's going on."

Gently, he moved her ankle off his lap. He stood up and paced around. "Damnit, Ellie, I don't want to give up yet. You've got to give people out here more time. They're slow to warm up to anybody."

"I don't know what to say." She pinched the bridge of her nose, hard. "Nora will get back to me soon, about the flights."

He turned his back to her, the line of his shoulders tense. She bit her lip. Why had he turned it into a breakup talk? He could have played along and given her a chance to catch her breath and think things over. When he went into the kitchen, took two beers out of the fridge and walked out of the loft door, she didn't say anything.

THE NEXT DAY was like salt rubbed into an open wound. Austin wasn't talking to her, except on the most basic level. She missed him horribly, even while he was standing right in front of her. Yet, perhaps the return of the sullen withdrawn man was where they'd been headed all along.

It was Sunday, and Austin's parents left early to drive into town for church. Ryder went with them, excited to see his friends. Austin left as well, telling her he was going to catch up with some work.

"Mama," Kinley said in her soft voice.

Ellie limped over with a plate of cut-up soft fruit to put on the coffee table. Austin had cleared a "baby zone" as he'd called it, between the couch and the fireplace in the living room area of the loft. The big window showed a panoramic view of open countryside, crisscrossed by fences, another barn, and a jagged line of mountains barely visible through fog.

"Time to call Nana," Ellie said. She held out a piece of banana toward Kinley, who grasped the fruit delicately with her index finger and thumb, grinned, then smooshed it in her hand. Ellie grabbed the waiting cloth.

The weekly video chat with her mother, always on Sunday, was becoming a rigid tradition. There had already been a flurry of texting between them to set up a time. Ellie propped her phone up on a chair, camera pointed down at the baby zone, took a deep breath, and hit the call button.

"There's my girl," answered her mother, in her breathless baby voice. "Kinley, baby, it's your nana. I can't wait to see you for Thanksgiving."

Kinley cocked her head, blinking up at the phone, then put one of Ryder's little metal cars in her mouth.

"No, Kinley, don't chew on that. Ellie, will you get that thing out of her mouth? Wait—are you in Sasha's house, dear? It seems much too quiet for that."

"Hi, Mom. I'm visiting Austin. We're at his ranch in eastern Oregon."

"What?"

Ellie waited a minute to let it sink in. "I sprained my ankle last Monday. He's been helping me out while I recover."

"Oh, my. Why didn't you call me? A sprain—did you see a doctor?"

"I did." Not answering the first question was better for both of them.

"How are you? You sound a little…different."

Ellie rubbed the back of her neck. "It's been a hard week. My ankle is better, and I'm walking on it a bit with the boot on. Mom, I'm sorry to be short, but I can't handle a lot of questions right now. The Buckleys, Nora and Brody, want to spend Thanksgiving with Kinley and I've agreed to meet up with them in Boise." She smoothed out a wrinkle in her sweatpants. "I'm not sure about Christmas. I'm sorry. Kinley and I will try to make it up there sometime before winter term starts."

"Oh." Her mother pursed her lips. "I haven't even met Austin."

"If you do meet him, I'm hoping you'll give him a super tough time. A little payback for how it's been going with his mother."

One of her mother's perfect eyebrows went up. "Ellie, it's the pink hair."

"And a hundred other things."

"Dear, you can win her over if you want to. That's your

superpower. Don't let a little country suspicion throw you off balance."

Ellie smiled, despite herself. Her superpower? "Well, another happening is I weaned Kinley. Felt like the right time. I didn't want her getting all of the painkillers I was taking. We're through the worst, I think."

They chatted on for another twenty minutes, mostly about Kinley. Her mother examined her naked ankle and reviewed her treatment plan, then said goodbye to go and do the big shop for Thanksgiving. Ellie hung up, a little lighter. Perhaps, she'd finally found a new footing with her mother.

She sat with Kinley, playing with her in the short bursts she wanted attention. After an hour, she reached for her crutch to get up on her feet and start the nap time routine.

Austin walked through the door. "Hang on," he said. "I'll be right there." He stepped into the kitchen and washed his hands.

"Hi," she said, as he walked over. "Thank you, but I can manage. I know you have a lot of work to do."

He gave her a level look. "Come on, chicklet. Let's get that bottle into you before you get any ideas about what you're missing." Kinley went with him willingly enough, patting his shoulder and whispering her ba-ba sounds.

Ellie tidied up the baby zone and managed to put away the fruit platter, even though she received the stink eye from Austin for walking without her crutches. Throwing up her hands, she went to the dining room table and opened her laptop.

A little while later, Austin closed Kinley's bedroom door gently, then deposited the baby monitor in front of Ellie. She grabbed his hand before he could walk away. "Thank you."

He stood rigid. She stood up and put her arms around his back. "Will you do me a favor?"

Breath whooshed out of him. "What's that?"

"Help me shower."

He turned and picked her up around the waist, then hauled her over to the bed. "In a bit."

She dropped down on the mattress and a second later he was on top of her, his mouth hard and demanding against hers. He yanked her sweatshirt off over her head. Her sweatpants were tugged down her hips until one leg was left bunched around her ankle boot. She flushed, heat rolling over her in a delicious wave. He squinted down at her, pulling off his clothes with quick smooth movements.

"You're gorgeous," she said, smiling up at him.

"And you're a handful," he growled, pushing up the knee of her good leg then putting his mouth between her legs. He lashed her with his tongue, pulling back and teasing just enough that she hovered on the edge, reaching down to pull at his short hair.

He crawled over her until the tip of his shaft nudged against her swollen, tingling opening. She rubbed against him and he plunged into her, hard, moving into a pumping rhythm, pounding her hips down into the bed. She closed her eyes and let the roller coaster take her, a breath-catching drop into bliss.

He collapsed on the bed next to her. After a minute of happy floating, Ellie said, "Feel better?"

"A bit." He reached out and took her hand in his big callused one.

"Good."

"My brother can drive your car over for you on the twenty-seventh. He's in Riverside now."

She rolled on her side to watch his face. "Thank you."

"Kinley's family are welcome here. I hope you'll change your mind."

She pressed her forehead into his shoulder.

CHAPTER NINETEEN

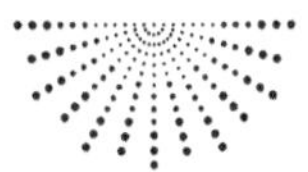

Austin found life taking on a new fullness with Ellie and Kinley there. It was addictive. Happy. Yet, she could take it all away at any moment. She'd leave him, and his son, worse off than they'd begun.

His father clapped him on the shoulder Tuesday afternoon. "Sweet girl you got there. Don't worry about your ma, she'll come around."

Austin finished ratcheting down the bolt on the tractor then stood up. He looked at his father, practically a reflection of himself aged twenty-five years forward. "Too late for that. Ellie don't feel welcome out here."

A grunt was his only reply.

By late Wednesday morning, the big house was filling up with the aromas of Thanksgiving pastry. His brother Buck swooped in, loud and cheerful as ever, his quiet fiancé, Randi, smiling wryly at his side.

"Darlin," Buck said to Randi, "look at that sweet baby. Isn't she the cutest thing you've ever seen?"

Randi rolled her eyes. "Yes. But most of them aren't that cute. And they cry, all the time."

"Don't you worry, darlin. Babies love me."

Kinley, it turned out, preferred Austin, which sweetened up his grumpy mood slightly. The baby rode around in his arms, gripping the front of his shirt. The Buckleys were flying into Boise on Thanksgiving Day and Ellie planned on being in Boise to meet them.

He glanced over at her, sitting in a chair with her foot up on an ottoman. Ryder sat on her lap, playing some game on his tablet. Her eyes turned toward his, that dimple peeking out on her smiling face.

"Chase is really staying in Vegas, Ma?" Buck tossed a nut in his mouth. He grinned at Kinley, who watched him with wary fascination.

"He is. Started that construction company and now is flipping another house." She sniffed, even though there was no mistaking the pride in her voice. They'd all been a little worried about Chase since his stint doing combat for the army. "Drinkin too much, sounds like to me."

The doorbell rang. They all glanced at each other. "I'll answer it, Ma," Austin said.

"No, I've got it." She put her towel down and walked out of the kitchen, Buck following her. In another moment, Austin heard his mother squeal in happy delight. His ex-wife walked into the room, his mother's arm around her shoulders.

"Hey, ya'all," said Becky. "I couldn't miss a Thanksgiving at the Montgomery's."

Austin glared at his mother, his entire body rigid. His ma shook her head slightly at him and guided Becky further into the kitchen. "Ryder, your mom is here," said his ma. "Come say hello."

Ryder was hugging Ellie and talking to her in an urgent low voice. Ellie patted his back and jerked her head toward Becky.

"Who's that?" Becky said in a tight voice.

"My girlfriend," Austin hissed. "Why the hell didn't you call me first?"

Kinley stuck her thumb in her mouth. Austin forced himself to take a deep breath. He patted the baby's back, walking over to where Ellie sat with Ryder still on her lap.

"Son, do you want to go say hello to your ma?"

Ryder pressed his mouth together. "Okay." He stood up and shuffled over into the kitchen, hands in his pockets.

"Austin," Ellie said, "I'm leaving. I'll go over to Boise today."

ELLIE COULDN'T CATCH her breath. Watching Becky walk in, with Dolly's arm around her shoulders, had landed in her stomach like a punch.

Becky stood nearly as tall as the men in her heeled boots, with long legs and wavy brown hair that cascaded down her back in a shimmering fall. Her face was sharp, and fierce, and glaring back at Ellie with narrowed eyes.

"Hey," Austin said, the muscle in his forehead twitching. "She's leaving."

Ellie pushed herself up onto her feet. "Ryder's over there talking to his mother for the first time in months. I'm not going to get in the way of that." Also, the inside of Dolly's house could have been a pressure chamber.

Ellie caught the eye of the young woman with Austin's brother, then waved her over. Austin stood with his hand over his face, Kinley patting his ear.

"Hi," Ellie said to Buck's fiancé. "I'm sorry to trouble you, but would you help me pack up my car?"

The pretty brunette pushed up her glasses. "Yes. I can do that. I'll grab Buck too." She walked back into the kitchen.

"Stay here," Ellie said to Austin. "Ryder needs you. And I don't want this to be awkward."

"Right," he growled. "Because you'd rather run away than admit to what's going on between us. And what I need barely deserves a second thought."

She flinched. "I'm sorry."

"Kinley needs her bottle." He grabbed the bag with the bottle gear in it and stalked away toward the kitchen, Kinley sucking her thumb and gripping the collar of his shirt.

Ellie used her crutches to swing her way out of the room, not bothering to say goodbye to Dolly.

Five hours later, when she at last pulled into the vacation house she'd rented in Boise, Kinley screaming in the back seat, Ellie put her head down against the steering wheel and closed her eyes. *Life is tough, but I'm tougher.* That didn't help. *Not all who wander are lost.* Nope, not that one either.

"Made it," she texted Austin, then forced herself to start moving. She doubted she'd be hearing back from him. Kinley was borderline inconsolable and refused to take her bottle for the next hour. Finally, Ellie had to sit with her, on the mattress she'd dragged onto the floor and surrounded with pillows because she didn't have a crib, until her baby at last fell asleep.

Ellie limped outside to unload a few more bags from the car, her ankle swollen up again and throbbing. She'd left the back hatch open, and a light dusting of snow had drifted in and coated her bags. Shivering, she loaded herself up with luggage, managed to close and lock the car, and went inside.

Hands opening, the bags dropped, spilling clothes across the floor. She collapsed on the couch. Her stomach was a tight, hard knot. She crossed her arms over her chest and tried to swallow away her dry mouth. *On my own.* It wouldn't be easy, obviously, but better than having the people she lived with resent and dislike her. Austin would be the worst.

His silent treatments were brutal, especially when he was the only other adult that talked to her.

She covered her face with her hands. More than anything else, she didn't want to hurt Austin and Ryder anymore. If she left them now, it would be better than leaving them later. Earlier that day, when she had said goodbye to Ryder, he'd thought she'd be coming back, and she hadn't tried to explain it to him. Wasn't it better to do this now?

The night stretched on, long and sleepless. In the morning, she was too shaky to pick up Kinley. Her ankle was so sore she couldn't see straight. Instead of driving to the airport, she had to arrange for a car to pick up the Buckleys and drive them to the vacation house.

When Nora and Brody Buckley shuffled in through the door around eleven, they both froze and stared at her. "Ellie," Nora said, "you look like you've been crying all morning." She scanned the room. "Where's Kinley?"

"Hi. Sorry, I think I'm almost done with crying. Kinley's napping."

Brody sniffed in his gruff way and dragged his suitcase off down the hall. Nora sat down next to her. She patted Ellie's shoulder. "Why are you crying? Tell sister Nora everything."

Ellie tried to smile, then blew her nose. "I left my boyfriend yesterday," she said nasally. "His ex-wife showed up, and his mother hates me, and I don't know what calving is. The ranch is too beautiful to believe and I'm like some rat that has snuck in and is stealing other people's cheese." Ellie covered her face.

"That didn't make sense."

"But I love Austin. And I love his six-year-old kid too. I miss them so much." She dissolved into sobs again.

Nora put an arm around her shoulder. "Ellie, I think you have it."

"What?"

"The attachment disease. You're not a solo swimmer kind of gal. If I'm a shark that eats up men like schools of minnows, or whatever, you're a horny dolphin that jumps around with a goofy grin on your face, screwing every chance you get."

Ellie snorted. "Dolphins aren't monogamous."

"Hush. Is the sex good?"

"The best."

"Call him."

"And then what?"

"Ask him to drive over here and bone—shit, just call the sorry jackass."

Ellie hugged Nora, who patted her awkwardly on the back. "Thanks for the shark talk. I'm going to step outside for a minute."

"Fine. Then pull yourself together. We have a reservation in two hours and I'm fucking starving."

Ellie pulled her jacket on and stepped outside. Austin's phone went to voice mail. "Hi," she said into the recording static. "I couldn't sleep last night, and I've been doing a lot of thinking. I really really miss you, and Ryder. I love you, Austin. Will you call me? We'll be at Shari's in two hours for dinner. I should probably try to nap…anyway, I'm not thinking very well but what I know is…leaving you is a mistake. I don't want to leave you." She hung up.

TWO HOURS LATER, Ellie, Kinley, and the Buckleys filed into the restaurant for Thanksgiving dinner. They took their seats at a booth table then all sagged.

"I can't believe she doesn't remember me," Nora said, yet again.

"She's a baby," said Brody, unbuttoning his suit jacket, his wispy white hair combed back. He smiled and waved at Kinley. She hid her face against Ellie's shoulder.

"You didn't talk to us for seven months, Nora." Ellie stirred her ice tea, glancing down at her phone again. "I barely remember you, and you used to be one of my best friends."

Nora snorted. "I'm supposed to be her favorite auntie. Didn't she like the designer baby clothes I sent?"

Ellie huffed, despite the dread tightening her stomach. Austin still hadn't called her back. "You're her only auntie, so the competition is low. And the clothes were great."

Nora fiddled with the napkin under her Bloody Mary. "I'm sorry, Ellie. That I stopped talking to you—it won't happen again. I have anger issues." Her father snorted and she glared at him, one eye squinted closed. "The school counselor used to call it the 'red zone,' which made me madder because I thought she was teasing me about my hair."

Ellie elbowed her gently. "You're forgiven."

"Will Kinley ever let me hold her?"

"I predict yes." Ellie rubbed Kinley's back. "But not right now. She's in a mood." Was she missing Austin too?

Brody cleared his throat. "Ellie, you have a home with us, whenever you want it."

Blurry-eyed, Ellie managed a wobbly smile. "Thank you. But don't start me crying again."

They fell into small talk. Ellie tried to force herself to be a better host, and to coax Kinley into at least looking at her relatives. All the while, though, missing Austin sat on her mind like a giant elephant she couldn't see past. He'd tried so hard, cared for her and Kinley while she lay in his bed a miserable lump, and she'd walked out on him. He was done with her.

The bread basket arrived at the table. Ellie held out

chunks to Kinley. Her own stomach was shut down. Austin hadn't ever said very much about his relationship with Ryder's mother, but she knew that Becky had walked out on him over and over. Was it any wonder that he wouldn't want to be with another woman that couldn't commit to him?

She'd go back to the ranch and talk to him. Ellie almost stood up right then, but took a deep breath instead. Nora gave her a look. *No regrets*, that was the motto she needed—she'd try.

"Ba-ba," Kinley shouted, jerking Ellie back into the present moment. Chubby little baby legs strained as Kinley managed to stand herself up on Ellie's lap, bracing her hands on the table. Ellie steadied her. "Ba-ba!" Kinley raised one hand in the air, gummed-up bread dripping from her fingers.

"Ellie, I'm here." Footsteps pounded down the aisle toward their table. Ryder jumped in front of them, grinning, his arms spread wide. "Hey, can I sit on your lap too?" He bounced up and down.

Austin appeared around a corner, carrying his hat in one hand, and a high chair in the other. "Howdy," he said. "Got room for a couple more?"

Kinley started crying, reaching out toward him, until Austin picked her up. Ryder said, "Ellie—Ellie." Nora and Brody watched it all with their mouths hanging open.

Ellie slid out of the booth and wrapped her arms around Austin, then pulled in Ryder too. "You guys," she said, choking. "I'm so glad to see you. But why are you here?"

"Well," Austin said, "Ryder and I preferred your company. I was a little put out with my ma for bringing in my ex, even though she swears she didn't know a thing to tell me. There were some words thrown around. Ryder's ma had a bit too much to drink, so, after I heard your message, we hightailed it out of there. Course, that was when my phone battery died."

Ryder handed her a napkin. "It's okay, Ellie. We're together now."

Austin kissed the top of her head. He glanced over at the Buckleys. "Let's get some pumpkin pie into her. Sugar helps when she leaks like this. Sound good, honey?"

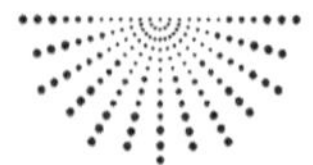

Austin spent the next two days showing Ellie and the Buckleys around Boise. The weather mostly cooperated, clear but cold. Kinley clung to him, dressed in a pink full-body puffer suit with bunny ears, generally wearing an expression of surprised disapproval. She cut another tooth, the thing finally poking out that Saturday morning.

Becky texted him as they walked around looking at street art downtown. He stared down at her name on his phone, the vein in his forehead starting to twitch.

Becky: Hey, I'm sorry about all that. I missed you guys and wasn't thinking.

He rubbed the top of his head. Kinley laid her cheek down on his shoulder, gnawing on a binky. Apologies from Becky were rare. Another message dinged in.

Becky: I'm glad you found somebody. Ryder even likes her and that's all that matters to me. If Ryder wants to, I can come out and do horse work with him, bout once a month during my off season. Teach him roping, to start. What do ya think?

He stared at his phone, blinking. This was a new side of Becky. A corner of his mouth quirked up—there was hope for them yet.

Austin: Fine by me. I'll talk to Ryder and Ellie about it. I think Ryder would like that, if you're not too hard on him. I'll let you know.

Ryder ran up to him. "Dad, I want to go back to the slide."

The big, five-story spiral slide in downtown Boise was always the highlight of any visit for Ryder. "Like I told you, son, it's closed. Hang tight. We're about done with Freak Alley then we'll hit Basque Block and get some grub. Trampoline Park's right after that."

"That's gonna be a million years." Ryder crossed his arms and stomped next to him.

"Ellie likes it here." The big outdoor gallery, full of graffiti murals, had her walking around with a sparkle in her eyes. The Buckleys had taken a few pictures and then wandered off to shop on the main street. They were all meeting up for dinner. He had to talk to Ellie, but it never seemed to be the right time.

Ryder sniffed. "I want to see Santa Claus."

"Okay. What are you gonna ask him for?"

"I want Ellie to stay for Christmas."

Austin hitched up Kinley higher in his arms. He wanted Ellie to stay too. "Hey, now, Old Santa does toys. He doesn't control people."

"When are we gonna ask her, Dad?"

"Soon." He needed to talk to Ellie about a whole slew of issues. They'd been too busy staying up late drinking wine with Nora and Brody, all crammed together in the small vacation house, for heavy conversation. Honestly, part of him was dreading it. He didn't know where her head was at, or how willing she'd be to keep trying long distance.

"Dad, are you procreating?"

Austin halted and stared down at Ryder. He blinked a couple of times. "Do you mean procrastinating?"

"Yeah, that."

"Ba-ba," said Kinley, leaning sideways to reach for the top of Ryder's hat.

"I'm givin Ellie a little time."

"What for?"

He switched his grip on Kinley. "Well, she has a lot of hard choices to make."

Ryder shoved his hands in his pockets. "Dad, it's been years."

Kinley started thumping her head against his chest. "Okay, time to go. Chicklet here has had enough."

"Yeah, Dad." Ryder jumped, then ran over to Ellie.

Austin started to shout at him, then with a kind of fatalism, he closed his mouth and let Ryder do his thing. Maybe his son understood something he didn't.

Ellie leaned over and listened carefully to Ryder. They talked, then they hugged. "Dad," Ryder shouted, "Ellie says yes to Christmas."

THEY ALL DECIDED to spend the last couple of days of the Buckleys' visit out at the ranch. "What's happening with your job?" Ellie asked Nora. Both of them were sprawled out in the lounge chairs on Austin's deck, drinking wine and watching the sun set.

"The pissers offered me more money and a bunch of

empty promises about my safety. After they threw in more PTO, I folded. So, I'll fly back with Dad on the Tuesday red-eye, and zombie work on Wednesday. Good times."

"I'm so glad you came. Kinley knows who you are now too. I think she really likes your hair."

Nora took a swallow, her face glum. "She's going to forget me again, isn't she?"

"Not if we do video chats."

"Come visit during the summer." Nora's head turned toward her. "We'll go down to Wildwood and hang out on the beach. Bring Ryder. He'd love it."

Ellie blinked at her. "I'm not sure where I'll be next summer."

Nora sniffed, shaking her head. "Look around, Ellie. Get your head out of the sand and go for it. There's Dolly waving at us—time for another insane meal cooked by your man. Does he think we're cows that need to be fattened up?"

Ellie got to her feet and grabbed her crutches. Her ankle was still sore, but she could walk on it for short distances. Nora's words replayed in her mind. She covered the icy ground slowly, alone because Nora had carried their wine glasses up to the barn kitchen.

She kept waiting for a sign, some portent that would signal what she should do next. The Buckleys loved the ranch. Dolly had surprised her by being incredibly welcoming to everyone, hosting every meal in her big house. There had been a shift in how Dolly treated her since she'd gone to Boise. Overall, though, Ellie could have been an alien dropped down into a corral filled with hungry cattle. She felt useless.

At the big house, Brody came in from his horseback ride with Austin and Ryder, ruddy-faced and grinning. Kinley called, "Mama," from her blanket in the living room where she'd been spending part of the afternoon with Dolly.

"She's such a sweetheart," Dolly said to Ellie, her face soft as she gazed down at Kinley. "Ellie, I'm so glad you're both here. I hope you know that."

Ellie stared at Dolly, her mouth hanging open. "Oh, thank you."

Dolly glanced around then turned back to Ellie. "You know, darlin, Austin doesn't tell me much. He's a private person. I barely knew you existed until he flew you out here."

"Right," Ellie said, at a loss for what else to say.

Dolly patted her hand. "What I'm tryin to say is, I'm sorry for not being as welcoming as I should've been. Austin set me straight when you left before Thanksgiving." She huffed. "Well, anyway, mothers tend to think they know best. I want my boy to be happy more than anything. Ryder too. It hit me, after you left, that's what you've done. I'd almost forgotten what contented looked like for Austin. So, this old woman is going to stay out of the way and mind her own business."

Ellie managed a wobbly smile and thanked her for hosting the Buckleys so generously. When Austin drove Nora and Brody to the airport on Tuesday, Ellie found herself spending a comfortable afternoon with Dolly and the kids. They put up Christmas decorations and baked cookies while a light dusting of snow fell outside.

Time passed. Ellie spent that first week after Thanksgiving buried under a mountain of design projects in addition to a pile of final exams to finish. Austin, Dolly, and Ms. Peggy too, all supported her through twelve-hour days of intense work.

After sending off the last file of coursework, at close to ten p.m., Ellie plopped over on the bed. "I did it. Celebrating would be good, or at least of shot of tequila, but I'm too tired."

Austin lowered his book next to her. "Good job. And you

didn't even blow up your computer, even though you pound on it like you're hammering in nails."

"My laptop needs to know who's in charge." Ellie pushed hair out of her face. "I hadn't realized before my injury how I can do everything online now. I gave a presentation to one of my professors through a Zoom meeting. I was so tempted to not wear pants."

Austin shook his head. "Bribing people with flashes of you in your skivvies is unethical. And unnecessary. You do good work, woman."

"You're only saying that because you want me to take my pants off for you." She rolled closer to him.

He put his book down. "The paradox is it's all true." He took her hand. "You can do good work, and I can take your pants off. When you're here with me."

She stared into his gray eyes, crinkled up at the corners in the dim glow from a lamp. Finishing a degree online was an option—but she'd have to change her major to something like business or marketing, and only have a minor in graphic design. There was also a campus three hours away in Bend that offered an arts, media, and technology bachelor's she was tepidly interested in. She kissed him instead of answering.

Over the next week, Kinley began crawling in earnest, gleefully pulling down anything she could reach. Ellie's ankle got a little better and Ryder started fretting about when she was going to leave after Christmas. Austin did his best to convince Ryder not to question Ellie about her plans, but the loft was too small to avoid overhearing their conversations.

The second week in December, Austin arranged a date night. Both of the kids would have dinner with Dolly and Chip then stay the night at the big house. "It's pretty amazing to live next to grandparents," Ellie said.

Austin flashed a big grin at her, then pulled her in for a

kiss. "I want to show you somethin. Bundle up and let's ride out on the four-wheeler."

They rode out together on one of his big ATVs, Ellie behind him on the seat hugging his back against her chest. He drove for a few minutes out to a rise that looked down on an open meadow, just out of sight of the hub of barns around the big house. Sunset cast long shadows across the wide-open country that rose into distant taupe and mauve mountains in the fading light. She hadn't been interested in landscape painting until she'd spent time on the ranch. Now she found herself studying how the hills receded and the colors desaturated in the distance, with an ever-changing sky. There was so much beauty in the rugged wild spaces.

Austin helped her off the four-wheeler. He held her hand, stopping her before she could walk forward toward the ledge. "There's a question out there for you. I've been wanting to ask you this for a while, but I've held back."

Her eyes widened. Sometimes, she had the ability to switch off thinking about the future. She'd done that for the last couple of weeks on the ranch. Her plan had been to stay until Christmas and then figure it out. Ellie took a deep breath. Her stomach did a somersault.

"Ryder's been workin on me. The kid puts himself first, and he wants what I want. We're allies in this. You're it for us, Ellie. And I think if Kinley could talk, she might say that her and I have a special bond too. She calls me 'ba-ba,' but she feels like my baby. I love her."

Her throat clenched. "She definitely loves you too."

"I'll take you however I can get you, but I'm going to be a little selfish here and push for what I want. Before you sprained your ankle, I was ready to be patient. But now, after living together for about a month, I understand what we have. We're a family, Ellie. A family that works really well together."

He hugged her in close. She buried her wet face against his jacket. "It's pretty crazy where life takes you sometimes."

Her knees bent, then straightened. Vague amorphous pros and cons swirled around in her mind like a dust devil whirlwind. The strangest thing was, the ranch was beginning to seem like home. Clearly, Austin had completely spoiled her with everything from his cooking to his foot rubs. Had the luxury gone to her head? *I'm only human.*

"Come here." He pulled her forward to the edge of the bluff. Down below them, in a rainbow of colors, he'd spray-painted, "I love you, Ellie. Will you stay with me?"

She stared down at the words, which reminded her of the Oregon Country Fair and also of the street art they'd seen in Boise. He hadn't known until she'd sprained her ankle. She exhaled—the injury had been it. Stressed out and in pain, she'd been too grumpy to recognize the sign. "Look around you," Nora had said, and something else not very kind she was trying to forget. Her shoulders dropped and she stood up straighter.

"I'm staying." She leaned forward and kissed him. "Now let's go celebrate. In bed. Date nights don't grow on trees."

EPILOGUE

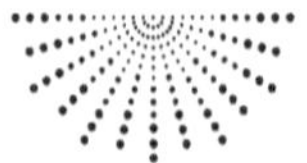

Two months later, Ellie sat at the dining room table in the loft, working on her laptop. Her phone lit up with a call from Mari. She carried her laptop, phone, and the baby monitor out to the stairs where she wouldn't wake up the kids.

"Dang, girl," Mari said. "I thought I was going to be mad at you for ignoring me for a minute. What's you doing?"

"Oh, you know, drinking tea, keeping up with my online classes, waiting for my hunky cowboy to stop working."

"Shut up. It's Friday night—don't you have a hoedown or some shit to go to?"

Ellie leaned back against the stairs and crossed her legs. "No. I'm a serious person now. It's pretty shocking."

Mari scoffed. "What, are you making more babies or something?"

"No. I mean, not that I know of. Kinley came along when I was on birth control though. Crap, Mari, now I'm worried."

Mari laughed gleefully. "Relax. But you better have me in the wedding. Maid of honor."

"What's with all the status quo pressure? I'm not even

thinking about it. Besides, all of those decisions would kill me."

"Girl, leave it to me. Maybe I should start a wedding planning business—I love those crazy parties; I just don't want to have one for myself any time soon."

"Uh huh. Who are you seeing now?"

Mari sighed. "Nobody. I almost slept with Greg the other night."

"What!"

"Yeah, we were both hammered, kind of passed out on the couch together with the television playing an infomercial over and over. We started kissing, this awful super slobbery mess, then he said my name and I sobered up enough to run out of there. Now we're not talking."

"Huh. I can sort of see it with you two. You could do with a nice guy, for a change."

"Never. By the way, I bought our Oregon Country Fair tickets. The plans are happening."

"What about spring break? Pippa is road tripping out with her new girlfriend. We're going to a hot spring. You could ride with them. Also, my mom, brother and stepdad are coming for Easter."

"Ahh. I guess you're happy then."

Ellie smiled. "I am. Sasha and I set up our web page for the fabric design business. We're still in phase one of your business plan, but we're getting there."

"I kind of want to sleep with Greg. Do you think I should do it?"

"Kind of? I don't know."

"Gotta go, my party people are here. I'll call you about spring break. Kiss that baby for me."

"Bye, Mari."

Ellie worked on the stairs for another hour. Her life was filling with work online, classwork and business. The idea of dropping out of college, and saving a mountain of money, was kicking around in her head. *But I'm so close...*She shut her laptop, setting it on the landing at the top of the steps.

Austin opened the door into the barn at the base of the stairs. He looked up at her and smiled. "Another calf tonight."

"Congratulations. Are you done with the baby watch?"

"Yes ma'am. I'm all yours, after I shower." He sprawled out on the steps next to her. "Not sure why you like sittin on these so much. Maybe you're part goat. They like perchin up on high places too. I had one as a kid that sat on top of a step ladder every chance he got."

She grinned down at him. "That would make me a nanny, right?"

"Or a doe."

"I just had an idea for a logo…"

Austin took her hand and kissed it. "I can't imagine life without you, Ellie. I have a big question I want to ask you soon. What I'm wonderin is, where do you want to be? Pick a continent."

She blinked a few times. "You mean like traveling?" She sat up straighter. "A vacation?"

"Yeah. I thought you'd like something like that."

Humming, she rolled on top of him. He chuckled, grabbing her bottom and sliding her down. She kissed him on the mouth. "I'd love it. But what a decision—I'm going to need a little while to think about it."

THE END

SIGN UP FOR MY AUTHOR
NEWSLETTER

Please help other readers find this book by leaving a review. Also, receive free sign-up bonuses, information about give-aways, coupons, and be the first to learn about new releases through my author newsletter. Sign up today!

www.annaalkire.com

ACKNOWLEDGMENTS

Biggest thanks to the two best guys in my life, my husband and my son, whose timely hugs and shoulder squeezes have powered my writing life. Love you.

Special thanks to my editors and beta readers. Thank you Manda Waller (copyedit), Peter Senftleben (proof), A.M. Vivian (beta), and Shelbie Kellum (beta).

And thank you to the fabulous illustrator, Ashley Santoro, who designed the cover.

ABOUT THE AUTHOR

Anna Alkire has been a long-term college student, a business owner, and a world traveler. Now "settled"—with a sigh and a cup of decaf—Anna lives in Washington state, where she splits her time between a husband who thinks the North Pole would be a great place to live, chasing her hurricane of a son, learning new handicrafts, and creating worlds full of the kind of romance and fun she most wants to read. Find more about her (and grab a freebie or two) at her website, annaalkire.com.

9 798986 388144